Complicated Favors:
A Turkish Affair

Copyright © 2006 Jeanne Reeder
All rights reserved.
ISBN: 1-4196-4941-8

To order additional copies, please visit www.createspace.com/3311639

JEANNE REEDER

COMPLICATED FAVORS: A TURKISH AFFAIR

2006

Complicated Favors:
A Turkish Affair

AUTHOR'S NOTE

Although this story is fiction and the characters unique to this novel, Turkish and Kurdish culture and history are presented as honestly as possible.

ACKNOWLEDGMENTS

Heartfelt thanks to my dear friend Barbara Fischer who introduced me to Turkey. Together we relived her memories and forged new ones.

My son, Alexander Reeder, has my deep gratitude for being my best critic and 'first read' for <u>Complicated Favors: A Turkish Affair</u>. My life-long friend Norma Phillips provided unbiased, astute editing. Jo Ladwig's intriguing questions resulted in helpful clarifications. As always, my perceptive friend Deanna Pledge provided encouragements as only another writer can do with such enthusiasm.

Jim and Perihan Masters of Izmir, Turkey, and Learning Practical Turkish fame, were of immense assistance with learning the Turkish language and providing suggestions within this text.

My husband, John Reeder, clearly has earned my high praise and appreciation for being an unerring source of support and patience in his acceptance of the many long hours of research and writing.

For Barbara Fischer, Whose Zest For Life Is An Inspiration To All Who Know Her

- 1 -
A good companion shortens the longest road
- turkish proverb -

The Turkish Airlines airbus was roomy, new, attractively decorated, and above all served good red Turkish wine. Knowing Turkey was a Muslim country, Charly had been concerned that this might be a non-alcoholic flight, but not as much so as Frances, who had brought a flask of Johnny Walker Red along just in case. Charly had read that Turkey was moving at an uneven pace toward westernization, distancing itself from the more fundamentalist leanings found in other Middle Eastern countries. *Ah,* she thought, *that's what being a secular Muslim country means: alcohol on airplanes is allowed.* She idly wondered what kind of growing pains Turkey might be facing and asked herself once again why was she going.

To be reminded she had but to glance at her seat-mate, Frances. *What a sweetie! Seventy years old and going strong.* After a forty-year absence, Frances was returning to Turkey to relive memories of her teaching days at Roberts College in Istanbul. She had wanted to share this country with which she still had close ties with her good friend.

Charly and Frances had been colleagues at a medium-sized liberal arts university and after leaving had continued to be best of friends. Frances had retired five years previously and had been using all of her newfound free time for traveling and reconnecting with old friends in exotic places. She and Charly had often traveled together in the summertime between semesters during their twenty years together at the university.

Charly had left the university two years ago and begun working as a private investigator, primarily in psychological forensic assessment. Charly figured that, at age fifty, leaving the routine of professorship had come at just the right time. She now had ample time to take cases of interest when the timing was convenient. Fortunately her father had made a killing in the stock market in the sixties by acting on a tip from a geologist that his team discovered oil on the North Slope in Alaska. He had parlayed the investment into millions, which Charly had inherited, meaning she did not have to work on a regular basis any longer and could choose her job commitments. This meant that, on occasion, she accepted work for various government agencies as an analyst; a facility for languages combined with her absorbing interest in Middle Eastern countries had led to a number of these assignments over the years.

It was during a CIA recruiter's trip to her college that Charly's life had veered from the routine and safety of professorship into the work of her dreams. She had been disappointed at first to learn that she was "too old" to work for the CIA, and after expressing herself rather strongly on that issue following the meeting, she and the recruiter had gone to dinner together.

A few weeks later she had received an invitation to participate in the agency's evaluation for analysts who worked off-the-book on special projects. Charly had learned this was a network of professionals with varied talents who could be tapped when needed. Testing scenarios had taken place over three days and had included the ability to analyze and synthesize. For part of the evaluation she was asked to provide an analysis of a situation after being presented with sets of information in different sensory modes such as visual, auditory, and olfactory. Another test had provided a set of information in the form of a crisis described in several disparate reports, and Charly had been asked to develop a method of verifying which was valid. Physical fitness levels were also evaluated and skill with firearms assessed. Charly had enormously enjoyed each challenge.

Then Charly had heard nothing more for a year—until one week before she and Frances were to leave on a vacation to hike around Petra in Jordan when she received a call from someone who had identified himself as a colleague of the recruiter. Would she be willing to make contact with someone at the hotel in which she would be staying? After finding out a few more details, her adventurous nature had asserted itself and she readily agreed. A knock on her door a few hours later by a nondescript accountant-looking type had provided more information, and that had been the beginning of a "sometimes" relationship. Charly never knew when she would be called upon, nor did she receive much notice.

Now, on the plane to Istanbul, Charly pondered previous trips she and Frances had taken together. Most had had a way of becoming a fact-finding escapade. Frances had always provided a perfect cover—a bit of a wise grandmother mixed with the joyfulness of youth and discovery. While Frances would be openly welcomed into homes and doted upon, Charly could quietly, almost unnoticed, gather information. Sometimes this had involved joining a group of men, disguised as one of them, as they held clandestine meetings or stood guard for hours, while Frances, meanwhile, was being fed and comfortably bunked down for the night. Frances was the honey to Charly's bee sting; Frances the silk glove to Charly's hammer. But those befriending Frances would have been shocked at the depth of information she was able to discern, which, joined with Charly's, made a complete picture.

However, this time Frances had insisted they book an organized tour, feeling that if it were left for others to control their schedule while in Turkey, they would get into less trouble. Fine with Charly. In fact, she had been glad to have the opportunity to control her own destiny for once.

At present Frances was lost in her own reverie of what lay ahead for the two of them, but along a line which would have surprised Charly. In fact, she was worried about just how to tell Charly that, while buying dates at their local Middle Eastern food market, the owner, Besim, upon learning that she and Charly were traveling to Turkey, had asked her to take a gift to his cousin. Frances had readily agreed, as this would be a good excuse to visit the "real people" of Turkey again, away from the tour for just a day or two. Consulting a map, she had been relieved to see that it didn't look too far from where the tour would be going to the home of Besim's cousin; just a side trip away in the mountains in the Hakkari region. Relieved, she had stopped by the Mosque Market to pick up the present the day before they left.

"I didn't wrap it so you could see what it was. And here is a note to go along with it." Besim had handed her the latest CD of a well-known rock band. "Do you like this band? You can listen to it if you want."

"Uh, no, I don't think I will, but thanks." Frances inwardly cringed as she thought of the hard-hitting music, which she could enjoy for no more than two minutes at a time. It certainly wasn't the gentle rhapsodies of the Great Masters, which she loved.

"If you don't mind, here's some paper to wrap it in when you get there. Customs officials don't like wrapped packages."

COMPLICATED FAVORS: A TURKISH AFFAIR

Somehow, I don't think Charly will be too happy about this! Frances had allowed this fleeting thought to escape for consideration at a later time.

The two women were curiously silent on this seven-hour flight. For Frances, memories of her three-year sojourn to Turkey in the 1960s occupied most of her thoughts. *Who would still know me at Roberts College? Anyone? Will my residence house on campus look any different? Will my favorite pide bakery still be at the bottom of the hill? Can I still find my way around Istanbul on the dolmus? I love that little bus. You meet such interesting people. Will the Hilton still have wonderful afternoon English Teas?*

Charly was busy trying to learn some colloquial phrases to go with her very passable if stilted Turkish. The tapes she had gotten from Learning Practical Turkish plus Frances' good memory of pronunciation had gotten her off to a credible start. Fortunately, hooking up with a couple of Turkish graduate students two months ago had really done the trick.

Some of her thoughts led invariably to the delicious food that might be encountered during their tour. Charly was an accomplished gourmet cook and wine connoisseur, and loved to taste foods from other cultures and then make her own versions of them. Frances was a frequent guest at her table, and provided kind critiques, as well as frequently supplying her own creative Middle Eastern fare.

As she closed her eyes to review Turkish vocabulary and their tour agenda, the images immediately came forcefully into Charly's consciousness again. This had begun three weeks ago when they had received their itinerary and Charly began reading Turkish travel books about the places they would be going, and accessing the Internet for the most interesting sounding side trips which covered places Frances had not visited forty years ago. Most of this research had been done in the beautiful early fall weather on her patio. The Oregon rains were yet to come and the pungent smell of pine was a fitting backdrop to the gaily blooming daisies.

Leaning back in the comfortable rocking lounge chair one afternoon, she had closed her eyes to the bright afternoon sun, absorbing the warmth of the mid-September day. No sooner had her eyes closed than vivid, colorful images appeared of robed people walking an uneven, stony street between two- to three-story block buildings. From the window sills of these dwellings, flowers perkily waved in the breeze, along with colorful lengths of cloth. Charly remembered thinking how unusual it was for her to be seeing what might pass as a dream as soon as she closed her eyes and certainly was not asleep. Curious, she continued to look around the scene, and soon found that people in the street had paused and were looking in her direction. A woman in Muslim attire, with head swathed but face bared, waved at her and began shouting to her in a language she did not understand. Several others started doing the same. She did not sense any anger in the shouts, only that they were trying to make her understand. It seemed that the longer she could not comprehend the louder and more agitated their arm waving became. Finally, several women unfurled a white cloth with writing on it. Charley recognized the Arabic script, but could not read it. She tried very diligently to do so, as it seemed so important to them that she understand. As she watched, one by one the figures stopped talking and waving, and faded away. She was puzzled by the fact that she had "watched" this scene while totally conscious of sitting on her patio, and had spent the remainder of the afternoon wondering what the people had been trying to convey.

COMPLICATED FAVORS: A TURKISH AFFAIR

When Charly went to bed that night and for the next few weeks before going to Turkey, she would no sooner close her eyes than similarly vivid images would appear. The women were always dressed in black garb to their shoes, with their heads covered and a scarf or *hijab* drawn over their foreheads. Men were robed, too, and wearing fezzes. The images never tried to talk with her again, but would walk along beside her over rocky, mountainous terrain. Sometimes they would be in the distance with camels or donkeys and would wave. At other times just their faces were close and they appeared to be gazing at her. At first when she was a bit scared or startled by what was happening, they would disappear all of a sudden. As they became familiar, Charly began to enjoy the images, thinking of them as an adventure. She was particularly fascinated with the multi-story structures, which seemed to come from the hillside itself, and the rugged pinnacles sometimes seen in the distance.

So the images are still with me, she thought now. *But what do they mean?*

Charly and Frances landed in Istanbul wide awake and dawdled their way along, changing money into Turkish lire, locating baggage, and getting lost on the way to customs. They were the last ones to go through, and the bored agent motioned for them to hurry to him, only to be followed by opening the door for them to exit. No customs check here! By the time they made it to the street and were looking for signs for the tour, it was evident that there was a van-load waiting none too patiently.

The drive to their hotel took about an hour, twice what it should have. The traffic was horrific, with lanes going from three to two or two to one with no apparent warning. This led to cars coming into an intersection at odd angles, all honking, with their drivers shouting and waving their fists as they jockeyed for position. After observing this wide-eyed for awhile, Charly voiced her amazement that there weren't any accidents. A closer look revealed most cars had multiple scratches and dents, none which prevented aggressive driving.

Check-in went smoothly but tediously because there were twelve arriving at the same time.

"Look how everyone is just sitting back, waiting for someone to hand them a key. Can't we just do it ourselves? It would be faster." Charly was getting very impatient. Graciously waiting was not one of her virtues as it was for Frances.

Frances, sitting calmly in an overstuffed chair, smiled. "You're supposed to just relax. This is a tour and they'll take care of us."

Charly rolled her eyes and continued fidgeting. "I hate just waiting."

"Well, you'll be doing it a lot on this tour. Adjust."

Charly scowled at Frances' flip, if logical, advice.

Their room was comfortable with twin beds and a European-style bathroom, complete with bidet. The view from their sixth story was of the roof across the street with various vintages of antennae. Below, two fresh fruit vendors were hawking their wares. An *abayah*-clad woman walked into the small grocery store across the street, cloth shopping bag in hand. On her heels was a woman in a smart suit clicking along in her high heels. *Ah, contrasts*, thought Charly.

It was three o'clock in the afternoon, seven in the morning at home.

"Tea time," Frances enthusiastically proclaimed.
"Hmm? How about a little nap?"
"No, no. It's time for tea. We're in Istanbul!" Frances' face was wiped clear of any fatigue. All that remained was unmitigated enthusiasm and anticipation.
"Okay," Charly gamely responded, as she could not resist.
"Where will we have this tea of yours?" *As if I don't know, Frances. You are so transparent!*
"At the Hilton, of course. That's where my friends and I would always go about once a month for a taste of the West. I'd get my hair done and we'd eat hamburgers. "
"Do you know how to get there from here?"
"No clue. I have no idea where we are."
At the desk they asked the clerk to call a cab for them to go to the Hilton. They were informed that it was close enough to walk. A cab would be a waste of money and the driver's time.
"Only a couple of blocks. Here, I'll draw a map."
The handwriting was barely decipherable, but being game they set out. They turned right and headed down a gently sloping street to Taksim Square, three blocks away. Every ten feet or so they were accosted by young boys with t-shirts for sale, robed woman selling homemade handicrafts, or street vendors holding up ripe figs or oranges. Alleys were dangerous places, as people parked their cars at odd angles, barely leaving enough room for a vehicle to pass through, which bicycles and small cars did at top speed. The sidewalks were awash with people of various ages and garb hurrying along and then suddenly dashing across the street, zig-zagging their way through traffic. Dominant were smells of cooking, gas and diesel exhaust, sweat, the noise of honking horns, yelling drivers, and hawkers shouting to get their attention.

Frances felt right at home as memories rushed back. At first she tried to politely engage the vendors in simple conversation, looking at what they proffered, and smiling. That led to the intensifying of the sell and drew others even from across the street to engage in boisterous competition. Frances' smiling "no" or "*hayir*" only seemed to encourage them.

Charly, on the other hand, did not feel charitable toward being swarmed, and employed the Turkish "no" consistently and unsmilingly. A quick tilting back of the head while *"tsk-tsking"* between the teeth worked wonders. After the initial attempt, Charly was not bothered again. Frances could not bring herself to "be so rude," so Charly took her arm and *tsk-tsked* their way to Taksim Square.

The roads did indeed merge at this intersection as the hotel clerk had said, and from all directions. They paused to take in this famous square designed nearly one hundred years ago. "This had been the branching point, thus *Taksim*, from the city's water distribution system," Frances shared.

Always the teacher, Charly thought with a smile.

Pointing to a statue on the opposite side of the square, Frances informed Charly, "That's Ataturk."

"Who?"

With only a touch of exasperation Frances informed Charly, "Ataturk was the founder of modern Turkey. You'll be hearing a lot about him, and seeing all the statues you can handle. We'll even visit his museum in Ankara. You'd better do some research, Charly."

Whoop-de-do! Statues and most museums were way down on Charly's list of what she found interesting. *I sure as the devil hope it's not going to be "that" kind of tour.*

Around the square was the Marmara Hotel, opera house (Ataturk Cultural Center), an open space which Frances pointed out had once been the reservoir, a park, and a variety of small and large shops, many of them eating establishments.

It was at this point that the hand-drawn map became useless. Frances and Charly stood on the street corner pointing at the map and word "Hilton" and asking for directions. Charly was learning that speaking with her tutors was entirely different than the quick pace of normal conversation. Charly just kept repeating *Hilton* whereas Frances would politely use her Turkish, which came back with amazing speed after forty years of nonuse. In response, they received an invitation to join an elderly bearded and robed gentleman for coffee in addition to slightly different pointed directions from each of several others they approached.

Determined, they dashed across the street, not appreciating the fact that in Turkey cars had the right-of-way. Taking the average of the directions, they found a pathway through the park and a little peace from the noise as they passed old men on benches and children playing on the grass. This soon came to an end, as the direction they wanted to go was blocked by a large fenced area around a nondescript two-story building. Armed guards could be seen patrolling the grounds within a gated entrance. Smiling and waving, Charly approached the nearest guard intending to ask for directions. Before she got within twenty yards, he placed the rifle across his chest and shouted something incomprehensible to Charly.

"Charly, get back here," demanded Frances. "He's told you to stop."

"Ask him for directions. Surely he can point us in the right direction. While you're at it, ask him what he's guarding."

"Are you crazy? There was just a bombing in Taksim Square last week. You'll get us arrested or shot. Let's go!" Frances stalked off.

Too tired to argue and not wanting a smudge on their first day, Charly veered away from the guards and the fence. Her curiosity was even more aroused as to what they were guarding. There were no signs to give a clue. Charly and Frances skirted around the large, guarded fenced area, having to walk on a dusty uneven path for two blocks.

With relief Frances soon spotted the towering Hilton logo a couple blocks away. The "short walk," according to the hotel clerk, had taken them one hour and they were more than ready for a traditional afternoon tea.

Frances led Charly through the elegant lobby to the patio and chose a seat overlooking the Bosporus a short distance away. She was disappointed that the once gorgeous open view was now slightly marred by a large multistory hotel, which they later learned was the recently built Swiss Hotel. Nevertheless, the view was a magnificent panorama of foliage and ships in the distance.

Earl Grey tea and the variety of delicious tiny sandwiches they nibbled on could have been consumed at any of the Hiltons around the world. This sameness was what had appealed to Frances in the 1960s as it was a taste of home amongst the Istanbul Middle Eastern flavors and sights. Around five, the clientele changed to the elegantly clad in search of cocktails. Charly and Frances easily made the transition to champagne and *mese* of nuts and cheese. Frances barely paused in her litany of memories of her life in Turkey.

"It was quite a trip on the *dolmus* to get here. Arnavutkoy American College for Girls, later called Roberts College, was perched high on a hill in the area of Bebek. We had a beautiful view of the Bosporus and the city. To get bread I'd walk to the most delicious bakery and buy *pide*. Of course, I couldn't make the walk back up the hill now!"

"Did you live at the college?"

"We teachers lived in a three-story house with a lovely sloping yard. It was convenient for all to stay up there, and much more fun to be all together. We were from several different countries and became good friends. We'd take trips together, driving to Syria, Lebanon, or Jordan and all over Turkey." And Frances continued relating several more adventures.

When they were finally ready to return to their hotel, the waiter presented them with an attractive array of their leftovers on a beautiful china dish, adding a bit more to make it a substantial repast. He seemed confused when they said they weren't staying at the hotel and should not take the china with them, so they finally generously tipped him and left with the gift in hand.

Deciding not to chance a walk back to the hotel at dusk, they commandeered a cab and were chagrined at the five minute ride.

They did not further endear themselves to their tour group as they were forty-five minutes late for the welcoming party. A few remembered that they had waited for them at the airport and scowled as they entered the room, interrupting the tour director's talk. Pretending not to notice anything was amiss, they found a seat and poured themselves a juice cocktail from the nearby pitcher.

Frances and Charly's pleasure-taking in observing others and exploring the unusual was at its peak. Their doctorates in human development and psychology had well-honed their skills and whetted life-long interest in human behavior. Despite being physically tired from their trip, they stayed up late sharing their impressions of their first day in Istanbul and of a few fellow tour members.

The *muezzin* began the first call to prayer for the day. Charly immediately became awake and opened the windows to let the sounds wash over her. Having heard the *muezzin,* the servant of the mosque, summon the faithful to prayer before, she found the call as mesmerizing and somehow comforting now as she had the first time. Charly was enchanted as additional *muezzin* began at different times throughout the city, their calls reaching a crescendo before fading to the last, single, elongated note. Frances just turned over, covering her head with the pillow, asking that Charly do her ablutions first. Somehow those extra minutes really seemed to help prepare her for the day.

Charly reminded herself not to drink the water, although brushing teeth was okay. There was a card in the bathroom extolling the wonderful treatment that had been done to the water, but still, "don't drink it."

The bus was waiting in front of the hotel to begin the tour. There was quite a gathering of merchants trying to interest tourists in buying brightly colored head scarves, baby booties, postcards, and t-shirts. Noting their momentary bemusement, a heavily mustached, well built, sturdy man with flashing brown eyes took Frances' arm and ushered her through the enthusiastic sales folks and onto the bus, all the while tossing his head back with the tsk-tsk sound as the crowd miraculously parted in front of the two of them. Charly walked closely in their wake and he handed her onto the bus as well. Frances thanked him politely in Turkish, *Tesekuradur,* which elicited surprise. Soon thereafter, their helper took the driver's seat, tour guide Kamil did his count, and the bus rolled out.

Kamil explained that he and the driver, Hakan, had teamed for over ten years. Hakan was married with two children and was a wonderful father and Kamil married with none.

Was that bit of information given so early to warn off thoughts of a vacation romance, Charly wondered. *But since Turkey is a Muslim country, husbands and wives would surely be loyal to marriage or face dire consequences, so why the warning? Or was jail time only for women? Maybe it was just friendly information.*

"Frances, is adultery a crime for both men and women in Turkey?"

"I think men were exempt a few years ago. There's a draft in the Turkish Parliament to equalize punishment and have it only a crime if a spouse accuses the other. A strong secular movement wants to decriminalize it altogether."

"But how about religious marriages? Isn't more than one wife sometimes allowed?"

"It would be a criminal act. Why all these questions?"

"I was just wondering why Kamil told us he and Hakan are married. It seemed kind of odd timing."

"Relax, Charly. Stop analyzing for once and just enjoy."

But Charly couldn't resist. As she looked around the bus, she wondered who might be interested in a dalliance, married or not. Of the twenty-five members of their tour, all but three others were married or with their husbands. Charly immediately discounted a large, unpleasant looking thirty-something girl-woman, and another who might be a possibility as she was loud, brash, with poorly dyed black coarse hair and wore very tight clothing on her beginning-to-sag fifth-decade body. *Her husband must have saved himself the embarrassment of traveling with her by remaining at home.* Charly found certain characteristics very off-putting, and that woman seemed to have them all wrapped up in one package. *God, but*

JEANNE REEDER

I hate to think of the inconvenience of being trapped with her on a bus for fifteen days. Mentally shrugging, she decided to not let such worrisome thoughts muddle around in her head any longer, and concentrated on the scenery of Istanbul as they headed toward the old area and the Topkapi Palace, Saint Sophia, and the Blue Mosque.

- 2 -
A small key opens big doors
- turkish proverb -

So far the trip had been much more interesting than Charly had originally anticipated. She had been entranced with the spectacular beauty and richness of the jewels and incredibly fine workmanship displayed in Topkapi Palace and the Blue Mosque. The magnificent cathedral, Hagia Sophia, built in the 500s A.D., was covered from the ground up with plaques of red, yellow, and green marble blended with the mosaics and friezes. Although such magnificence greatly impressed her, it was the more everyday things that captured her heart. History pulsed through the crumbling wall of the viaduct. The varying sizes, colors, and materials of the minarets from which the muezzin called the prayers five times a day drew her attention and imagination.

Charly was intrigued with the contrast of dress on the streets, the friendly smiles and quick offers of assistance or tea. It was as if Turkish tea was the answer to all ills, including sneezes, bad humor, or too much rain. And it was interesting to whom they would offer it. Always to Frances, and it seemed to Charly only to her because she was with Frances. The Turks seemed to revere older women. Charly never saw them proffer tea to a rude tourist or one too busy swinging his head around sightseeing to bother to smile or try a greeting in Turkish.

She was feeling at home in Turkey and developing a clearer understanding why Frances loved it so.

By the fourth evening Charly was sure she had read the signs correctly. Hakan would squeeze her hand briefly and make quick eye contact as he helped her off the bus *It hasn't just been my imagination!* As they arrived at their hotel for the night in a small town near Bursa, Charly experimentally lightly squeezed Hakan's hand back, which was met with a quick nod. *Well, this could change things a bit. But how risky? After all, he is married and I'm certainly not looking for another involvement so soon. Oh well, a little flirtation might enliven things a bit. I wonder if there are any cultural rules? I can't ask Frances, that's for sure!*

Charly thought about Hakan while showering away the day's grime, but no revelations illuminated her dilemma. *I'm just going to adopt a wait-and-see philosophy, as foreign as it is to my nature!*

Her thoughts turned to the infamous Turkish bath later in the evening. Kamil had told the group that the waters on these grounds had been favorites of the sultanate families for many centuries. The hotel where they were staying had been built over the ruins with that in mind.

As Charly was selecting her dessert from the generously supplied buffet that evening, Hakan came close to her, almost at her elbow. Eying the array of sweets, but not looking at her, he asked her to meet him for tea after dinner. *"Birbardak cay incer misiniz?"* Charly looked at him in surprise. He must have thought she didn't understand. Since he spoke only sketchy English, he then pointed to himself, then her, saying *"cay"* and pointing toward the lobby, asking the question again in Turkish. Intrigued, Charly quickly nodded yes. After this couple of seconds "conversation," each returned to respective tables, he with his usual companion Kamil, and Charly with

Frances and some new friends from the tour. Charly wondered, *Did anyone notice anything? No.* They were animatedly enjoying their getting acquainted conversation and did not look up when she returned.

Charly was quiet as she wondered if she should meet him at all, and secondly, whether to include Frances. She had come on this trip to be Frances' companion, friend, and handy arm as they traversed uneven stone paths, not for herself. The idea of her having adventures beyond the tour, much less entering into a flirtation, had never numbered among her expectations. They had agreed to just relax this trip, not put themselves into an undercover situational analysis mode. Charly had made a conscious and firm (or so she thought) decision to remain unencumbered for this trip.

Charly had lost her husband the previous year in a traffic accident, and had not been interested in entering the dating game or a relationship which might hinder her freedom. Her marriage had been one of mutual respect and enjoyment, and one which encouraged exploring new horizons, just not those of a sexual nature. They had been very close, many had said "like two peas in a pod." She missed him, thought she probably always would, and felt a little guilty that it was less than what she had felt six months ago. She was rediscovering what it meant to no longer have a significant other to take into account in making decisions.

But I'm no longer married, so no restrictions. Whoa, girl, you're getting way ahead of yourself, Charly admonished. *We're only talking about tea!*

Thus chastised, Charly righteously and quietly got Frances' attention. "Hakan wants us to have *cay* with him after dinner. Frances readily agreed before returning to her storytelling. *Well, that should solve it all*, Charly thought.

After dinner, Frances and Charly adjourned to the darkened section of the lobby which the bar occupied. They ensconced themselves on a low couch, mostly hidden from passersby by verdant, low-hanging plants. When the waiter took their orders, they did not hesitate, ordering *rakı*, the delicious Turkish licorice flavored liquor which Frances already loved from previous visits and Charly had needed no time to develop a taste. They talked little, just sharing tidbits about those they had met. Giving Hakan a bit more time to join them, they had another *rakı*. Shrugging off his lack of appearing to a misunderstanding, they finally returned to their room.

Frances prepared for bed while Charly donned her swimsuit and headed for the indoor pool area, hoping it wasn't too late for the infamous Turkish bath. With a tip of the hat to modesty since she was in Turkey, Charly donned a t-shirt over her suit, knowing they had towels at the pool reception desk

The night was soft, nearly warm, and silent as she walked through the dimly lit flower gardens to the Turkish bath and mineral pool area, passing no one on the way. There were only a few people in the pools. Five middle-aged men stood in a circle conversing in the larger pool, and as Charly gently slipped into the water and began back stroke laps they stopped talking and stared. After three laps, she felt sufficiently like an intruder to shift over to the smaller, round pool, which had a beautiful cascading fountain in the middle. The water was warmer here, and she immersed to her chin, thinking how good it felt to be pampering her body with the same healing minerals that had soothed sultans over generations. Perceiving movement in the water, she opened one eye to see a young entwined couple peering around the fountain from the other side. Charly smiled and nodded and they ducked back.

Feeling this just was not to be her night for peaceful reflection, Charly abandoned the pool area and went to the desk to ask if she could make an appointment for the Turkish bath. The young Turkish Adonis shook his head, saying "too late." Noticing her obvious disappointment, the attendant shrugged and motioned her to follow him. Luckily she had learned that in Turkish a hand movement away from the body meant someone was beckoning, just the opposite of what the gesture meant in most Western countries. Passing through a small room housing a hot tub with one male occupant, he opened a door to an empty, highly misted steam room.

The large marble surface in the middle, perhaps twelve feet square and two feet high, was surrounded by a contiguous marble sitting area. Charly gently lowered herself onto the warmed bench and closed her eyes. Surrounded by the peace of solitude and warmth, she could feel the tensions of the bus ride and worry that Frances might catapult herself off the edge of some rocky pathway gradually fade.

Her thoughts turned to Hakan, idly wondering why he had not joined them for a drink after dinner. *Was it because Frances joined me? Well, hadn't I been told that single ladies should never go out alone in Turkey? And that Turkish men look very differently upon the direct glances and friendliness of American women than do our countrymen? "Scratch a Turk and find a romantic poet" was one of those supposed cultural truisms I read about before I came here. Turkish poetry and stories are well known for being titillating descriptive of longing and lusty love. So why am I thinking of that now?! What should I do, if anything, about Hakan?*

Charly allowed herself to daydream about the possibilities, which she found arousing and very pleasant. Deciding not to censor thoughts of this man with the flashing brown eyes, she was well into a delicious fantasy of sharing glasses of wine with him in the darkened gardens of this exotic resort hotel when the door opened and a slender Mediterranean appearing man in a brief bikini slid onto the bench nearest the door. They glanced at one another, nodded, and quickly looked away. After several minutes, the misty steam descended once again and Charly returned to her daydream, only slightly irritated by the interruption.

The intruder began dipping hot water from a nearby receptacle into which water lightly streamed, splashing it on the marble around him, causing steam to rise. Following his lead, Charly did the same and soon the room was dense with steam.

Standing, he walked the two feet to the flat marble in the center of the room and patted his hand, then laid face down. He motioned for her to do the same, and returned to the bench.

Thinking it was part of a Turkish bath ritual, Charly mimicked him and was pleasantly surprised by its warmth. She scooted toward the center and relaxed, absorbing the pleasant feeling engulfing the length of her body.

After a few minutes she was surprised by hot water being thrown on the marble pedestal and gently lapping against her. The sensuousness of this caressing water increased as it swirled against her from every angle, particularly between her slightly parted legs. Deep relaxation induced an almost hypnotic state.

She sensed that the illusive stranger had sat beside her and soon felt his hands massaging in what was to her a unique fashion, tapping with the five fingers held together, beginning with her back. As he proceeded to thoroughly massage, Charly guessed he was a professional who had come in at the request of the attendant on duty. It occasionally flitted across her mind that she should refuse these ministrations, but the pleasure brought to relaxing muscles was too keen. Thus reassured, she allowed herself to sink deep into a jelly state of pure enjoyment, and seemed to float on the intense steam over the warmed, wet marble.

Charly felt him shift his weight and straddle her, which had the effect to bring her into sharp awareness. When she felt his erection upon her bathing-suited hips, she abruptly turned over, unintentionally knocking him to the tiled floor. She nearly laughed at his startled expression as he sat shaking his head. Several thoughts simultaneously flitted through her drugged mind. He had done her a favor by the massage, but what would the price be? It was important to her to save face, so she smiled, held out her hand to him, and slapped the marble several times. Giving her an unsmiling, wary look, he got up and lay down on the marble pedestal.

Following his earlier example, Charly splashed the very hot water all around him, being sure no spot was left out. *If it felt as good to him as me, he should have the experience, too. Favors should be returned.*

She then began the massage, but the more typical kneading of muscles and using the two handed chop on the thighs. His body was firm and muscled without an ounce of extra fat. Short, fairly sparse body hair covered his body. He would occasionally moan, so she assumed she was doing an okay job.

After a few minutes, hoping to verify that he was a professional working in the Turkish bath area, she asked him if he worked at the resort. These were the first words spoken between them.

"No, I am a tour guide," he said with a heavy Turkish accent.

Oops! Charly said nothing further to him.

Charly continued to silently massage him until she had given as good as she had received. When completed, she slapped the marble twice, and said "Okay" and got up, extending her hand as a token of deed-done, and they shook hands.

Charly walked to the door of the steam room and turned the knob. After several tugs she realized the door was locked. He stood behind her; she could feel his warmth and just the breath of a touch. Again she twisted the knob and tugged but without results. *Terrific*, she thought, *what now?* Straightening to her five-feet-seven-inch height, she turned to face him and stomped her foot. "Open!"

He looked at her for a long moment, finally reaching over the door sill, retrieving a key, and unlocking the door.

Charly flounced ahead of him to retrieve her towel, room key, and t-shirt on one of the chairs on the other side of the pool. Her decorous extraction was somewhat hindered by slipping on the wet tiled floor a few times as she was noticing that no one was in either of the pools and the lights were now a lot dimmer.

When she walked into the anteroom with the attendant's desk, that, too, was unattended and darkened. She glanced at the clock: 10:45. She remembered reading that the Turkish baths closed at 10, a little before the time she had asked the attendant about the area. *What a stupid mistake,* she admonished herself. *I've behaved just the opposite of what the advice has been: don't go without a companion at night and never look a Turkish stranger in the eyes. I've certainly done both of these tonight and more. I wonder if touching means some sort of promising.*

The door leading to the hallway was unlocked, and Charly quickly exited, heading toward her room via dimly lit gardens. She heard the key turn, locking the outer door to the bath area. She could hear her companion of the steam room close behind her, but since exiting that room hadn't acknowledged him.

When she paused at the door with her key in hand, he faced her, saying "now you like full-body massage my room? Very good."

Even knowing how good it might be, and certainly exciting, she replied, "No thank you. I am tired and need to sleep. Besides, my roommate is waiting up for me."

He shrugged, they shook hands again, and he walked toward the staircase. Charly followed him with her eyes, wondering where her adventurous spirit was lurking, while at the same time being grateful that a potentially explosive situation in the steam room hadn't detonated.

Charly turned the key to her room and opened it, finding Frances poking her head from the bath, saying, "How was it?" Charly started laughing and sat on the edge of the tub while she told Frances her story.

Frances immediately blamed herself for not going. "I knew better. I've lived here before." But she also laughed with Charly, sensing her embarrassment for allowing herself to get into a potentially negative situation. They made a pact not to tell anyone.

It took a long time for Charly to fall asleep that night, as she alternately felt embarrassed and foolish for putting herself in that situation. But she also felt proud of the way she had handled it. After all, it had been an enjoyable adventure. And not a small part of her wondered what would have been if she had taken him up on his offer.

And where was Hakan?

The next morning after the usual Turkish breakfast of cucumbers, tomato wedges, feta, yoghurt, walnuts, boiled egg, honey-sweetened pastry and Turkish tea, they went quickly to the bus. Charly glanced around, wondering if she would encounter the stranger of last night and hoping she would not. *God, what if I find him talking with Hakan or Kamil? How would they react if he told them about last night? I'll hide! Damn, I can feel myself flush. From embarrassment, no less. Where did that come from? Maybe I just feel foolish. God, I sound like a teenager. Stop it!*

Arriving at the bus without sign of him, she breathed a sign of relief. Hakan handed Frances onto the bus as he had been doing for the first two days of the tour, but quickly walked away leaving Charly to contemplate his rigid back.

The remainder of the day she saw little of the scenery as her thoughts were with Hakan and why he was ignoring her. *Is he angry because Frances and I waited for him last night, instead of just me? Did he feel I was toying with him? Why am I dwelling on this rejection and why are his feelings so important to me? I feel a connection with him, for whatever reason. It feels like I've known him before. Maybe I should confront him in his own language since he doesn't speak English. But I'd really rather neither he nor Kamil know yet that I understand their side comments in Turkish. I'd probably mispronounce something and make it worse. Frances says I speak Turkish with an Arabic accent. Weird!* Charly spent most of the day using her palm-held electronic dictionary, opening a file for phrases which might relate to this quandary.

After correcting a few of Charly's pronunciations, Frances looked at her curiously. *I wonder why Charly is interested in getting down the accent right for "Are you angry?" Who did she offend now? Oh, well, none of my business.*

Late that afternoon Charly left Frances drinking tea with several others and went in search of Hakan. Finally finding him wandering alone around an ancient crumbling grave site, she approached him without speaking. They solemnly gazed at one another.

"I waited for you last night."

Hakan nodded, saying, "Yes, you and Frances."

"It is difficult. Frances and I are friends. I am sorry, *Uzgunum.*"

They slowly smiled timidly at each other and nodded. Both sensing a truce, they walked away, separately. When it was time to board, Hakan handed Charly onto the bus, giving her hand the now familiar and anticipated squeeze, which she reciprocated.

That evening Hakan and Charly again met at the dessert table and she asked him, through gestures and use of nouns, to have a drink with her and Frances after dinner. Ruefully smiling, he nodded.

Frances and Charly drank *rakı* and wrote postcards while they waited for Hakan to appear. He did not pause as he passed their table in the small bar when exiting the dining room until Frances called his name. "Hakan! Please join us."

They spent a pleasurable and mildly frustrating hour with Frances using her forty-year-old surprisingly good Turkish. Charly followed the conversational flow fairly well and tried to master her computer dictionary for terms she did not know. Of course that was impossible, as most base words had an ending or prefix. It went much more smoothly for Charly when she put away that crutch, relaxed, and actively joined the conversation. Her pronunciation was hilarious, and Frances kept trying to correct her as Hakan bemusedly just shook his head. They may not have learned much about each other but there was a lot of laughter and kindly gazing at one another along with the silences. Hakan showed them a photo of his two lovely teenage daughters. When asked about his wife, he did not seem to understand and shook his head.

As they left the bar together, the waiter came up to Hakan, kissing him on both cheeks. Hakan shrugged and said to Charly and Frances, "Turkish way."

Riding up together on the elevator Hakan and Charly stood to the side only a hair's breadth between their shoulders, hips and fingertips—close enough to feel the electric warmth. They stared straight ahead, as did Frances as she faced the elevator door. When Hakan exited a floor below theirs it was difficult for Charly not to follow him. *This trip might prove interesting after all,* Charly thought.

- 3 -
Study from new books, learn from old teachers
- turkish proverb -

Charly was fairly bubbling with enthusiasm. "I had no idea Bursa was a city of gardens and parks. Quite a contrast to Istanbul! On the outskirts there were a lot of fruit trees. Peaches? And the Green Mosque complex was fascinating. It's a beautiful city!"

Frances enthusiastically agreed. "It was the first capital of the Ottoman Empire. I guess this was logical, as it was the center of the silk trade. The first silk cocoons were brought here with the caravans of the Silk Road. And now, it's also the center for towel manufacturing."

"I'm so excited about seeing the beautiful silks and cotton products. If Turkish towels weren't so heavy I'd take a couple home, or maybe a large absorbent robe. What about you, Frances?"

"I'm looking for silk pillow shams and some scarves for friends back home. Something easy to pack."

"Did you visit here when you lived in Istanbul?"

"It's my first time in Bursa. I've been wanting to see this ancient capital, and of course visit the infamous bazaar. I heard it's been here since the early caravans came through."

Kamil made an announcement to the group just before the bus came to a stop at the Silk Bazaar. "You must return in exactly two hours to this spot. Set your watches. It's too crowded here for the bus to wait for stragglers. If you are left, you have to get back to the hotel on your own. This is a huge structure resembling a maze. Look for landmarks so you can find your way back. Don't just look at all the pretty things you want to buy or you'll get lost."

The side street leading into the bazaar was busy with merchants who had set up their kiosks to tempt those going in or for a final sale from those departing. A young boy sat on a wooden stool in front of his silk scarves and pillow covers, hands clasped, head bowed. Next to him was an old, bent man in white robes and beard loudly extolling his wares and waving silk scarves to entice.

As usual Frances and Charly were hungry and decided that eating was first on their agenda at the bazaar. They approached one of the many gendarmes serving as community or bazaar police asking where the restaurants were. Quickly surmising from his blank look and big smile that he understood no English, Frances managed to get their needs across. He beckoned them to follow and led the way through alleyways within the bazaar, making over a dozen turns. At first they tried to note landmarks, as Kamil had instructed, but soon became so turned around they concentrated solely on keeping their guide in sight.

The gendarme passed several cafés before finally stopping in an alleyway with two small tables. In front of a stall where the cooking was done stood a heavily mustached, bearded, tall, and toned man of around sixty wearing a fez and beaming from ear to ear. He and their escort shared the traditional embrace and kissed cheeks.

Charly and Frances were left in the hands of their host, Agah, who referred to a board with menu items in Turkish. As Frances applied herself to translating, Charly saw that behind the partially glassed-in window of the kitchen was a large skillet with what was rapidly becoming her favorite dish: Turkish goulash made with lamb, tomatoes, onions, and hot green peppers, and served along with *pide* and a salad rich with olive oil and lemon juice, with sliced lemons and additional hot peppers on the side. Charly thought this had to be one of the most satisfying dishes ever invented.

Agah turned to Frances. "And you, dear lady, must have *Iskender Kebap.*"

Frances clapped her hands. "Yes! The famous Bursa dish. I've had it elsewhere, but I must have it in Bursa!"

"So what's this *Iskender Kebap?*"

"You'll see. You've already had versions of it. Translated, it's Alexander's Roast Lamb. You know, lamb roasted on a spit, but very special because it's raised on the nearby thyme-covered slopes of Mount Uludag. You'd probably know it because of its ski resort south of here. Anyway, it's named for a chef from Bursa who created it about one-hundred-forty years ago. The lamb is spread atop diced flat *pide* bread, then topped with spicy tomato sauce and browned butter, served with a dollop of yoghurt on the side."

"My God, that sounds delicious! Will you let me taste?"

Frances laughed. "Of course!"

Their Kurdish host was impressed with Frances' knowledge of this famous Bursa dish. "Although *Iskender Kebap* is now served throughout Turkey in many restaurants, the best is still made in Bursa. Be warned: it's addictive!"

As soon as they were seated at one of the two tables, Turkish tea was placed in front of them.

Agah only delayed his joining them long enough to give the order to the cook. He spoke in heavily accented but very good English and proceeded to relate how he had learned the language so well and had enough money to buy his bazaar café.

"I come from a tiny village near Diyarbakir. Do you know the American air base near there? There was an American pilot who was traveling around the area with Turks on reconnaissance and came into my father's café for coffee. I was a young man then working with my father. I served him coffee. The Turkish soldiers roughed us up trying to get information, but the American calmed them down and got them to leave.

"He returned the next day, alone, and using simple Turkish, apologized. I offered to share the hookah I was enjoying with my friends. That was the beginning. Over the next two years he came by a lot. There was a lot of trouble in our area with smuggling drugs, and the Turkish military were always harassing our villagers. They destroyed two nearby villages. Our American friend would talk with them and assure them we were good people who did not harbor criminals, and they left us alone.

"Soon after he returned to America, the Turks burned our village and killed many. My family and I fled to Diyarbakir. It's a big city with many Kurdish refugees. Once we left, we no longer wrote to our American friend. He retired, returned to Turkey, and tried to visit, but our village had been destroyed. It took him one month to track us down. He gave us money as a gift before he returned to America. He said it was the only way he knew how to repay our kindness to him when he was a lonely soldier in a strange land. He told me to use it to start a business."

Beaming, Agah spread his arms wide to encompass his tiny café of which he was immensely proud.

Charly expressed her curiosity. "Have you Kurds been behaving yourselves lately?"

Perhaps this was a rude question by some standards, and clearly Frances thought so, judging by the outraged glare she gave Charly. But Charly was spurred by her wariness of Turkey's repression of the Kurds, which began with Kemal Ataturk's election as President of Turkey in 1923. Ataturk was revered throughout Turkey, by the Turks, not the Kurdish or religious Muslims.

Without even a slight pause to reflect, Agah responded. "You must mean the recent bombings in Istanbul, don't you? Yes, there are still terrorists, probably mostly PKK, who continue fighting for their rights with violence. But do you know why we religious Muslims are so angry?"

"Well, I know that he gave women the right to vote," Frances quickly responded. "Why would this anger them?"

"Not that part, my lady, although surely a lot of husbands were put out for awhile! Nor did the Law of Surnames upset many, epitomized by Mustafa Kemal being given the name Kemal Ataturk, Father of Turkey. No, I mean the changes which hit Turkey at its very core. It was the laws banning Islam as the state religion, of it being illegal for children to attend religious schools, and even taking away our language."

"What do you mean, taking away your language? You mean outlawing Kurdish?" Charly ventured.

"Turkish was made not only the official language, but the only language which could be spoken in public. Prior to that, Ottoman Turkish was spoken and written for all civil, religious, and military matters."

"What's the difference?"

"Arabic was the primary language of religious matters as Persian was of art, refined literature, and diplomacy. Administration of the Ottoman Empire used Turkish mixed with those two."

"I remember that being discussed when I was teaching here," Francis said, nodding her head. "The grandparents of the children usually spoke more Arabic than Turkish. The parents wanted the children to learn English as a second language. I always thought that with such close Arab neighbors, Persian or Arabic would have been a more practical choice."

"Yes, a common problem. Ataturk himself went around to the villages, holding audiences in the parks to teach the new Turkish alphabet to the children. A whole new vocabulary was devised by a government appointed Committee of Scholars."

"You must have been a child when all this was going on. Do you remember it at all?"

"I remember the celebrations when public outrage finally resulted in the overthrow of Ataturk's law that Islamic call to worship and public readings of the Quran be in Turkish, and we once again resorted to Arabic. I remember very well the anger, most of all the anger that we could not attend school in our own language. Anger that due to the Hat Law men could not wear the fez or women the headscarf in public."

"After all these years, it's just the same, isn't it?" Charly prompted.

"And that is what fuels the PKK and other terrorists who have resorted to violence to win freedom. Now for the first time we have a pro-Muslim party in the majority in Parliament. Between that and Turkey wanting to join the European Union, many of us are hopeful for the first time. Until there is more equality, one can expect terrorist acts from small factions."

Agah gazed at Frances and Charly as they listened with great empathy. *These are people I can trust.* He learned through their questions and reactions that this empathy sprang from their being strong individualists who did not believe the government had a right to dictate attire, language, or religion, although Frances was having a more difficult time reconciling this than Charly. *Interesting because Frances voices agreement with Ataturk, but shows in her heart otherwise.*

The delicious food and scintillating conversation went well beyond the two-hour limit and they hadn't even had a chance to shop. Noting the dilemma, Agah insisted upon closing his closet café and taking them to his friends' shops.

The next hour sped by as they looked through beautiful silk scarves, shirts, pillow covers, and luxurious Bursa toweling while sipping tea each shop owner provided. This common practice greatly increased the time necessary to decide what to purchase. Some tourists refused the offer of a stool and the *cay*, briskly doing their business with a minimum of social interaction. Participating in this cultural ritual had become as important to Frances and Charly as what they bought.

Bargaining for the price went better than they had previously experienced at other places. It probably helped to have Agah lurking close by, trying on a shirt Frances wanted for her brother-in-law, and playfully draping a dozen silk scarves around his shoulders and prancing around the shop.

In high spirits, the three new friends walked toward the exit arm-in-arm through the alleyways when space allowed. They passed a couple from the tour group who had also obviously missed the bus. They stared at Charly and Frances, startled to see them with the distinguished Kurd but nodded and walked by as they waved packages at one another.

Before bidding them goodbye, Agah asked if he could meet them before dinner to continue their conversation. Because they already had plans with new tour friends for before dinner drinks in their room, Charly suggested they meet after dinner. Frances quickly glanced at her, shaking her head. Charly chose to ignore her, and they agreed to meet in the lobby bar at ten o'clock.

Putting them in a cab, Agah negotiated the price to their hotel with the driver who appeared quite deferential. The cab took off like a bat out of hell, tires, then brakes, squealing and nearly missing a young boy pushing a cart piled high with brightly colored clothing who was intent upon his tourist prey across the street.

Frances seems lost in thought, or maybe she's just terrified of the erratic driving. "Why so quiet Frances?"

"I was thinking about a village near Diyarbakir. I want to take a side trip there."

"You mean leave the tour?"

"Only for a couple of days."

"Frances, what's up? What aren't you saying? And why all of a sudden?"

Okay, this is it. I can't delay telling Charly any longer. Frances took a deep breath and began her explanation. "You know Besim at the Mosque Market at home?"

"Well, of course! But what does he have to do with anything?" *I wonder if this is one of Frances' famous diversions to avoid the topic?*

"He gave me a gift before we left. A CD."

""Well, that's nice. Turkish music?" Mentally shrugging, Charly turned to watch a street vendor shaking his fist at a car that had almost hit him.

"Not for me. For his cousin in Turkey."

Charly snapped her wandering attention back to Frances. "But you barely know Besim! We're not supposed to transport gifts from strangers."

Frances was indignant. "He's not a stranger, Charly! I've been shopping there for several years."

Charly shook her head. *No use arguing. I've learned that long ago. When she "'knows," she "knows."*

Changing tactics to safer ground, Charly continued trying to get the full story. "How are you supposed to get to these people? Are they here in Bursa? Istanbul? Have you called them?"

"Besim said they live in a small village near the Sat-Cilo Mountains in the Hakkari region. I thought you might like to go visit."

And just like that, Charly thought, Frances has it all settled in her mind. Just a little side trip.

"Have you arranged this with Kamil? To leave the tour?"

"Well, not yet. But I will." *That wasn't so difficult. Charly didn't throw me out of the cab in disgust, anyway. I know I should have told her before we left home, but why add complication before it's necessary?*

Charly sat back in her seat, exasperated, mulling over this new dimension to their trip. Soon, the beginning of a grin tugged at her lips. *I just cannot be upset over such clearly Frances-behavior. I love her too much to upset this trip for her.* Now putting her mind in gear to find a solution, she felt easier. *How on earth can we deliver the gift for Besim?*

They arrived at their hotel after twenty harrowing minutes of dodging other vehicles and aggressively nosing the car into traffic as the lanes abruptly went from two to one, then back again. Unclenching their hands, which had been holding tightly onto the side of the car and the back of the front seat, they paid the two million Turkish lira, and with relief for being in one piece, exited the cab.

"So, will you go with me?"

"Let's look into it, Frances. We'll see what we can do about it."

There was just time for a quick shower and change into one of the several long-sleeved sweaters each brought and their "good" pair of slacks. A knock on the door announced the arrival of the ice and extra glasses, on the heels of which appeared two friends carrying various types of *mese* and their own choice of libation. Charly put aside her concern with Frances' revelation to enjoy the evening.

After pouring drinks, they settled down to share their reactions of their day in Bursa before the dinner hour for their tour group. As Charly wrapped herself around her rakı, she caught the eye of Megan. Megan was a well-traveled woman in her early sixties who kept in well-toned condition by meditating, practicing yoga daily, and taking long, rapid hikes through the hilly Welsh countryside near her home. She was a psychologist teaching at a local university who also practiced Reiki, a mystical form of healing which fascinated Charly. Megan sensed there was something more to share later. After this moment of recognition, they returned their attention to the others, entering an ongoing discussion of their purchases in the Silk Bazaar and their degree of prowess at bargaining.

Gwen, a white-haired, jovial nurse from Florida, was particularly quiet as she drank her Coke. During the short time knowing her, they had all felt the good feeling brought on by her gentle smile, but not tonight. One by one awareness of her preoccupation quieted the others.

"Gwen, why so pensive?"

"I just read an e-mail from my son. The U.S. has placed our military and embassy personnel in Turkey on Delta alert. He wants me to come home."

"That's the highest status, isn't it? Why now?" inquired Megan.

"I accessed the U.S. State Department website and pulled this up." Gwen unfolded a printout and handed it to Megan.

Megan read aloud. "'The U.S. Government has indications that individuals may be planning terrorist actions against United States citizens and interests in the Persian Gulf, the Arabian Peninsula, and Turkey. U.S. citizens should exercise caution in considering travel to these areas at this time. American citizens in the region should avoid large crowds and demonstrations, maintain a low profile, and take appropriate steps to reduce their vulnerability. Americans should vary routes and times for all required travel and treat mail from unfamiliar sources with suspicion.'"

"It's dated today and expires in three months, on January 17."

Frances turned on the television to BBC and within a few minutes a similar announcement was made.

Each reacted in a similar fashion, realizing that there was nothing they could do but be vigilantly alert to suspicion of a terrorist act and continue the practice of not going out alone. The absurdity of being able to pick out a terrorist in a crowd got them chuckling as Charly's descriptions of searching the street for poorly dressed, swarthy, bearded Arabs carrying a bomb under their robes became increasingly absurd. They all agreed to watch BBC more regularly as they made their way to the elevator for dinner. Talk turned to favorite desserts they hoped would be available tonight.

We sound so light-hearted, Charly thought. *But I know we're all worried. None of us will go home, so all we can do is trust the protection of our tour. Wish I had my gun, just in case.* Charly noticed that Gwen had quietly removed the USA pin she always wore.

Kamil did not inform the tour group of the heightened alert.

- 4 -
No matter where you go destiny follows you
- turkish proverb -

It was 9:30 by the time they left the dining room. Frances and Gwen pleaded tiredness and went to their rooms. Megan and Charly headed to the lobby bar in view of the entrance to the hotel. Even though they had not known each other long, they had shared several discussions of mysticism, Jung, Freud, dream interpretations, and the possibility of a past life. They had a strong empathic response toward each other. Enjoying a rakı, eschewing *mese*, Charly filled Megan in on the Silk Bazaar experience, her encounter with Agah, and the plans for tonight.

"Are you game to stay and talk with Agah if he comes?"

"You bet. Wouldn't miss it. But in view of the Delta alert, isn't this the kind of thing they are warning against, meeting with strangers?" asked Megan.

"Very likely. But wait until you meet Agah. You'll be sympathetic to the Kurdish cause, too, once you've heard his story."

"Well, I already am. The Kurds in Turkey have been repressed for a long time, all in the name of westernization. They're not even counted in the census! But I don't want to spend the night in jail if someone from the Turkish military comes in and takes offense."

"Don't worry about it. We're just going to be able to learn firsthand what we only read about," encouraged Charly.

At that point, Agah walked up to the table and Charly rose to greet him and introduce Megan.

"I do not have much time. My friends are here for a demonstration tomorrow and we need to meet beforehand. I am sorry I did not know about it when I met you earlier."

Noting Charly's disappointment, he continued. "Since you are interested in the plight of we Kurds, please come with me. Who knows? You may even want to join us tomorrow." At this, he chuckled.

Charly and Megan exchanged a glance, Megan shrugged, smiled, and said, "why not?"

Feeling adventurous, fortified by a good dinner and rakı, they rose of one accord and left money on the table. They were walking toward the exit as Hakan was leaving the dining room. Charly's eyes met Hakan's, and she paused. Feeling a tug on her sleeve, she resumed walking toward the exit with Megan and Agah.

The night was chilled by the drizzling rain, and Charly pulled her newly purchased Turkish wool shawl around her. Not having brought a coat to Turkey in October was a definite error but helped justify the purchase.

They walked several blocks along the dimly lit streets before entering a small store selling bottled water, juices, milk, and a variety of snack foods. It was similar to many they had seen in every town on this trip so far. The man at the counter nodded and they continued to the back.

Asking them to remain in the main area, Agah pulled aside a curtain. Before it closed Charly glimpsed several bearded men wearing fezzes. After a lengthy monologue, angry voices erupted. Charly wished they spoke in Turkish so she could understand. Megan was just as lost, as Kurdish wasn't one of her several dialects either.

"Must be Kurdish."

"I think that's a given, Charly. Logical, don't you think?"

Charly just rolled her eyes.

Agah replied to the angry men with just as much vigor. After several minutes of these exchanges, the voices lowered. Agah came back to them, handed each an *abayah*, a long robe with hood. Donning them, they entered, sitting on the cushions indicated behind the men. No one was introduced.

"We try to speak English, but is not so good," the man who appeared to be the group leader told them.

One by one, with varying degrees of English mastery, they told them tales of their families' persecution in their home village, now reduced to rubble.

All were from the same village in the Hakkari region. They were visiting in the old section of Istanbul, which had an enclave of Kurds. One man had been born in southeastern Turkey. The other four had fled Iraq after the Gulf War because of the stepped up persecution by Saddam Hussein. One of them described murders in the middle of the night and of dozens in a neighboring village dying by an attack with poisonous gas. One never knew who was next.

"Our Kurdish brothers in Turkey welcomed us into their villages. They let us stay with them until we could build shelters of our own."

With Agah translating freely, their story of oppression continued.

"It soon became apparent that the Turkish government expected us to assimilate into their culture, abandoning our own. We could not do this. Our souls are with Islam. Our best chance of survival was to maintain our Kurdish language and culture. Refusal to stop wearing the fez meant harassment, arrest, and torture, which we endured. Agitation grew as small groups of men met to discuss what could be done. Some wanted to comply outwardly at least, but in their hearts and homes to practice Kurdish ways. Others spoke of daring terrorist acts to force not only Turkey but other governments to appreciate and assist in remedying their plight. Out of this rose the infamous terrorist Öcalan.

"He was a strong leader who banded the fragmented groups together. Some of us joined the PKK, others not. No matter. They destroyed our homes anyway. They killed our young men. We started to rebuild. They came back. We had to leave. Many deaths of the Turkish soldiers occurred which did not gain the PKK sympathy, but fear, anger, and reprisals. "

The mention of Hakkari pricked Charly's interest as that was near where Frances was to deliver the small gift from Besim.

Excusing her entry into the conversation, Charly remarked, "*Affedersiniz*. My friend has a gift to deliver in the village of Mehvit. Perhaps you know the person to whom it goes."

This was met with silence as eyes opened wider and the men looked at one another. All began taking in Kurdish at the same time. After several minutes, Agah asked her how she had received the package, the person's name, contents of the package, and her plans for delivery.

"A friend in my friend's hometown gave her a gift for his cousin. He thought the personal touch of a friend from America delivering it would mean a lot to his family. The name of the family is Raif."

"What is in the package?"

"Music."

"How will she get there?"

"*Bilmiyorum*, I don't know. Take a bus or rent a car from Konya, I guess."

They were clearly dissatisfied with the vagueness of no delivery plan and thought she must be lying.

"Why aren't you telling us more?"

Another interrupted, "She is a mule for the CIA. She is working with the Turkish government and is testing us."

Murmuring assent, they all nodded and stood up.

The spokesman for the group announced, "We will accompany you to the hotel to get the package and deliver it for your friend. It is too dangerous for you two women to go there."

Not liking this high-handed attitude, Charly stood, bowed, and politely declined. *"Teşekkürler, hayir."* I want to deliver it to his family myself. Besim is a good friend." Only a slight exaggeration, as she thought about the owner of the mosque grocery store.

After exchanging looks with the others, Agah shrugged, smiled, and said, "It's time to go now. I will walk you back. You will be safe with me."

The walk back was quiet, each busy with his or her own thoughts. Charly finally broke the silence, first asking what his friends were so upset about, to which Agah responded that they were just trying to help.

"What's the demonstration tomorrow?"

"The Democratic People's Party, the DEHAP, is pro-Islamic. They are trying to gain seats in Parliament and are staging demonstrations for their cause. "

They passed only a couple of people. Most shops were closed.

Hakan sat alone at the table in the bar area, watching the entrance to the hotel, wondering where Charly had gone and why. He had recognized that her escort was Kurdish, but had been unable to follow them. As he was headed toward the exit Kamil had waylaid him, saying that one of the group had left her purse on the bus. Now all he could do was await Charly's return.

Hakan laughed at himself. *I thought this was going to be just another boring tour, driving the bus while Kamil pontificates. Mischief or worse by the Kurdish terrorists has been at a reduced level since Öcalan's capture. I was lulled by it. You dummy! Why do you think there's a new elevated countrywide security alert? I should have been more alert, instead of mesmerized by Charly's eyes. I like the way she dresses, too. In that tiny suitcase she carries, out come the most attractive outfits. Her close-fitting pants and her body-hugging sweaters define a slim, almost boyish body. Ah, but what lies beneath is no boy! I've seen the light in her eyes. Ah, ipsiz, you jerk! I've been better trained than that. Damn, I goofed. First time a woman has interfered with my training. Allah! I wonder what that means.*

He shook his head, feeling very uncomfortable with these thoughts. While waiting, he had called his unit commander and asked him to check out Charly. As a matter of course as security intelligence officer, he had everyone's passport number and could check on them if indicated.

Who would have thought! Charly has worked as an operative with the CIA. There is no indication that she is working on an operation here. Usually we're told and do all we can to cooperate. If so, I would have been informed she was on my tour. I've got to find out what's going on here.

Hakan rationalized his concern. He felt he had a right, of sorts, to notice and care as he sensed the beginning of an undetermined relationship with Charly. It was more than just an obligation because she was on his tour or that it was his job as an agent to perceive a dangerous situation and prevent its development.

COMPLICATED FAVORS: A TURKISH AFFAIR

Damn, here's that circle again. Admit it, man, your attraction to her has clouded your observations. I wonder if her trip is related to some mission and not just a nice trip with her friend. I was resentful of them sticking so close together, but maybe she was just avoiding me. Showing up with Frances for a drink after dinner, when I had only asked Charly, really made me angry. Why did it affect me so much? Pretending only to speak a few words in English certainly didn't work to my advantage with the invitation to Charly the other night.

Hakan's undercover role had gotten in the way in communicating his intentions to Charly. Experience had taught him that by pretending not to speak another's language he usually gleaned more information.

Hakan felt that if he were ever alone with Charly, he could rapidly determine the extent of his interest in her. He visualized her beautifully expressive green eyes and felt himself becoming aroused. He ordered another rakı and indulged himself in erotic thoughts of the two of them together as he became increasingly uncomfortable.

Thus absorbed, he almost missed her as she and Megan strode into the hotel. Scanning the lobby, Charly immediately noticed Hakan. Their eyes locked. Charly automatically took a few steps in his direction, remembered Megan, and quickly said she would talk to her in the morning.

"But I thought we would talk over what happened tonight. Let's go to my room for a drink."

Megan noticed Hakan across the room. "Ah, I see. Okay, see you for breakfast. *Hoşçakalın!*" Megan winked, waved, and walked toward the elevator without a backward glance.

Whatever is or isn't going on between them isn't my business, but, she thought, *good for them.* Although fifty, Charly was a lot younger than that in appearance and energy, and was certainly daring. Having known her for only a few days, Megan was nevertheless aware that with Charly a relationship with Hakan could easily develop beyond casual dalliance. Her intuition as half-Arab told her their souls recognized each other. *As did ours. Jealous, am I? No, just wishful thinking. Inclinations aren't in sync this time around—maybe in our next life.*

Hakan followed Charly's approach to the table, rising to pull out a chair for her while continuing to hold her gaze. He noticed her face was flushing, as he felt his was also. When both were seated, the waiter automatically brought them each a rakı and more pistachios. It was several minutes before they broke their silence.

Abruptly his mood altered and with barely concealed anger he confronted Charly. "Tonight, who was the stranger? You could be hurt. How do you know him? Why did you go with him?" Hakan's brown eyes flashed and there was no softness in him now.

At first Charly started to take offense at his audacity to question her. She had a strong aversion to being controlled or having things demanded of her. *How dare he? It isn't any of his business.* But underneath his anger she could sense his concern for her. *Otherwise, why be so angry?*

"My, my, but your English has improved," Charly responded in Turkish.

At first Hakan stiffened, blustered a bit, but said nothing. As if he had made some decision, he turned his hand over and gently intertwined their fingers, expressively rolling his eyes before once again capturing her gaze. His anger left as quickly as it had come.

"Looks like we both have been playing a game, Charly. Which language shall it be?"

"More privacy for now if we speak English, so let's go with that."

Charly smiled and poured a little water into her rakı, watching it turn murky. *Maybe that is what Hakan and I are like. Maybe there is just too much clouding understanding between us.*

Hakan and Charly sat silently for a few minutes nibbling on pistachios and sipping rakı.

Knowing that he deserved an explanation, Charly proceeded to describe how she and Frances had met Agah and about the night's meeting. She emphasized wanting to learn about the Kurds and omitted reference to the package.

Hakan refrained from interrupting her discourse, although his active body language indicated his agitation, frequently shifting, raising his hands and arms, and rolling his eyes. When she was finished, attempting to use even tones, he explained to her that what she had done was dangerous.

"Even in your country, you would not go with strangers. Why do you do so here?"

"I felt I could trust Agah. And originally we were going to just stay here. When he said he had a meeting, I didn't want to lose the opportunity to talk with him. I thought I could gain more understanding about the Kurdish plight from his friends."

"You cannot know anyone well enough to go off with him just by talking for an hour, particularly we Turks."

"Ha! And what makes you men from Turkey so special? Besides, he's a Kurd not a Turk."

"For starters, men view women differently. We treasure them. We like to keep them safe. The Kurds, who tend to be more strict adherents of Islam, view women who don't wear the head covering with disrespect. They treat them differently. Did these men actually allow you to sit with them?"

"They asked us to wear *abayahs* and to sit behind them. They were polite to us."

"I think they figured that as foreigners you might help them plead their case to your government. They want sympathizers to their cause. "

"We don't have any clout with the government. They were mistaken on that point."

"Actually, the more sympathizers the better. Word gets spread that way."

Hakan continued, "You were lucky, Charly. Turkish men are known for our courtly ways and reverence for women. But occasionally nice looking men befriend a single woman and offer to buy her tea and show her around. And some do just that. There are other instances, far too many recently, involving women being drugged and kidnapped for ransom, or raped."

This just confirmed what the State Department warnings had included about traveling in Turkey. Charly had just ignored it, thinking her judgment was good enough. Besides, she thought her training in hand-to-hand combat situations would protect her. She did not share this with Hakan. Instead she said, "But I wasn't alone. Megan was with me."

At that ludicrous comment, Hakan threw his head back and laughed, shaking his head. Recognizing the absurdity, Charly joined him.

Hakan knew that with Charly's background and training she knew better. He wondered to himself why they were hiding so much from each other.

The silence expanded as each busied themselves in their own thoughts. Neither felt enough trust in the other to divulge secrets and intentions. Much had been revealed tonight, making each restless.

- 5 -
Dogs bark but the caravan goes on
- turkish proverb -

Charly had wanted to prolong their time together and sensed that Hakan did, too. The tug toward one another was gaining strength, almost palpable now. Charly opted to return to her room for a hot shower despite knowledge of the folk lore about cold diminishing an aroused state.

Charly wanted to savor her developing feelings toward Hakan. Perhaps she could even begin to sort them out in some realistic manner. Thus resolved, she opened the window. As the brisk breeze touched her, she snuggled into bed. Sleep quickly nudged aside the "what-ifs."

Charly was awakened in the middle of the night. Listening, she heard a faint clicking sound. And again. The breeze had stopped. No motion from the partially opened drape. With the dim light from the window, Charly could see Frances' sleeping and unmoving outline; no sound from her. Could it be water dripping from her shower? Now fully alert, she heard the sound shift from a slight click to the clank of metal and a soft thud. *That was it,* Charly thought, *the safety chain on the door; I remember fastening it before my shower.*

Tugging the top sheet loose and draping it over one arm, Charly quietly slipped from bed. With growing curiosity she crept to the bathroom whose door was adjacent to the entry.

A dim light shone under the crack in the door at the bottom and side. Why so dim, she wondered, then remembered that to save energy many hotels in Turkey only turned on safety lights after midnight in the hallways and lobby areas. *Why such an idle thought now? Should I yell and scare whoever it is away?* More curious than afraid, she peeked around the bathroom doorjamb. Charly noticed a metal file was extended into the opening and successfully unhooking the chain from its lock. She ducked her head back. More light filtered in as the door slowly opened. Frances' light snoring gave false evidence that the room's occupants slept.

Immediately to the right of the door was an open closet with a low bench on which Frances and Charly had put their luggage. Pen point flashlights in hand, two figures were bending over the cases, one apiece. *I wonder why they don't just take Frances' purse and run? Or my pouch with the passport lying right on top of my case?*

Irritation finally overcame her curiosity and she looked around for a weapon. Nothing. Spotting Frances' perfume bottle she quietly loosened the top. Holding onto it with one hand, Charly held the bed sheet in the other. Letting forth with a horrific bellow of the bull moose, she lunged forward, simultaneously dousing them with the perfume and tossing the sheet over their heads just as they were turning.

Frances sat straight up in bed and flicked on the light. "Good God, what is that? Charly, did you fall?"

Seeing the commotion she reflexively got up and lunged into them. There was a tangle of the three bodies among the sheet and a strong reeking of perfume. Frances started flailing at them, shouting, "Run, Charly. I've got them. Get Kamil!"

At this point, Charly was laughing so hard she couldn't have gone anywhere. *Oh, but for a camera,* she thought.

The two men untangled themselves and dashed from the room, each leaving their dislodged fez among the sheet and Frances. Charly dashed after them.

At the noise, doors were timidly being cracked. Hakan appeared, recognized Charly, and also gave chase to the two intruders. By the time he ran to the bottom of the one flight of stairs, the two were fleeing through the main hotel door. A sleepy-eyed attendant at the desk gazed on in bleary bewilderment at the sight of the two men, *thoubs* flowing, followed by a man and woman in boxer shorts and t-shirts. *Acayipbir sey!* he thought. Strange indeed.

"Call security!" Hakan shouted as he ran past.

Dashing outside, Hakan saw them leap onto motorcycles. One started immediately and zoomed away. The second cycle's motor did not catch. By the third attempt Hakan had grabbed him around the neck from behind, the cycle and both men falling in a heap. Dashing up, Charly saw the intruder lying unconscious. Two gendarmes assigned to the hotel arrived to witness Hakan slapping him awake.

"Face down! Hands on head!"

Hakan quickly complied, kicking the other man over onto his belly.

"What's going on here? Who are you?" shouted one of the hotel security men.

"This is Hakan, our tour driver." Charly walked over to stand by Hakan. "The other guy broke into my room."

"We'll see." Hakan and the intruder were handcuffed, pulled up, and led back to the hotel. Charly ran ahead and asked the desk clerk to connect her to Kamil's room.

"Kamil, there's been a bit of a mess. Come to the lobby with identification for Hakan. I'll explain when you get here."

When he couldn't get any details from Charly and she unceremoniously slammed down the phone, he quickly dressed, gathered papers, and hurried to the lobby.

After seeing the designation on the copy of Hakan's national ID card of state security division, the police were solicitous and immediately uncuffed him.

"Now can you tell me what's going on? Hakan?"

Hakan looked at Charly.

"Well, somebody, please!"

After the story was related, Kamil still looked puzzled, but did not pursue questioning.

The gendarmes carefully listened and took notes, assuring them that the captured intruder would be jailed and would soon identify his accomplice. They treated the incident as a routine room break-in.

When Kamil, Hakan, and Charly returned to her room, Frances was pacing the floor and greeted them with "well, what was all that about?"

"Are you okay, Frances?" countered Charly.

"I will be when you tell me what's going on."

"That's what I want to know, too," Kamil and Hakan both voiced.

They collapsed into chairs in the sweetly reeking room. Frances poured them each a glass of restorative rakı.

"Why did you waste all my good Pavlova perfume, Charly? Do you know how difficult it is to find?" Frances tried to maintain a sternly prissy manner, but after a couple of moments, couldn't keep from grinning.

Frances and Charly began chuckling as they described how the theft was aborted.

Hakan did not join in the hilarity. Wearing a deep scowl and opening his arms wide, he uttered, "What? Why? What were they looking for? Is anything missing?"

Not having any of these answers, they looked through the suitcases and purses. Nothing appeared to have been taken.

Standing close to Hakan, Charly felt the heat from his skin and inhaled the mix of sweat and his lemon cologne. Almost involuntarily she leaned closer, grazing his arm with hers. A shiver went through both as they shifted apart and returned to the task at hand.

Coming to the CD, which was wrapped in decorative paper, he asked what it was.

"Oh, I'm delivering this for a friend," responded Frances.

Hakan's questions came fast and furious: who had given her the package, what was it, to whom was it to go, where, plans for delivery, etc. The more answers he heard, the more agitated he became. *I cannot believe that this well-traveled, intelligent professor could be so naive. Has she even read the security warnings?*

Shaking his head, he glared at Charly. "Why didn't you stop her? Or at least find out what was on the tape? You should be well aware of terrorist plots in our country!"

Before Charly could reply, Frances stood up for her friend. "Charly didn't know. I just told her this afternoon. Besides, Besim is my friend. Friends do favors." She gave him a tight-lipped smile and said no more.

Reassuringly, Charly patted her knee, knowing from past experience that the subject was closed for the obstinate Frances.

The standard action was to report her as a potential security risk the next morning. Obviously they wouldn't do that. It was clear to Hakan she had been caught by her good heart. But the Kurdish family Raif, to whom she was to deliver this in Mehvit, had long been under surveillance and was well known in the military security. It was generally believed that his group had caused many deaths, including a good friend of his.

With a nod of approval from Charly, Hakan revealed to Kamil what he had discovered about Charly's occasional work with special ops in nearby Jordan and Iran. Her fluency in two Arabic dialects and more than rudimentary Turkish came to light.

"Hakan, I'm curious. Why did you even think of checking Charly's background through your ops sources?"

"Charly and Megan left the hotel with a stranger tonight. Any association between tourists and Kurds automatically comes under suspicion. "

Kamil listened in disbelief. "Why didn't you call me?"

"I knew you were editing your play on a deadline, Kamil. I thought it could wait until tomorrow."

Kamil replied with a knowing grin which had a tinge of a scowl. "It's more than that I think, Hakan!"

Kamil shook his head, a bit befuddled over the incidents of the last twelve hours. Even though he was no longer a security agent, this was how he and Hakan had met. He had spent four years while at Istanbul University infiltrating student activist groups with ties to the PKK. And yet, he had no clue what had been going on. *It makes me wonder how Hakan happened to ferret out these details and I was oblivious. But, I don't think I really want to know.*

Kamil mulled over what he knew. The Hakkari region was a staging area for terrorists. Mehvit was a small village deep in that mix. Down to his marrow he was convinced Frances had merely done a silly thing, a nice thing, without thinking. There was no clandestine intention. Maybe she was unaware of the world-wide security announcement to never deliver a package for anyone where there is a terrorist alert. *But maybe Frances' misguided kindness could work to our government's advantage. I wonder what Hakan will think of such an idea?*

Hakan had also been deep in thought of the alternatives. Thinking of Charly. Worrying. He came out of his reverie, hearing the silence. Then, at the first lightening of dawn, came the sweet and, to him, peaceful sound of the first prayer of the day through the open window.

Frances and Charly had fallen asleep. Hakan and Kamil nodded as if in accord, and quietly left their room, taking the CD. An agent picked it up from Hakan's room fifteen minutes later for analysis.

The next day was what the tour referred to as an "at leisure" day; members of the group were on their own to select tours from several the hotel offered. Thus, it was a welcome day off from tour responsibilities for Kamil and Hakan. And it provided good sleep-in possibilities for the travel weary. Those six a.m. wake-up calls could try the most pleasant tourist.

Kamil and Hakan met at nine for breakfast, seating themselves as usual well away from their group. Both had been thinking of possibilities.

"Kamil, I want the package to be delivered. It could provide just the innocent cover we need to get a look around."

"I knew you would. I concur. It's too good of an opportunity to pass up. But it would put Frances in danger. Or would you go alone?"

"Well, first, she wants to go. Second, she's going to be stubborn about it. And Charly will insist on going."

Kamil was concerned. "I can see Charly adjusting to it if a mission becomes difficult, but Frances?"

"If it's just a simple delivery, no problem. You've seen how well she gets along and how children in particular flock to her. It would be a big plus. Charly says she picks up incredible details about a community through them. But, from what I've gleaned from Charly, if it gets violent, Frances prefers to hear about it later, not be part of it."

"Ha, you're right about all that," agreed Kamil. "I've seen her with children, too. It's the unknown I'm concerned about. You'll give them both a choice?"

Hakan nodded agreement. "They both will be insulted if we don't. Besides, it's Frances' gift to deliver. Let's wait until we get the CD analysis. We'll have a better idea then."

"Under whose auspices will you work?"

"My unit already contacted me this morning about why I wanted the security information about Charly. They are as good as usual in sniffing out even some unplanned operation. I wanted to discuss it with you before them. "

"Well, thanks," Kamil sarcastically remarked. "I assume that after last night, you'll want to leave sooner rather than later. Maybe we could—"

Hakan interrupted, taking out his cell phone. "And here's the call now."

"Hakan here. Anything on it?"

Kamil listened in growing frustration as the conversation went on, with only cryptic questions from Hakan. Obviously it wasn't a "clean" CD.

Hakan scowled as he closed his cell. "Complications. There was music all right, along with a longer than usual pause between songs. Barely discernible, they said. What was between songs was encrypted and they haven't been able to break it. Yet. "

"That puts a whole new light on it. Does this mean it's confiscated?"

"Well, no. They've been wanting some intelligence on the village for a long time. To them, this is their chance. They consider Charly a plus because gathering information and synthesizing it is her expertise. It's how she contributed on the special ops missions in Jordan and Iran. Forensic analysis of the village is what they need."

"Is it urgent?"

"Urgent enough to want Charly and I to go ahead. Apparently there are a lot of encrypted messages flying around emails right now from that region. Something is being planned that has our military intelligence, MIT, spooked."

"And Mehvit houses PKK?"

"They're unclear, Kamil. They used to be active terrorists. You know the history on the Raif family. But someone pinpointed from that region has been feeding MIT intelligence which has proved helpful. "

"Sounds like it's enough to arouse curiosity."

"Yes, enough to send us in."

"And what did they say about Frances?"

"They thought she would provide a great diversion and come up with valuable details. But there's an unknown risk, and she's not trained."

"I'm going to be interested in how you're going to work that out, Hakan!"

"Yes, me too."

Kamil and Hakan spent the next two hours working through the details, finally settling upon a workable plan.

The tour would continue until Konya, two days hence, where there was a local man who could fill in as a driver. Charly would explain her departure as a side trip which had been previously arranged.

Hakan called Charly's room, awakening them. "Join Kamil and me for lunch. We have a plan."

Charly was delighted to actually be able to deliver the package, but quickly sobered when she heard of the possible encumbering dangers. Decidedly, it was not to be a pleasant social visit, which she had anticipated when Frances told her about the gift. However, it didn't take her long to adjust to the new information and embrace the adventure.

Back to familiar turf, Charly thought. *And this was to have been a vacation away from all that. Just a casual trip for two old friends. Ha!*

Although Frances wanted to go along, Special Forces work had never been a part of her and Charly's mutual investigative work. The delivery did not sound like it would be the comfortable adventuring which she had been looking forward to. Besides, it would be impractical for her to go along due to the rough hiking and donkey riding through the mountains that would be necessary to access the small village.

Donkey riding? Did Hakan say that or did I make it up?

Frances was torn. Part of her was secretly relieved not to go along, as she wanted to see the changes made to Ephesus over the past forty years. On the other hand, hadn't she had similar adventures with her friends years ago here?

I love these little out-of-the-way villages. The people are always so friendly and offer tea.

As the planning flowed around her, Frances reminisced about the time she and three of her girlfriends had gone in their car through southeastern Turkey on their way to Lebanon where they did their international banking at the American School. Approaching a tiny village they had noticed a small group of children playing beside the road. In Turkish Frances had asked, "Where are your mothers?" The children eagerly took the three

Westerners where their mothers were preparing the midday meal. One of her friends was a nurse and immediately noticed that one of the children had a festering sore. After asking permission, which was readily given, several children were examined and sulfa was administered to aid the healing. They had eaten their meal with the mothers and children and drank a delicious tea of which they had consumed copious amounts. After bidding boisterous and respectful goodbyes, the three were on their way once more on the rough roads. A couple of miles beyond the village, the driver, Ann, commented that she needed to pull over as she was so sleepy she couldn't keep her eyes open. The other two had agreed. After sleeping for a couple of hours, they went on their way, discussing what could have made them so sleepy. Spontaneously they began laughing as they remembered passing the poppy fields. It was a custom in southeastern Turkish villages to give honored guests opium in their tea in celebration of new friendships.

Frances didn't share this memory with the others. She just smiled to herself about those special days. *Maybe it's time for another one!*

Kamil, Hakan, and Charly were stopped in mid-sentence as Frances broke her reverie. "Well, Charly, we have three days to enjoy ourselves before we leave. We visit Cappadocia tomorrow and I've never been. It sounds like your type of place. Your imagination can go wild! Now, let's go back to the Silk Bazaar and do some of the shopping we missed yesterday."

With that, she got up from the table. "Come on, come on! The day is edging forward." Charly shrugged and left the dining room with her.

- 6 -
Stretch your feet according to your blanket
- turkish proverb -

"Oh my God, is it real?" Charly sat mesmerized as the bus drove through the area of Goreme.

Frances was looking just as awestruck. "It looks like something Disney would have designed."

The fairy chimneys loomed from the sandy ground in tall cones. In the distance openings to caves several stories above could be seen. From some, brightly colored material was waving in the breeze, perhaps clothes, a bed covering, or rug.

Kamil explained some of the history of the area. "For thousands of years, people lived in these caves, carving themselves homes and leading a community life. In the 1950s, the government condemned them as living spaces. The constant filtering of dust particles and cracking of the soft stone were a safety hazard. The government built the dwellers modern homes nearby in the hills where they could still see the enchanting formations. As soon as the officials left the area, many people moved back into their old homes, giving up their modern conveniences like running water and flushing toilets. Ancestral homes meant more.

"Historical accounts say that a traveler many centuries ago saw smoke coming from some formation tops, but there was no sign of people. He thought fairies were living in the region in what he called 'fairies chimneys' when he wrote home."

Charly sighed. "I can just imagine them dancing about."

"I'm sure you can, Charly!" Frances thought that if anyone could, bet on Charly. She had always admired her interesting mix of toughness and feyness.

The group continued into the valley near Uchisar known as the Valley of the Pigeons. Here, thousands of pigeon houses had been carved into the soft *tufa*. Since ancient times this area has been a rich source of food and fertilizer. Although most were now in disuse, some farmers still insisted that this was why Cappadocia was said to have the sweetest fruit.

The valley was perfect for hiking and viewing above ground caves. Charly, Frances, and Megan immediately began the climb up the narrow path, exploring cave openings as they went. They had been advised not to go inside as there was constant silting of the *tufa,* and areas which had fallen through. When they got to the top, perhaps six stories high, they perched on the cliff's edge and sipped their bottled water. They were quiet for a long time. Fellow travelers had opted to stay on the valley floor, and no sounds floated up to them. Only the wind whistling through cave openings and the occasional scattering of rocks by some small creature broke the silence. Each of them was mesmerized by the uniqueness of the landscape. Charly felt something more, a tug on her soul. It felt to her as if ancients were whispering. She felt an energy sweep through her that gave her goose-bumps even on such a hot day. In silent accord, Megan and Charly stood and voiced the ancient mantra of "om," softly first, then soaring. It was given as a sign of recognition of the souls which had passed through, and a sign of joy for being there.

Frances got to her feet, and said, "Well, that was eerie! I bet you scared everything off within miles. What was that all about anyway? I'm hungry. Let's go."

The spell broken, they laughed as they carefully began their descent. Charly noticed three armed soldiers in the distance guarding the road which led farther into the hills.

Before lunch they stopped at Kaymakli, one of the larger of the many underground cities in the area.

"Go ahead, Charly," Frances said. "I don't think I want to chance navigating the tunnels. Kamil said we'll have to crawl some of the time. Just don't wander off down there or you'll get lost."

After descending just a couple of levels, Charly thought Frances had made the right decision. *I sure wish a few others would have listened to Kamil's warnings. I don't even feel sorry for those two ahead of me who are scared to death at the steepness, confined space, and dim light. They should have known better themselves. Besides, they're holding the rest of us up. Five more levels until they can turn around!*

Charly soon forgot her grumblings as she got ahead of the slower ones at the next level. Then she had more time at each landing to look around at what had been home to those hiding from persecution centuries ago: bedrooms, wine cellars, storage rooms, a church; each space had its own function. Ventilation was through natural vents or chimneys. There were blackened areas where cooking fires had been built. Wandering away from the group, Charly stepped through a portal into another room, then through the next doorway. Utter darkness. *If only I had a flashlight! I can sure see how someone could get lost with all the twists and turns, no entry ways in a straight row.*

She felt her way back and asked Kamil to borrow his spare flashlight.

"If I gave you my spare, you'd just go off on your own. You can't do that, Charly. So, no, you cannot have it."

Charly shrugged, not surprised at Kamil's response. *I'll come back on my own. Someday.*

They arrived in time for lunch at their last stop of the day in the Goreme National Park. Before touring, they were happy to make use of modern facilities and money exchange.

Charly and Megan walked slowly with Frances up the steep, natural pathway littered with stones ready to turn the ankle at a careless step. This site, as were most in Turkey, was definitely not conducive to those who didn't have good balance and sure footing. Someone in a wheelchair would have had to abandon visiting most sites.

As they walked into one of the many chapels carved out of the hillside, they were awestruck with the frescoes adorning the sides of the caves, very dimly lit with one hanging bulb only slightly helped by Kamil's flashlight. As Charley edged to the side to get a better view, Frances grabbed her arm. "Look out! There's a hole where you are about to step. Shine your flashlight over here for a minute, Kamil," requested Frances, still holding onto Charly.

Indeed there was a gaping hole, perhaps two feet in diameter. Its depth was greater than the flashlight penetrated. Kamil explained that with all of these caves, below or above ground, major decaying was constantly occurring. The dozen people in one small area of the cave, blocked the low light, and the pitfalls couldn't be seen.

"Walk carefully, dragging your feet a little," he recommended, "then you can catch yourself."

Charly softly exclaimed to Frances, "Good lord, he seems unconcerned. If this were at home, the site would be closed for fear of an accident and the lawsuit which would surely come."

Returning their attention to the frescoes, Frances remarked, "Look at those colors. Isn't it wonderful how they have lasted centuries with some only fading a little? But what a tragedy about the eyes!"

Kamil explained that when the Muslims had driven the Christians out they had gouged out the eyes of the angels, throwing rocks at them if they could not be reached. They felt it was bad luck and against Islam to have such icons. Charly wondered if it were similar to the Afghanistan government decreeing the destruction of the Buddhas, even the one six stories high. The United Nations' pleas to spare such statues of great import to the world had not been heeded.

After viewing a couple more chapels, Kamil gave the group an hour to explore on their own. Megan, Frances, and Charly split up at this point, agreeing to meet back at the bus.

As she climbed, Charly found the narrowing pathways becoming increasingly steep. Ladders had been placed to access more remote cave dwellings. Finding herself alone, Charly seated herself yoga fashion in a dusty rock/clay doorway and, breathing deeply, looked around. It was rare to have moments alone and she really felt she needed to re-center, to get in touch with her inner self. She felt a little battered by being with others so much, meeting their needs, listening, talking, helping. *There are too many voices and demands. I need to listen to my own for awhile.*

The energy emanating from this Cappadocia area was deeply affecting her, changing her perceptions, intensifying them. This change had begun within hours of arriving in Istanbul, and had gradually increased until reaching this near crescendo level. *This is what it looked like in my dream before the trip. The dwellings, cliffs, and a feeling of some message which I couldn't understand. And now there is even more clearly an awareness I can't explain—just strong feelings.* Something was changing within her. It felt like a major chemical or neurological imbalance resulting in intensifying her sensitivity to her surroundings and her strong attraction and affinity to Hakan. She could not see him from this distance, but the bus was visible in the parking lot. She closed her eyes to meditate for a while in the silence.

Megan could see Charly from her vantage point on the cliffs several hundred yards away. *She's seeking solace, too. I hope she isn't denying the strong pull of this area for her. She almost vibrates with repressed excitement. My soul feels at peace here, but my heritage makes it logical. I live in both worlds. There's something pulling Charly to do so, too. But can she? Should she? It would be much easier on her if she were more like Frances—eagerly seeing everything but not letting it become part of her.*

Frances had chosen to walk along the more gently sloping path to the other side of the area. She was alone, the voices of fellow travelers having trailed away. A light wind kicked up dust. She drew her coat more firmly around her.

Sensing something, her gazed lifted. A young boy was leading a camel along the path on the hillside toward the narrow valley below. She was drawn to the poignant simplicity of the scene. As the camel and the boy slowly meandered along a narrow and barely visible dirt path, Frances began a slow and careful descent to intercept them. Hearing the falling stones Frances dislodged, the boy looked up, paused, and watched her approach.

"Günaydın! It is a hot day," Frances said as she held out a dollar bill and asked if she could have a ride on the camel.

He had not done this before. *Should I? The lady looks nice, like my grandmother. And, I would love an American dollar. That's over one million lire!* The boy grinned with thoughts of what he would buy and had the camel kneel. "I am Abdar. Please. I will take you for a ride on the camel."

Frances settled atop the camel's bony back. No sooner had she done this than the camel stumbled to its feet, jerking its head. Catching the boy unawares he dropped the one rope loosely looped around the camel's head and the camel took off running along the rocky path. Frances leaned forward, hugging as well as she could the neck of the camel, laughing delightedly, ignoring the pungent scent.

"Hold tight!" Abdar ran after them as fast as he could. *Allah! I am in real trouble.*

The camel's path took it down the valley and around another hill. Looking back, Frances could no longer see the boy or the hilltop she had descended. Thinking that the hour Kamil had given them to explore must be about over, worry began to set in, but the camel did not respond to any of the threats or admonishments she was issuing. Ahead were more caves which had been carved into the hillside, but these were not peopled by tourists. As suddenly as the camel had begun its flight, it stopped, and Frances went flying over its head.

The fall knocked the wind out of her. As soon as she could breathe again, she stood. Feeling something warm trickling on her leg, she looked down and saw that the leg of her slacks had been torn to reveal a long, deep gash. By then, she was surrounded by Kurdish women all seeming to comment at once.

The oldest (certainly the most wrinkled), walked up to Frances, stopping when she was an arm's length away. She and Frances grinned at each other, nodded, and the elderly woman knelt to look at the cut on her leg. Speaking rapidly, a woman got on either side of her and held Frances' elbows as they led her to the cooking fire and helped her sit upon a large stone serving as a bench.

Frances was handed strong, hot tea to drink while the elder of the group washed her cut leg. Another woman had appeared with an earthenware container holding a thick yellow substance. It was smeared liberally on the cut, then bound with what looked like straw tightly woven into flexible strands a yard long.

While they were bandaging her leg, Frances noticed brightly colored head-scarves and blankets dangling from the caves, presumably for airing. What smelled like a lamb and garlic mixture was emanating from a large pot over the fire. It was at this point that Frances' adrenaline surge left her. She must have looked pale of a sudden, as she was gently lowered from sitting on the rock to leaning against it, with a blanket thrown around her. For some reason she felt safe here and nodded off.

When Frances awoke it was to the sound of rhythmic chanting and low talking among men and women in a language she was just beginning to learn, thought beautiful, but did not understand. *It must be Kurdish*, she thought. Opening her eyes but not moving her body, she recognized the boy who had haplessly allowed her the camel ride. He was sitting very close by her side. Noticing she was awake and smiling at him, he brought a bowl of steaming meat and rice and a piece of flatbread. Although the women frequently glanced her way, the singing and talk continued as she gratefully ate the deliciously spicy food and drank more hot tea.

It was now dusk and the full impact of what had happened hit her. Charly must be frantic by now. Not having a watch, she guessed that at least five hours had passed. She got up to go, saying in Turkish that she must find the tour group. Her leg was stiff and she almost fell. Not having brought her purse and thus paper and pencil, Frances wrote the names Hakan, Kamil, and Iyilik Tours in the sand and pointed to the boy, Abdar, and the direction from which she had come. "Yes, I understand. I will go look for them." After a few words with the elder woman, he scampered off, without the camel this time.

Abdar returned within thirty minutes with Hakan striding long and purposefully beside him. He looked determined and angry, with eyes flashing and intensity permeating his demeanor. Frances stood with the old woman quickly appearing by her side and engaged Hakan's flashing eyes as he came to stand within three feet of her. Casting his gaze to the old woman, they engaged in rapid Kurdish laced with some agitation.

Hakan knelt and began gently unwrapping the bandage to see for himself what the old woman had told him. "Your cut is deep, Frances, and some muscle may be torn. You need stitches. I'll report in and a jeep will come for us."

Hakan took out a mobile phone and told the rest of the search party his coordinates. "Handy little things, aren't they? The gendarmerie passed them out to the search team."

"Where's Charly?"

"She's out there searching too." Simultaneously, through his mobile came a whoop of delight. Charly had heard the good news.

Within five minutes three jeeps drove up. Charly leaped out and rushed to Frances. "Well, that took nerve! Not even inviting me on your adventuring." She reached out and gave Frances a bear hug. "Let's go to the doctor."

The gendarme insisted on taking Frances to the hospital to be checked out thoroughly. Frances needed not only twenty stitches, inside and outside the wound, but had bruised ribs as well.

The physician insisted she stay overnight and Frances reluctantly demurred. In her room they piled blankets on her and brought hot broth and rice. The painkiller administered before treating the wound took hold along with the shock, and she drifted into a sound sleep with Charly holding her hand.

Leaving Frances' room, Charly motioned for Hakan and Kamil to join her, and they returned to their hotel. As in one accord, they stopped at the now empty lounge area, ordering rakı. When they'd added only a little water and taken a sip, they discussed how Frances' accident would affect their plans.

"Obviously, she cannot go with Charly and me now," began Hakan. "I think it is for the best. It will be easier for two of us to disappear."

"You mean our cover will be easier, don't you?"

"Right. We won't need to portray ourselves as tourists with a guide. With your training, we can blend in and not be noticed. Otherwise, we'd have to be out in the open."

"I agree. This will give us a lot more freedom, particularly if we are to work within your security unit, rather than just stumble across this remote village."

Kamil was concerned about Frances. "But will she comply? I can just see her, bandages-be-damned, insisting she go along."

"Frances and I have certainly had our share of adventures before, but they were mostly investigating cases where forensic interviewing is required, looking for interrelationships, patterns. Frances is superb at that. She'll meet someone for the first time, and within a few minutes they will be telling her their life story. I have a feeling that from what Hakan has said, more specific training may be involved this time, emphasis on 'may.' Frances has never handled a gun before, as she is opposed to violence."

"But surely you've had to use a gun before on your cases," Kamil incredulously inquired.

"Well, of course. And I did. But, Frances just shifted her focus at those times, making herself scarce. She is remarkable at seeing the positive side of things, what she wants to see."

Hakan finished his rakı. "I'm off to bed now. We'll talk with her tomorrow. In light of what you have said, I see no reason to postpone our leaving the tour. Okay?"

In agreement, they rode the elevator together, parting ways at their floor.

The next morning, Charly awakened once more to the haunting canting of the *muezzin*. The sonorous Arabic flowed over her, bringing tranquility. She missed not having to rouse Frances, only to have her say, "You use the bathroom first." Frances soaked up every bit of extra sleep she could.

Um, Charly thought, *if hospitals are anything like those in the States, she will be roused from sleep early, and won't like it one bit. I can just hear her grousing.*

With that thought Charly laughed, then quietly listened as the strains of the first call to prayer faded away from the last one to join.

First on the agenda was breakfast, then a visit with Frances. Of course everyone had heard about her disappearance and reappearance, and wanted to know some details. Once they were assured she was safe, Charly soon had everyone laughing at Frances' antics.

The day's agenda had shifted slightly, with more free time available to select day tours of choice, thus freeing Hakan.

Kamil ended up involved with the local gendarmerie who were conducting a census. Traffic on all roads would be stopped without the permit on display giving them exemption to travel. All residents were to remain in their homes. Nomads had specific places to report. Army personnel and gendarmerie were positioned on all roads and on city and village streets to be sure everyone complied. Even though Kamil's group consisted of non-Turkish tourists, each had to fill out a form in order for the tour bus to receive its permission to be on the road the next day. This meant that Kamil had to hunt each group member down, verifying information such as age, citizenship, and if they had running water in their homes.

Hakan and Charly went to the hospital to check on Frances. Not surprisingly, she had several nurses in her room and was entertaining them in Turkish with the adventure of yesterday. There was a festive air about the room, certainly not that of an injured person.

After listening a few minutes, Charly walked in saying, "My, don't we feel good today!"

The group around her bed parted, and there sat Frances, propped up, leg slightly elevated. Her hair was meticulous, she wore lipstick, a bit of rouge, and a brightly colored scarf Charly had never seen before around her neck.

"Well, what kept you? I've been up for ages."

When Charly and Frances were alone, Charly broached the topic of the departure from the tour.

"Frances, the doctor says your leg will be fine. But it and your bruised ribs will bother you for awhile."

"Tell me about it! I dread it when I have to get up to go to the bathroom. But guess what? Megan has agreed to stay with me for a few days, and we'll fly to meet the tour in Antalya.

Between you and me, I think she just wanted more time here. You know how she is about these energy fields of hers. So, I'm sorry, but you and Hakan will have to go on without me. Will that be a problem?"

"No, that'll be just fine, Frances." Charly hid a secret grin. "In view of all this, we'll leave tomorrow. With things thrown topsy-turvy with your fall, there will be less suspicion cast on our leaving."

They spent the next hour in relaxed chitchat about their trip so far and their new friends. Frances would end the tour in Istanbul with the group and await Charly's return at her favorite hotel, the Hilton.

The nurse came in to change the IV pain medication and antibiotic, indicating it was time for her to rest. When the nurse left, Frances voiced emotion, directly referring for the first time to Charly's leaving the tour. Taking Charly's hand, her eyes flooded with tears as she simply advised, "Don't take risks and stay close to Hakan." Charly bent to kiss Frances as she struggled to hide her own tears.

- 7 -
A pound is sixteen ounces wherever you go
- turkish proverb -

Charly heard a faint tapping on her door. It was still dark. Cappadocia would soon be awakened by the *muezzin's* call. She knew it was Hakan, as they had planned to leave with as little notice as possible. Charly quickly slipped into the modest long skirt and long-sleeved full shirt which came below the knees. Everything else was packed and waiting by the door.

The lights in the hotel were dimmed very low and there was no one in the main lobby area. The Turkish conservation of energy served well for their clandestine departure.

It promised to be a beautiful day as the stars filled the sky, only beginning to disappear as the sun cast its first glow in the eastern horizon. They would be facing that glaring sun on the drive toward southeastern Turkey. Only a few cursory words were spoken as they shared the thermos of hot tea Hakan had thoughtfully brought along. Although a million questions were bursting inside Charly, she decided that not everyone was a morning person, so at least for the moment she chose to keep thoughts to herself.

Each was preoccupied with thoughts about the mission. Charly was both excited and apprehensive. There was much more potential for adventure than if she had remained on the tour. Prior to this she had worked as part of a U.S. military operation on two Middle East operations. Both had been with ops people within the country as part of the team. And there had been at least one or two within the group with whom she had previously teamed or trained.

Charly thought about ways in which today was entirely different. *First, it might not turn into an "operation." There might simply be a drop off. Secondly, I'm not with any team member I know. So, there is a major trust issue. And third,* she ticked off to herself, *being attracted to someone and flirting is one thing. It's quite another to begin a mission with him. Too many unknowns.*

Perhaps this will just be an "in and out." I'll deliver the CD to this nice old lady who will love it. She'll give us some tea and cake and we'll be on our way. Ha! Even I can't buy that fantasy. It's likely not just a tape of music at all. The space between songs has Hakan concerned enough to pursue it. I hope MIT can decode it before we arrive.

Frances' naiveté at least has led to spicing up the tour. I bet that was her intention all along. Probably! She's damned lucky not to be jailed.

Hakan was pondering his own tugs of apprehension. He had doubts about Charly. Even though she had been on several missions with Special Forces over the years, he had no clue what they had entailed. Perhaps she had just taught some class in forensics or was along as an observer. Somehow he thought there was more involved. *I guess I should be thinking more about that and asking her about it, rather than spending time as I am wondering about how it would be to touch her. Now. How would she respond if I leaned into her so my arm brushed her breast? Accidentally, of course. Maybe she would snuggle closer and rub—aw, no. I can't do this.*

Squirming in his seat, Hakan tried to ease the pressure of his responding body. Embarrassed that his thoughts might become heard, he increased his speed and abruptly passed the slow moving truck they had been following up the incline for several miles.

Charly gave him an inquisitive look, then went back to her reverie.

"Hungry?"

"Always!" Charly quickly responded, as she usually did, to inquiries about food.

Hakan pulled into a rest stop restaurant, where there were several cars and a bus getting washed by hand by some young boys.

They placed their order at the counter, which displayed choices of various kinds of cheese *borek*. Charly was delighted to see these favorite pastries of hers as well as *pogaca* and ordered one of each. The cheese *borek* was light and melted in her mouth. As expected, the *pogaca* was a chewy version of *pide* stuffed with sour cream and parsley. The very strong Turkish black tea served in a tulip-shaped glass jolted her awake. She ate more than her share of the grapes although she limited herself to one fig, knowing from experience the uncomfortable results of indulging in more.

Hakan was enjoying watching her quickly consume her breakfast, licking her fingers. *Certainly no dainty professor, here*, he thought. *But she did wince at the strength of the tea. Time will change that.*

Other than voicing mutual pleasure in the food, there was no conversation. Within thirty minutes they were back on the road.

The rest of the day was uneventful as they drove through broad valleys with large fields of cotton, where women in colorful scarves and ankle-length attire were picking by hand.

Hakan informed her that the higher quality of cotton for which Turkey was well known came from this hand-picking method of harvesting as fewer strands were broken. At the end of the day trucks picked up the loads of cotton and the women piled on the back of either the truck or wagon, whichever the land owner could afford. Later in the day Charly saw such trucks; the women looked tired but rode proudly with straight backs as the wind from the moving vehicle cooled them, and the sleeves of their blouses billowed.

They stopped at another rest stop for spicy kebabs wrapped inside delicious *pide* from the stand. While eating and drinking Coca-Cola they walked to stretch out legs and unkink muscles. Nothing else was in view but the occasional hut on the side of a hill. Only a few cars passed. A steady wind blew up dust from the loose, sandy soil. In mid-summer it would be one hundred degrees Fahrenheit here, thought Charly, thankful for the seventy-degree fall weather.

As night fell they found themselves tired and hungry again after the long day. Hakan knew of a small hotel in the next village. As they drew nearer Charly donned her long, colorful scarf of reds, looping then tying it around her neck in the back, making sure it came down onto her forehead above her eye brows. They were entering the more conservative part of Turkey where she felt it was more respectful to honor the locals' customs than hers. Hakan noted that her hair was covered and pulled the shawl from the backseat and draped it around her shoulders. He reached over to gently pat her leg and let his hand rest there for an almost imperceptible moment.

Strange, but in the donning of the scarf, she somehow felt closer to Hakan and to the reality of their being alone. Feelings of shyness and awkwardness washed over her, which, thank goodness, she thought, were fleeting. She chuckled aloud as she thought maybe she would appear more authentic if she could conjure up those feelings at will. Hakan, misunderstanding, commented that she made a good-looking Turkish woman. Charly didn't correct him.

On the outskirts of the small town a makeshift barrier had been erected, manned by two uniformed men with rifles. Checkpoints were frequent in Turkey, increasing the closer the proximity to eastern Turkey. Anticipating this in their earlier planning, Charly was to remain silent. Hakan had quickly become acquainted with her frequent, direct, and outspoken manner. Charly was tired and didn't feel like being delayed from a hot bath any longer, so a backseat role sounded just fine.

Hakan slowed and pulled onto the side of the road. One of the soldiers approached and asked for their identity cards. He seemed surprised when Charly gave him her passport. This stimulated a barrage of questions about where they were going and why. Hakan explained that she had hired him to take a driving tour to southeastern Turkey. This led to comments about "crazy Americans" and an exchange of Turkish lira.

Before waving them on, the soldier warned about not traveling after dark due to the increased rebel movement. Evidently there was another uprising among Kurdish terrorists in the region.

They drove slowly into the small town, where a few hotel and restaurant signs were scattered along the main and side streets. None were large multi-story Hiltons, but rather two- or three-story concrete block structures. Headlights illuminated gaily painted scenes on some of them. Hakan stopped at one on a side street, which didn't seem to Charly any better than the rest, but he seemed to know where he was going.

"I've heard from some friends that this is clean and even has a Turkish bath, or at least a steam room."

"Wonderful. I hoped we haven't missed the hours for women."

When she had discovered that many more hours were available to men than women in the baths, resentment at such inequality had infuriated Charly. Guessing this, Hakan just chuckled as they got their packs from the trunk.

The lobby had simple, whitewashed walls covered with painted vines. Colorfully woven Turkish rugs covered most of the stone floor.

Seated at a table which served as a reception desk, a stooped, white-haired man with deeply bronzed, lined skin greeted them in Kurdish with polite curiosity. "Welcome. Have you had a pleasant journey?"

And thus ensued an energetic conversation about the weather, security stops, and if they had been troubled by the census the week before. Selim was impressed that an American traveler would seek his hotel and was eager to please. He firmly insisted they try a nearby restaurant "for the best lamb in the region."

Charly enjoyed the friendliness displayed by nearly all she had met in Turkey. But now she was hungry, tired, and not wanting to linger.

As quickly as he could, Hakan procured two rooms. Each held a twin bed with brightly colored cotton coverlets and shelves on which to place suitcases and clothes. The room had the ever present lemony scent the Turks loved so much. Verbena was touted to be cleansing, and when appropriate, an aphrodisiac. The floors were highly polished. Selim had given them a shared bathroom, otherwise, they would have had to make do with one down the hall.

After a quick freshening, they walked a few doors from the hotel for dinner. It was a simple place with only half-dozen or so tables, a wooden floor, and no other customers.

"Sorry, we are closed," a young boy sweeping the floor told them.

"Why so early?" inquired Hakan.

"Tomorrow my cousin is getting married. Soon he will come with his friends to drink for his last night. So, no more customers tonight." He walked over and turned off the light in the window and door.

"Ah, I see." Hakan explained to Charly that this small establishment likely did not have special permission to serve rakı, so needed to close to do so.

A pretty, full-bodied woman with long dark hair peeking from under a bright yellow scarf came from the kitchen area and looked inquisitively at them.

"My name is Hakan, and this is Charly. We have been traveling all day and are very hungry. Selim from the hotel thought you might serve us. Maybe he did not know you were closing tonight."

Noticing a twinkle in her eye and a glance at the door, Hakan turned. In walked Selim.

"Ah, Bihter, my most good daughter, have you not served them a rakı yet?" Selim good-naturedly chided.

"Come, come. Sit with me," he offered as he pulled out three chairs and motioned to Hakan and Charly.

Shaking her head with a broad smile on her face, Bihter reached under the counter for the rakı, which she brought, along with water, ice, and glasses.

After rakı and delicious spicy lamb patties with rice, Charly was drooping and ready to return to her room. The wedding party was just beginning to drift in and after initial curiosity, welcomed the strangers. After a few toasts, they departed to shouted invitations to join the wedding party tomorrow.

Hakan insisted they relax in the *hamam*.

"Oh, but all I want to do is go to sleep. I'm so tired."

"But that's why you need the hot steam," countered Hakan, "to soothe your aches and relax you so you can have pleasant dreams. There is nothing like the *halvet* to do that."

Approaching the door leading into the steam bath, they found no light shining underneath and that it was locked. Charly had been a little disappointed the establishment was too small to have a masseuse, but no steam tonight further dismayed her.

"Well, that's too bad." Charly turned, heading toward the stairs leading to her room.

Hakan challenged, "Let's see if we can find the key," and started rummaging through a drawer in the desk.

"We can't do that!"

"Yes, here it is." Hakan proudly displayed the key.

Noticing Charly's frown he added, "Selim whispered to me where it was just before we left. Don't worry so much."

There was one small dressing area curtained off. Hakan and Charly took turns undressing and wrapped the provided toweling around them. Adjoining was a steam room large enough for four people to comfortably sit on benches around three sides. There were several buckets with dippers and four open hot coal beds. They began dumping ladles full of water onto the coals, and soon the warm room became thick with steam. They had positioned themselves on adjacent benches, so semi-reclined in the privacy of the veil of steam, only rousing to toss more water. It was silent except for the occasional hiss of water.

Charly dozed, in a state of pure lassitude, floating. Coming slowly back to reality, she became aware of the sole of her foot being gently massaged. Drifting through her mind was something she'd read about the bottom of the foot containing all the nerve endings for the body. She didn't want to open her eyes as it felt so incredibly good and she didn't want it to stop. *Am I dreaming? Talk about dreams being wish fulfillments!*

Uttering a soft, satisfied moan, she gradually opened her eyes. Her towel had slipped to her waist and her head was cradled on her arm. Hakan had her foot on his thigh and with his eyes closed was massaging it. The steam lent an ethereal feeling to the scene and Charly felt like she was in a trance. Becoming aware of her gaze, Hakan opened his eyes, meeting hers with the intensity she had felt on other occasions. They were aware of one another's desire expressed with that gaze. Hakan gently squeezed her foot and released it. In turn, Charly sat upright, tugging her towel back into place.

After several minutes of silence and reorienting themselves, they simultaneously rose and returned to the dressing room taking turns again dressing. Without touching or speaking, they walked back to their rooms. Reaching her room first, she lightly laid her hand on Hakan's cheek. He turned his head to kiss her open palm, holding it with his for a few seconds before releasing it. With a touch of his hand to his heart, he walked toward his door.

What was all that! she wondered, quickly brushing her teeth with the bottled water and taking a quick shower. As she sank into the smooth citrus fragrant sheets it seemed like every nerve ending was tingling with sensitivity even to the lightness of the sheet. *I so wish he would come through the adjoining door.* Charly daydreamed about the explosion of the senses as they would greedily explore one another. *But is this what I want? It would certainly be a complication to both of our lives. Hakan is married* with two girls, and my husband died only the year before. Maybe he just misses his wife. So we could just have a simple, uncomplicated affair, or just sex. That would be really very nice. Flirting with a married man is one thing, but perhaps jeopardizing his marriage is another. That's not fair. And I'm not ready for complications right now.* Charly fell asleep thinking *keep it simple,* and spent the night in a lusty dream world.

Hakan did not fall asleep so easily that night. With all his being he wanted to go to Charly and plunge into her yielding warmth. *But would she be receptive? They were drawn to each other, that was clear, but committing with such intimacy was a big step. For me it is, anyway, and I bet for Charly, too. I don't think she's at all prudish, but it's clear she has high standards set for herself. Maybe she loved her husband too much to ever love another man. Love?! Where did that come from? Lust would be more like it. Is it just a matter of time until we give in to our desires? Charly must think I am such a fraud, as she thinks I'm married. Kamil told everyone that to dampen anyone's interest in either of us. True, I do have two teenage daughters. It's a bad time for them to be without their mother. My being gone so much doesn't help either. I hope they're getting along okay staying with their mother's sister and family.*

Hakan fell asleep wondering what his daughters were dreaming.

Arising with the *muezzin* call at dawn, they met at breakfast, which was provided by a bleary-eyed Selim. Charly, who seldom ate yoghurt at home, eagerly tucked into the dish, which she had garnished with walnuts. Turkish *cay* was always welcome. They glanced awkwardly at one another across the table, and said little as they ate.

As they began their drive, Charly reached over and laid her hand on Hakan's leg. Immediately Hakan reciprocated and thus they rested for a few minutes. After a simultaneous squeeze, their eyes met. The longing was there along with confusion around the edges but they both seemed to relax into a peaceful silence as the sun rose above the high barren hills to the east.

At Charly's urging, Hakan began talking a bit about himself and his involvement with the MIT, Turkey's secret intelligence agency. For fifteen years since the late 1980s, terrorist groups had actively sought Kurdish rights through violent acts. Innocent civilians in crowded urban areas were targeted as well as the sabotage and killing of the Turkish soldiers. Although most of the terrorists had fled into the bordering mountains of Iran and Iraq, they were still a force to be reckoned with. There had been a message from the Eastern Command Center on Hakan's laptop this morning that they still had not broken all the encryption. There was just enough information to advise that they should proceed with extreme caution.

"I'm concerned we'll be going into a dangerous situation."

"And, you are just finding this out?" Charly incredulously asked.

"Well, at first my section thought we could do reconnaissance in the area as we delivered the package. A good cover. But the information I received this morning changed all that. Evidently there are coordinates contained within the CD, but they don't know yet to what it refers. They're still working on the rest."

They fell silent as they absorbed this new information and adjusted their perspective. What was actually in the package became of paramount importance.

"It doesn't sound as innocent as we had hoped. Definitely a message but terrorist related?"

"We won't know if we don't continue. What do you say, Charly?"

"Well, I don't want to go back. Let's just do it and see what happens," blustered Charly, full well knowing the foolishness of that approach. It wasn't as if she hadn't done this before, getting herself into tricky situations as she had investigated some very unsavory characters. She shuddered when she thought how the tables had been turned five years ago when she was trying to locate a child taken by his Saudi father, who had returned with the boy to his home country. She had ended up kidnapped herself and spent three months rehabilitating from a painful gunshot wound. That's when she had refreshed her skills with her .45 magnum, and carried it on all future cases, or was provided with one. But she had no weapon now. She hadn't thought she'd need one, and had made no arrangements.

"I haven't seen you carrying a weapon. But you have one with you, right?"

"Of course. Pull up the floor mat under your feet."

Inside were a Walther, a sheathed knife, and a GPS receiver. "Not much. I'm surprised."

"Basics. I can boost the fire power when I need to through my contacts. We'll need more than that for certain when we make the delivery. How well can you shoot?"

"Expert ambidextrous in rifle, but sharpshooter sustained fire with a pistol. Slow fire events only with both."

"Impressive." Hakan was clearly taken aback. "How did you get so good?"

"My father was a hunter in Alaska where I grew up. I was an only child and my father treated me as his sidekick. He gave me my first .22 on my sixth birthday and he taught me to shoot at empty cans at our cabin. When I could hit five in succession at fifty feet he took me ptarmigan hunting."

"Ptarmigan? What's that?"

"A very tasty bird, like a grouse. We hunt them in winter when they're white. That's part of the trick, just being able to see them against the snow. Dad insisted I learn to shoot all small animals in the head so they wouldn't suffer."

"And so they wouldn't bleed out into the meat," added Hakan.

"Ha! Yes, that too."

"What else did you hunt?"

"Until I was ten he only let me go on small game hunts for ptarmigan and rabbit, and in the summer, ducks. Then he gave me a choice between using his 30.06 or .300 Winchester magnum on my first big game hunt, for moose. I'd been practicing for six months with both, but much preferred the .300. I sure got sore shoulders from both, but I could handle the recoil in the mag better. "

"Well, did you get one?"

"Yeah. Nice rack, too. It was late in the day by the time we dressed it out, so we hung it in a tree and pitched camp. We hung bells on the bottom, and lucky we did. In the middle of the night the cow bells started ringing. We grabbed our guns and could just make out a big grizzly trying to paw it down. Lucky for the long daylight hours, we could clearly see. He was getting pretty mad being thwarted, and his growls increased as we tried to scare him away by beating on pans. Dad told me that if he charged us, it would be my shot. I dropped my pan and spoon, and took off the safety. Within seconds the bear turned, pawing in the air, bawling. As suddenly, he charged. I got him through the eye, which should have brought him down. I chambered another bullet, shot again, and he came down within three feet of where I stood. I glanced down and Dad and his long-standing hunting partner had taken aim and were still in position."

"Were you scared?"

"It happened too fast. Besides I had two great shots and figured they'd back me. I think about that trip a lot."

"You were really close to your dad, weren't you?"

Charly agreed and shared a few more stories, lasting until it was time for lunch. Hakan delighted in her enthusiastic recounting of the life he had known nothing about until now.

- 8 -
A carefree head is to be found only on a scarecrow
- turkish proverb -

I told my contact in this region we'd be coming by to discuss whether or not to continue. It depends to some extent on other operations in the area. If we continue, we have to have a plan as it doesn't seem as simple as we had at first thought."

The sun was high when Hakan turned off the two paved lanes onto a narrow rutted dirt road and wound his way toward the nearby hills. After a few miles, when the road turned more into a path, they saw a compound up ahead and sheep milling around. The structures of stone and cement blended with the colors on the hillside.

When they came to a stop, the silence was only broken by the occasional bleating of the sheep. Five men holding Uzis appeared as soon as they got out of the jeep. A burly, barrel-chested older man with a beard walked toward Hakan, booming out his name.

"Hakan, so you've arrived. Welcome, welcome." He proceeded to kiss Hakan on both cheeks.

Turning to Charly, he explained, "Turkish custom!"

Everyone laughed, as much in relief of tension than anything else. The guards lowered their weapons and faded into the background of the low shrubs.

"Well, you've really gotten yourself one going now, don't you?" The man holding the Uzi spoke in Kurdish, looking at Charly.

"I only know a few words in Kurdish, please speak Turkish." Charly surprised him, and quickly glanced at Hakan, who nodded.

Charly extended her hand, which was firmly clasped by his warm, broad one, as Hakan introduced her to Cevik.

"*Merhaba*, Cevik, *memnunoldum.*"

"And I am happy to meet you, too, Charly," responded Cevik, using lightly accented English.

Cevik led them through a tall, heavy gate into a courtyard surrounded by one-story high stone walls. Scattered throughout the courtyard were several small concrete buildings with very high windows. *No peeking in these,* Charly absently thought.

A woman in a long dress and headscarf appeared, warmly greeting Hakan as her wide smile extended to Charly. In heavily accented English, she invited, "Please come. I am Gulperi." At her bidding they sat on embroidered pillows around a low wooden table. Soon, warm flat bread, lamb sausages, chunks of tomatoes and yoghurt were brought, along with lemonade. After some initial conversation in Turkish, they switched to Kurdish. Being lulled by the rhythm of the language, but not understanding, Charly tried to read body language and guess. Frustrated, she soon drifted with her own thoughts.

Gulperi, what a lovely name, thought Charly. *Rose fairy in Turkish—an omen of some sort?*

Charley believed in synchronicity, that things happened for a reason, often connected to the historical past. She got lost in her thoughts of change and her feelings of being here before; here in this barren and beautiful country of eastern Turkey.

Many didn't find high desert regions desirable, but to Charly it felt like home. In graduate school in Oregon, she had often escaped to the high desert of Christmas Valley, riding horseback alone at dawn and dusk. The peacefulness had seemed to settle her. She had quickly made friends with a few locals, finding a niche that no one back in the valley knew about. Privacy and special spaces were important to her.

Charly came back to the present with Hakan nudging her elbow and asking if she wanted more lemonade. Surprisingly her plate was empty and she was no longer hungry. Glad to see they had reverted to Turkish, Charly asked if they had settled on a plan yet.

Cevik responded to her slightly huffy question. "I'm sorry we spoke in Kurdish, but we needed to find out more about you and the situation. I felt it was better to do so in a language you did not understand. But Hakan has reassured me you can be trusted. So, no more secrets."

Charly simply nodded, as she probably would have done the same.

Then the questions came fast and furious concerning her fitness level, martial arts training, what experiences had she with weapons, explosives, and on and on.

Charly chuckled, "Oh, oh, this sounds like war!"

Cevik explained, "It seems to us and to our intelligence command post that you could be very helpful to us. We've been looking for a way in with the Raif family, and you have it with your CD to deliver."

"But," broke in Hakan, "it could be dangerous. I wouldn't want you to do it unless you have a chance of getting out, in case they suspect you."

"Suspect me? But I haven't done anything to arouse suspicion."

"Well, you have. MIT is alerted because you have a package to deliver in southeastern Turkey in a Kurdish village where known terrorists reside. This is against Turkish law, but they want you to go in, with me as escort. They want us to observe the people in the village. Now MIT is asking for more. "

The group was silent as Charly looked at each grim face.

"Why is this important for you?"

Gulperi answered, "We are tired of the Kurdish terrorists, of the PKK, trying to tear our country apart. Thirty thousand people have been killed by them in the last fifteen years. Some of the dead were tourists like yourself who were in a popular tour spot, others were our gendarmerie, police and military, and then there were innocent civilians, women and children who were caught in the crossfire or maimed by bombs. It is time for this violence to end."

As Gulperi paused, Charly commented, "You are Kurdish yourself."

"Yes, and for a while we thought the PKK was the answer. But there have been many Kurdish terrorists who have infiltrated from Iraq, Syria, and Iran. The violence has escalated. We want rights for the Kurdish people. We want to be recognized as a minority in Turkey, with citizenship rights. We are proud of our language. We want to give our children a Kurdish name to be proud of, not just to be used around fellow Kurds."

Becoming increasingly passionate in what she was saying, Gulperi continued. "We want our schools to teach in Kurdish, we want a radio program in our own language."

Gulperi leaned across the table and tightly grasped Charly's hand. "Please help us."

Charly accepted the challenge. "What I would be doing for you is a small part in your overall struggle, but I will do what I can."

Hakan's eyes held Charly's. "Are you sure?"

"That I will try, yes. But I need to know the plan."

"We've received some information which contradicts your office," began Cevik. "We get intelligence quicker than you do."

Hakan did not take offense. "No big surprise there. It takes a while for information to filter through various agents and be vetted. We have a lot more bureaucracy than you do."

"And that's the way we like it. Usually we can gain more trust and have more freedom when we don't have to follow the rules in everything."

"So, what contradictory information have you heard?"

"We've been hearing that the Raif family has broken with the PKK and has been working with the village guards in mountain communities to quell the violence. It's from good sources, but needs to be checked out. If so, that could give us tremendous advantage in ferreting out terrorists."

"This certainly changes the complexion of things," commented Charly. "So this might be a straightforward trip after all?"

"Might, might not. We've been wanting someone to verify. From what I know about you, this is your area of forensic expertise, Charly?"

"True! Looks like you've found us!"

It was agreed that Charly and Hakan would spend the next three days preparing her in case there was trouble.

"We need to first assess your skills, then hone them," Cevik explained.

Cevik's compound was the base for a training camp for mountainous counter-insurgence. Charly's quasi-fluency with Turkish would be helpful, but she needed to develop basic Kurdish.

Three days, right! Charly simultaneously felt exhilarated and nervousness at the challenge of the next few days.

After lunch, Charly changed into fatigues. Hakan, Charly, and Cevik walked up a trail into the mountains. As they walked around an outcropping a plateau came into view.

"Well, will you look at that?" exclaimed Charly as an elaborate obstacle course on the cliff side emerged. Dead ahead was a target range.

"Let's start you with the weapons first. What have you used?" asked Cevik.

"Hunting with a .300 mag with scope, and qualify for expert. I am not as accurate with pistols, sharpshooter, sustained fire event. Practice? At a range several times a year. I feel pretty rusty with pistols."

While she was talking, Cevik motioned for a human image target to be set up at two hundred yards. "Take your choice," he said, referring to four rifles brought out by a fit-looking soldier.

"Good, it has a scope. Accuracy checked for what distance?"

"Two hundred yards."

"And here we go." After loading, Charly assumed the standing position and put five shots in rapid succession into the chest area.

"Well, I wouldn't want to meet you across a field!" Hakan was clearly surprised.

"Now, let's see what you can do with a pistol."

"What model Glock do you have?"

"Good choice. They're less prone to corrosion and jamming in this dust we have here. What have you used?"

"Glock 21"

"I bet you'll like this Glock 30, then. It's lighter and more compact. I'd like you to try it and the Sig .228 or the .229, which can handle a larger caliber."

"Do you have the comp version of the Glock? I've learned to like the less recoil because of the attachment to re-direct the propellant gases."

"Yes, and we have the laser mounted, too. But it's the 32C."

"Then you don't have to line up the target with the sites. Cool!"

They spent the next three hours trying, then selecting and practicing with what would be Charley's pistol of choice, as well as introducing her to the AK-47. No surprise, she wasn't as proficient with the smaller weapon, but at least could hit the target at a good distance.

Cevik was impressed. "That's enough for now. You've done remarkably well. I had no idea you would be so skillful with guns. I had the background on you regarding your being a professor and forensic analyst but these other details were not included."

The sun was hitting the tops of the surrounding mountains, and now that her practicing was over, Charly felt the chill as the day cooled.

"My arms feel like they are ready to come off," Charly commented to Hakan as they walked the path down to the compound.

Hakan had been taken aback at her accuracy in using the guns against the target figure. He was learning a new side to her. Some of it was consistent, like her assertiveness, willingness to risk, and spontaneity. But until today he hadn't seen the hard side of her, the intensity of purpose upon her face during practice, her persistence in getting it just right. But now she was tired, and his feelings softened toward her, for now putting aside the glimpse of a warrior.

"How about a hot shower?" Hakan offered.

"And a clean set of clothes!" she agreed.

As they shared the evening meal with Cevik and Gulperi, conversation revolved around the day's success and how to orchestrate the remaining allotted two days. Charly was able to unwind the remaining tension that had lingered after her shower. Although she realized how absurd it was, she felt at home with friends.

After helping Gulperi clean up, Hakan asked if she'd like to take a walk before bed. She picked up a bottle of rakı and water along with a glass and followed him out the door.

"Ah, I see you are a woman with a man's taste," Cevik commented as he spotted her holdings.

"Man or woman, I could do with a drink after the pace of today."

Hakan and Charly nodded to the occasional soldier on watch as they walked to a flat rock which overlooked the valley. A quarter moon had just emerged over the mountains across the valley. It was chilly and Charly pulled her jacket closer, then poured some rakı with just a splash of water. They sat without talking, absorbing the silence and the occasional tumbling of stones as some small animal scurried on some unknown adventure.

"I think I can sleep now," Charly said after some time had passed. "I was so wound up today. This afternoon I finally realized this trip is no game, no frolic. And it doesn't frighten me. I want to do it. I'm excited by it. And, Hakan, I want to be with you."

They leaned into each other, drank the last sip of rakı, and headed back down the path.

It seemed as if she had just gotten to sleep when Gulperi was shaking her shoulder, urging her to get up. It was still dark and Charly needed some convincing.

"They want you for the next step in your training."

Charly became immediately alert, a characteristic from childhood which she'd found a blessing more than once. She dressed in clean shirt but the dirty fatigues from yesterday, and entered the kitchen where she could hear Hakan and Cevik quietly talking.

Declining the forever present hot tea but pouring some juice, she inquired, "Okay, so what is so important that you get me up well before dawn?"

Charly stood by the window noting that the stars were still out, but the moon had disappeared behind the mountains. Nevertheless, they cast enough light to make out the shapes of buildings and forms.

"We need to see how much of a friend darkness is to you. Many times when we are on surveillance or need to get out of a tough spot, it's at night. We want to see how you can hunt and evade in the darkness."

Charly had been on enough hunting trips to know the importance of getting up in the dark to get into the best place for the kill. Ever since she was small, she had felt that darkness was her friend, suffering none of the usual childhood fears of the bogeyman in the dark corners. Her ability to identify the origin, distance, and direction of sounds had been highly developed from childhood. "Okay, I'm ready—bring it on!"

Cevik blindfolded Charly and guided her, sometimes climbing, other times descending, doubling back and around enough so that she lost her sense of direction. When the blindfold was taken off, she found she was on a wide ledge about 2,000 feet above the valley.

"You aren't going to make it easy for me, are you?" The mountains prevented her from seeing Cevik's compound.

"Your goal is to find your way home, but you are going to be tracked. To be successful you must elude capture by my soldiers. They'll give you a fifteen-minute head start. They know these mountains, which are new to you." At that, Cevik pointed behind them. Someone flashed a light half again as far up the mountain. "You've got two hours to be back at the compound by dawn."

Hakan handed her a canteen, and he and Cevik leaned back against the rocks. "Here's a pellet gun. When you see your trackers, shoot them, and you'll see a stain of florescent yellow appear. "

"How about a pair of night goggles?"

"Ha! On your way, Charly, and good luck."

Giving them a thumbs-up as she hooked the gun's strap over her shoulder she walked around the jutting rock, squatted, closing her eyes. At first, the silence roared, then individual sounds became apparent A scurrying behind her and a pebble being dislodged must be a small rodent. The owl hooting and goats bleating in the distance needed to be blocked out, and the focus only for footfalls, a metal clank, a cough or sniffle, or rocks being dislodged.

Having spent just a couple of minutes attuning her listening, she opened her eyes and tried to assess where she was in relation to the compound. Knowing her pursuers would still be too far away to hear, she chambered a pellet.

Carefully working her way down the rocky mountain path, she was careful to lighten each step before putting her weight on it. If not, she knew in the darkness it would be easy to turn an ankle or send a rock careening, both of which would give away her position. Her plan was to find a hiding place so she could observe what the two trackers were doing. If lucky, maybe she could reverse positions and they would lead her to the compound with no "kills."

The path she was following led her around the mountain rather than down, and it quickly narrowed. As she cautiously felt along the rock rising steeply on her left in order to avoid the drop off, her hand felt space. *What's this*, she thought, glad she had caught herself before falling sideways. She couldn't see anything but increased blackness in a small area. Carefully exploring, she found there was a foot or so wide crevice. *I wonder if this could be a hiding place?* Thus pondering she edged her way into it, keeping the rifle to her left so nothing would reflect. She could just make it in sideways, glad of her slender build and small breasts. It went back about four feet before narrowing and preventing passage. The stars cast light into the space for about a foot, so she moved into the shadow and waited, straining to hear.

Charly lost track of the passage of time. *I guess I'll know it's too long when my muscles stiffen.* With this in mind she frequently scrunched her toes and did small rolls with her shoulders.

Did I imagine that? Ah, there it is again. A soft footfall, I bet. Yes, there he is, stealthily, making only the whisper of sound, walking past. Where is the other one? She waited what seemed like ten minutes, seeing or hearing no one else. *Aw, shit, they separated—of course!* Charly slowly crept from her protection, and paused. Sensing no one, she continued along the path.

Abruptly, the path dead-ended into rock and curved to the right. It was negotiable but steep. She paused here searching the darkness for the path below. Her stomach clenched as she caught a glimpse of movement below. It had registered a split second as she was scanning the terrain. *Interesting how it's easier to catch a movement sometimes out of the corner of your eye than when directly looking at it. There—he's emerging from behind the boulder. At least it's a man and not a goat! I've got him.*

She had to urge herself to go slowly and as carefully as before, for even though she was now a tracker, she was still being tracked. *Double trouble.* It was difficult on the rocks, as there were many loose ones which needed to be avoided. It seemed easier to see more on this open side and away from the mountain cliffs. Occasionally there were bushes to grab or a larger boulder, to make the downward trek seem safer. Charly paused every few minutes and listened. It was heartening to see occasional glimpses of the man in front of her. She could tell now that the path he was following was a zigzag pattern to the valley below. Thus, his way was easier than cutting across, but more time consuming. *And that is just what I'll do. I'll cut him off.* Charly felt a surge of energy. There was a dry creek bed from spring mountain run-off which ran to the left of the tracked one's path.

Although there were a lot of pebbles in the depression where the water flowed, Charly quickly found that the sides were worn fairly smooth. She was able to travel at a faster pace than on the path. Fortunately, the creek bed provided partial cover as it had bushes growing on the sides. About halfway down to the valley, she paused to quiet her breathing and listen. *The night is so still. Not even a breeze. How nice it would be to have bacon, eggs, and a cinnamon roll about now.* With this idle thought skirting through, she realized she was hungry and quickly pushed this distraction to the side. *What have I missed since I've been daydreaming?*

COMPLICATED FAVORS: A TURKISH AFFAIR

Realizing that distractions could be costly, she refocused and immediately heard the sound of a boot hitting a rock at the same time a rabbit went scurrying within a couple of feet of her. Still in the crouching position, she raised her rifle to her shoulder and slowly rose up halfway. The bushes were thinner here, but still above her head. *Shh, here he comes. Easy now. Just wait.* He passed her, walking slowly. *Now!* Just as he passed, Charly carefully but quickly aimed, pulling the trigger almost in one movement.

A shoulder hit just as he was turning in her direction, having heard the slight click of safety-off. *Lesson # 1, keep the safety off,* she berated herself. Although she wanted to shout gleefully, she remained silent so as not to reveal her position to the other tracker. Charly parted the bushes and strode to where the casualty stood grinning rather foolishly.

I've been bested by a woman.. Damn! he thought. They shook hands and Omar sat down to wait until dawn so as not to provide false distractions.

As Charly walked away, she could smell chocolate. *Unfair!* she silently shouted.

One more to go. She was imaging herself walking into the compound at dawn, with two successful "kills." She figured the tracker just shot had been heading in the right direction, so continued on this path.

Charly rounded the outcropping and met face-to-face with Malmud who stood there grinning.

"Oh, shit," she said aloud as she held out her hand.

"Didn't expect that, did you? Have some chocolate?"

As if on cue, a golden hue began to embrace the valley below. Tracker Two gave a quick hoot of an owl, and in a few minutes Tracker One joined them.

Omar and Malmud shared their chocolate with Charly as she queried when they had picked her up.

"Oh, we tried a technique we've used before, taking parallel paths, occasionally hooting to give our position. We figured you'd take the path down, so Malmud followed you. If you got one of us, we figured you'd never expect the other to be so close by. Immediately after a kill, most people relax their guard just a bit while they congratulate themselves. That's what we depended on. One might fail, but not both of us."

Although chagrined that their plan had worked so easily on her, she admitted they had bested her with a well-designed plan. "Hell, I'm a psychologist. I should have expected something like that. My cockiness got me that time."

"*Evet*," said Omar, agreeing. "But we've had many more years of experience and know these mountains well. Psychological training is as important as physical in our line of work."

All three were in good spirits, periodically taking turns hooting and laughing as they hiked down the mountain as dawn broke, casting the compound in first light.

"What's going on? We could hear you a mile away!" Cevik turned from doing calisthenics with about twenty men.

They surrounded the band of three as they clapped Charly on the back and chided Omar for the patch of yellow he was wearing on his shoulder. Hakan was standing to one side, smiling.

Hakan joined Charly as she continued on her way toward Cevik's house. Shoulders brushing they walked in silence for a dozen steps before Hakan spoke. "You did well, Charly. I'm proud of you." Their eyes locked and Charly saw sincere admiration in his.

But what right did he have to be proud? she simultaneously thought while at the same time wanting to grab him and hold tightly, partially out of exhilaration from her training, and because of the unspoken deep feelings she saw there. Their gazes held, both savoring this intimacy. Her senses were heightened already but she shivered with this new assault.

Gulperi stood watching them for a moment frowning, concerned that complications may loom for both of them. And not just for this upcoming mission. She thought of Hakan as a brother, and had loved his first wife, her cousin. She had been so different than Charly, so feminine and soft. Gulperi worried. *I like Charly but she is a westerner and only transient. They must keep on the path of friendship, no more. Perhaps he'll be driven away from feelings as he sees how she can be like one of the men. Oh, Allah, I'm so petty. Forgive me.*

"Charly, you're back! Come inside for breakfast," invited Gulperi, and thus the moment was shattered. Hakan returned to Cevik and his men, who were now on a ropes course.

After a shower, change of clothes, and food, Charly went in search of Cevik. She spent the rest of the day training with his men as they alternately climbed in different terrain, donned heavy packs and repeated the trail, dropped and shot, and practiced with sniper rifles.

They shared rations that night at dusk near the crest of a nearby mountain, huddled in an area which kept out the brisk, cool wind. They all talked quietly as they critiqued their own and the others' performances that day. They were equally as hard on Charly as on their own. Many commented on her stamina and her quickness not to repeat the same mistake twice.

Charly did not feel like a woman among men, but rather a soldier with them. *Thank Allah for the many hours of aerobics and private boot camp twice a year,* she thought. *The yoga has certainly improved my balance. Now if it would only snow, maybe I could make use of my skiing skills as well. Oops, better be careful of what I think. Winter can't be that far away.*

As a group they tucked the empty food packages into their packs and headed back to the compound. No training now, just a well pleased unit going home.

An exhausted Charly slept the sleep of the dead, awakening at dawn refreshed. She joined Cevik, Hakan, and Gulperi at the table, where Gulperi quickly poured her Turkish *cay*.

Cevik laid out the day. "More target practicing this morning. You need extra work on accuracy with pistols. As a sniper you more than pass muster. That won't take long. You need to demonstrate you can mount and use the AN/PVS night vision device and the M68 close-combat optic sight. You've had a lot of experience with scopes, but these have unique properties. You need to know them by heart, as in the field there's no learning time. Have you ever targeted with a stinger missile?"

Charly shook her head. "I just know about them, their effectiveness to shoot aircraft out of the sky, like the TWA flight. They're heat seeking, and have a long range."

Cevik explained: "The nose of the missile actually has an infrared digital camera. The target must be visible near the center of the sensor. Its range is about five miles, or a flying target as high as eleven hundred feet. We'll introduce it to you this morning, and have you try it. It's about one-fourth of your weight. "

"Why would we need to take along a stinger?" inquired Charly.

"You won't. And you likely won't need to acquire one. But, those you are seeking may have them. RPGs are on my list to acquaint you with, too. You and Hakan may have to recognize and disable them if necessary. Hakan already knows, of course."

"Of course," Charly echoed, realizing how much she would have to rely on herself, not her partner.

"After lunch we'll map out our trip, Charly. We leave tomorrow."

In the afternoon they perused both topographical maps and ones with roads and pathways. Current gendarmerie blockades were marked on the map as well as known strongholds of the different terrorist groups. They were on their way to Hakkari province, which lies on the border with Iraq and Syria, via Diyarbakir. The area was still under a state of emergency, set by Turkey in 1987 due to the high level of PKK terrorist activities. Both Turkish gendarmes and the military monitored checkpoints and roads throughout southeastern Turkey.

At dinner this last night each of the four seemed thoughtful. The mood was subdued as conversation veered from tomorrow's journey to more personal discussion. As they shared a bottle of rakı, each spoke of their parents, grandparents, and of the characteristics they most admired. Each of the grandparents had been farmers, but with different crops and animals. It was as if on this last night, they wanted to invoke their ancestors' spirits to the table. This was not unusual among tribesmen as a way to gain courage, and maybe a sense of protection.

Hakan and Charly walked an easy path to a nearby ridge and quietly watched the sun settle behind the mountains. The colors were subdued, a mix of pale yellow and lavender as it got later. Charly reached for Hakan's hand and leaned into his shoulder. And thus they sat, gaining warmth from each other as the night cooled. As the night sky became brilliant with stars the tension between them built until it could no longer be ignored. Charly lifted Hakan's hand and softly rubbed her cheek against it. They turned toward one another, their entwined hands caught between them as their lips met. At first the kiss was soft and sweet, then deepened as their hands separated and wound around each other. They held each other closely, tightly, as their hands wandered over the other's hair, face and back. Sounds of pleasure spoke of their increased passion for each other. At the point both knew neared the overpowering need for completion, they broke apart, looking into each other's eyes for an answer.

Do we really want this?
Oh, God, yes. I am aching for him. I want him now.
I have to stop now, or I never will. I want all of her.
But what about his wife?

Aloud, Hakan abruptly admitted, "My wife is dead."

"What are you saying? You've led me to believe you were married. Kamil said you were married and had two children. You've shown me pictures of your girls. Are they fiction, too?"

"I do have two daughters. I'm sorry. I should have said something before. But with this barrier I thought we were safer."

"But you have no right to decide for me!" Charly spoke harshly, jumping up and folding her arms around herself, suddenly chilled. "Goodnight." Charly stomped down the path.

The earlier momentum of increasing closeness was shattered as they each dealt alone with the inescapable fact of the existence of "other" and deception.

Neither one slept well that night, and rose at dawn to eat with Gulperi and Cevik. Gulperi inferred Charly's preoccupation and distancing was due to tension related to their mission.

Before they left, Hakan checked his email and sent a coded message that they were on their way.

- 9 -
Thorns and roses grow on the same tree
- turkish proverb -

Before they had driven a mile, Charly and Hakan began clearing the air from the misunderstanding of the night before.

"Charly, I'm sorry I hurt your feelings. I should have told you right away."

"I had no right to get mad like that. It made me realize that I've allowed myself to become too fond of you, too close to you. I'd built a fiction. My reaction was clearly out of line."

"We have some trust, Charly. And I don't know what else yet. Maybe we were both building unrealistic expectations, and this is just what caught fire."

Sounds like Hakan is distancing himself. But he's right. Back off, Charly.

I wonder if Charly wants to put some space between us. Being thrown into constant contact and trying to form a relationship on such bizarre grounds as this has thrown us into a place I have never before experienced. I know I'm very attracted to her, but now is not the time to push it.

I hope we can just let things evolve rather than analyze too much. Did I just think that? Bizarre! Talk about being out of character. Charly mentally shook her head at herself.

"Hakan, please tell me about your wife."

And Hakan obliged, and spoke of how they met and his memories of her.

Lutfiye had been from a traditional Muslim family, dressed traditionally, and was shy as a Muslim woman should be. He remembered her walking along the path at the university with her girlfriends, giggling, eyes cast downward. There was something that set her apart, perhaps the graceful way she moved. When he found out her name, Lutfiye, he thought her name was fitting, for it meant a good and well-behaved woman. He was Muslim but secular in beliefs, like his family and most of his friends. Because of her religious beliefs, he could not ask her out. She seemed so serious one moment, and happy and laughing the next. This contrast intrigued him. He could only see her in the company of her friends, but he was smitten. He learned from her friends that she was interested in him, too.

He would be graduating soon and would then continue into formal training in military security. His parents had been badgering him that it was time to seek a wife, but did not support his interest in Lutfiye. She was too young, only seventeen, and probably didn't even know how to cook, his mother Ahu pointed out.

His father weighed in with his views. "Well, maybe that's just the thing. She can learn to be the wife Hakan wants, and you can teach her to cook."

Reaching consensus, his mother approached Lutfiye's mother who also had her reservations in that Hakan was not a devout Muslim and would expose her daughter to liberal ways. The conversation went on for quite some time as more female relatives joined them, entering into the discussion with more enthusiasm and volubility than practical solutions. Being vastly outnumbered, Ahu left in time to prepare dinner with increased opposition in her heart.

When Hakan arrived home, his beautiful mother's eyes were hot with indignation as she related what had transpired. More than ever she wanted Hakan to turn his attentions elsewhere, to a woman who would match him in spirit and in the political belief to maintain Turkey as secular, in accordance with Ataturk. She wanted him to marry one as free as Ahu herself to dress as she wished, drink rakı if she wished, and have a career. Ahu was a teacher of literature in high school and loved the freedom it gave her to have her own money and develop friendships on her own beyond her husband.

"Mother, I love you. Your mother named you well as Ahu, meaning beautiful eyes. I don't want to see disappointment in them, but I want to marry Lutfiye." Tears had sprung to her expressive eyes, but were not shed.

A week later Ahu returned to the home of Lutfiye for the official visit. This was to be her first look at Lutfiye. As tradition demanded, Lutfiye served tea and sweets to the fifteen female guests, to show her skill and grace in this deceptively simple hospitality. The women took off their *chador* when they entered the receiving room whose windows had been carefully shuttered to the outside.

Ahu got her first look at Lutfiye's beautiful long curling hair and graceful, well-kept hands. The pale yellow dress she wore was stylish and demure, showing off her full bosom and round hips. Ahu looked for sultriness in her eyes and saw only shyness. Oh-oh, she thought, Hakan will be surprised, and not pleasantly, in bed. Someone of her looks should be a tiger in loving her man, but she knew this would not be the case. Clearly, though, she was good and decent, even though,

Ahu thought snidely, she will get as sloppy as her mother is in twenty years.

They agreed upon the exchange of gifts. Two days from now, Lutfiye, her mother, and Ahu herself would go to the best shops in Izmir to choose jewels and clothes for Lutfiye, as was the dowry tradition among the most traditional Turks. Hakan's family would pay. Gifts would also be purchased by Lutfiye's family for Hakan. The day of the wedding these would all be displayed and the honor of both families judged on the matching of these two young people. Lutfiye's family lived in a country village and kept sheep. There were also three prize sheep presented as gifts at the wedding.

And their marriage had been good, not exciting, but good. They had two daughters and their births were uneventful. She was built to breed, her mother had said. Lutfiye and her family wanted many children, but Hakan insisted on only two. He kept track of her cycle and avoided her fertile times. Luckily for him it had worked. It had been as his mother had predicted. Lutfiye kept a clean, well-organized home, with dinner ready soon after Hakan walked in the door. She knew he liked wine with dinner and rakı and although she didn't complain, she did not serve it. He would pour it himself and she would sit at the table with him, often in silence. She never complained about the weeks at a time he would be gone or his uncertain schedule. Hakan grew comfortable with the certainty of what to expect, even in bed. She never did get comfortable undressing in front of him but did not resist him when he pulled the sheet aside. She never turned him away except during her period or in the last half of pregnancy.

"I later learned from her sister that Lutfiye was jealous of the pretty tourists I met while driving my bus. She understood this was a cover for my job with military security.

The dangerous aspects did not worry her because she had faith in my skills and in the will of Allah. But another woman is always the fear of a Turkish woman. In her heart, though, she knew I would always return to her, that to me, a bond is sacred and our children more precious than life itself. And thus, she would lull herself into the security of a married woman."

Against his wishes, Lutfiye became pregnant for the third time. Early on she suffered dizziness and periodic abdominal pain, but would not see the doctor, opting to take herbal remedies instead. "This is the burden of a woman," her mother repeatedly told them both.

When Hakan came home from a two-week encampment, Lutfiye was in bed with severe pain and was very pale. Hakan insisted she see a physician, carrying her to the car. He took her to the emergency entrance. By then, Lutfiye was going into shock. It was a tubular pregnancy, which had ruptured. The shock caused by internal bleeding and infection throughout her system was too much. Antibiotics did not help. She died two days later.

"And your daughters?"

"They live with Lutfiye's sister's family. It is their main home now as I travel too much to provide one for them. They stay with me when I return. Our places are within a couple blocks of the other."

Hakan's story took all morning, with many pauses and a lot of reflection. Charly listened in silence, not interrupting. When he reached the end, she reached over and placed her hand on his knee, a gesture in which he immediately took comfort, and held it. Thus they silently rode, each lost in thought.

The two-hundred-fifty-mile trip southeast to Diyarbakir was over a fairly good road, but it still took them until late afternoon. They uneventfully went though five checkpoints, two of which were close to the city. One had to watch out for sheep as they nosed their way onto the roadway. The scores of apricot groves spoke loud praise of this fertile valley. All of this was background to their private cocoon of Hakan's revelations.

- 10 -
An open door invites callers
- turkish proverb -

Charly could see that it would not be difficult to find a hotel in this city of nearly one million. Hakan turned down side streets, driving through increasingly quiet neighborhoods until he pulled to a stop in front of a small three-story concrete building with a discreet hotel sign. As they walked to the door with their two bags they saw no one else on the street. Lights shone from windows in the pale yellow glow of dusk. Thus welcomed, they entered a beautifully appointed lobby area with local *kilim* carpets and polished wood. All of the signs were in Kurdish with no nod to another language, including Turkish.

A woman in traditional clothing, head covered, greeted them, and Hakan asked for two rooms. After showing identification, they were each given a key and directions.

As it turned out, the rooms were connecting. Charly was pleased as the threat of danger or uncertainty made her uneasy. Charly was just beginning to wonder about the folly of it all. Always before, the fact of her government behind a mission gave a sense of security. *No U.S. task force this time.* She'd like to be near someone who understood cultural ramifications. *It will be comforting to have Hakan so close.*

Charly was entranced with her room, with the sheer silk curtains hanging from the four posters drawn back to reveal a fluffy duvet of deep red. The walls were covered with deep red woven material with geometrical patterns in beige and yellows. Turkoman carpets were scattered on the wooden floors. The feeling of tranquil lushness took Charly into another time of sultanates. The bath was simple with a shower, but the burnished faucets shone like gold.

They took time for quick showers, then headed out for dinner. They decided to go to the Selim Amca Restaurant, which was famous for its regional lamb. And they weren't disappointed with the garlic flavored chunks of roasted meat, rice, eggplant and tomatoes. Even though they were deep into traditional Muslim territory, part of the city was cosmopolitan, and liquor was served in designated places. With dinner they tried the local red wine, finding it a little harsh, but it easily disappeared.

Before returning to the hotel they strolled through the city streets heading for a park a few blocks away. "Excuse me a minute," said Hakan as he dashed to a store which was just closing. Talking rapidly, the shopkeeper opened up the door again, and Hakan emerged a few minutes later carrying a single flower. "For you," he said as he handed Charly the perfect deep red rose. Slowly she touched it to her cheek, feeling its soft velvet, and inhaled its strong muskiness. "It's so beautiful, Hakan. Thank you." And she raised the rose to his cheek and gently stroked. Hakan turned his head so his lips momentarily touched the rose. When he put his arm about her waist to stroll on, she reciprocated. And thus entwined they walked up a gently sloping hill to the tiny park.

This is a pattern I could get used to enjoying. Like the Turks of old, Hakan can be fierce or gentle. Underneath resides a courtly romantic.

COMPLICATED FAVORS: A TURKISH AFFAIR

At the neighborhood park entrance there was a statue of a beautiful girl with a fairy perched on her shoulder.

"Do you know of this statue? It is famous to us. No? Well, let me tell you a story.

"There was once a beautiful young girl who was lost in the hills. Bandits from a neighboring village found her, bound her, and were carrying her off to marry one of their sons. She was very frightened but brave, and did not cry. She pretended to have fainted and to be very weak. That night when all were sleeping, she opened her eyes, plucked the knife from a scabbard of the nearest man, and cut her ropes. She sneaked out of the tent without anyone hearing her. But she did not recognize the surrounding hillside. She was lost. She began to pray. Feeling something on her shoulder, she glanced in the pool of water in which the villagers bathed. There perched this delightfully sprightly creature with wings and carrying a rose. She flew off as soon as she was noticed. Thinking she had just imagined the fairy, the girl began walking. Having taken no more than a step she noticed something glowing. Looking more closely she saw it was a rose petal, and then she saw a trail of them. As soon as she was past, the petals would blow away. Thus she walked through the night, eventually finding herself on the edge of her village. There were no more petals. The sun was casting its first glow upon the earth."

"A beautiful story! I love it. Is this *gulperi*, the rose fairy?"

"Yes. Every little girl knows this story. I've told it to my daughters many, many times. They are in search of their own rose fairy."

A light drizzle started to fall, so soft it was like a mist. That, the rose, and Hakan's fanciful tale combined to weave a magical space for the two of them.

"You are my *gulperi*," said Hakan.

The tension between them was palatable and both felt as if their bodies were vibrating. Simultaneously they drew closer and their lips touched. The gentle kiss belied the underlying power of their feelings. Overwhelmed by their desire to be together, they left the park.

As they neared the exit, they drew apart from entwined arms and walked side by side. They did not want to arouse suspicion, and romantic behavior in public was condemned. They were fortunate they had not been seen. Kurds had been known to toss a can of soda or whatever was handy at public displays of affection in sometimes painful disapproval.

Silently they took the elevator to their floor and unlocked Charley's door. She walked to the window and gazed at the city's wall, thinking. *Do I really want this? Yes! What about consequences? I don't care. I want him too much to even think about that now. I can deal later with whatever it is. Not now.* Turning, she saw Hakan standing between the dresser and the bed. She thought he must be wondering what she would do, and he was. He gave passing thought of his dead wife to whom he had pledged loyalty. *That's over now*, he thought with a touch of sadness.

Walking to him, Charly touched the rose to her lips, then his, then turned, laying it gently on the dresser. *I should put it in water. Not now.* That simple gesture melted whatever reservations lingered, and it became now for them, their night, their time.

Charley slowly removed her sweater, pleased for some reason that she never wore a bra. She was taut with desire. Hakan had slipped out of his coat. She unbuttoned and removed his shirt and t-shirt. The absence of words was not noticed by either of them. His chest was covered with a pelt of short dark hair which felt soft and wiry at the same time as she skimmed her hand from neck to belt buckle.

Hakan gently caressed her face, and said their first words since they left the park. "You are so beautiful. Your eyes touch my soul." And they kissed passionately, without urgency, hungry to give and receive caresses.

Charly slowly stepped back, dropping her hands to remove her slacks and underwear. Her hands went to Hakan's belt buckle and she slowly and deliberately removed the remainder of his clothing. Hakan gently moved his hands in circular motion from breasts to navel and below. Over and over. *Who are you, woman, that I want you so much? Who are you that I can't wait?*

Charly could no longer resist and bent, capturing him with moist lips and tongue. Their need for one another burst into flames and they lay upon the bed. Charly felt liquid and she surrendered her soul to him. Sensing this, and knowing his will was hers, he gently kissed her, before joining their bodies. And here, urgent demands were made and met and silence was broken with the call of the other's name and praise of the gods which had made this possible. They were swept away, increasingly brought to their limits when they soared together over the mountains and became one. *"Never like this,"* is how it felt to them. It was like coming home. They stayed as one as they dozed.

Charly woke first and was aware of his weight, which was heavy but felt good. It was difficult for her to remain still as her hips wanted to move even closer. The internal pull became stronger. Hakan slowly awakened. Motions matched in rhythm. And they quickly and quietly found the pleasure again of release. Shifting on the bed to cuddle front to back they fell into a deep sleep.

Some hours later Charly awakened and slipped quietly into the shower. As hot water cascaded over her, she touched her body where Hakan had and closed her eyes as her body tingled with remembrance. *Why does it feel so right?* she wondered. *There can be no going back after this. I can't pretend it didn't happen. I don't know how long we'll be together, but I want every minute I can. What are the complications? It feels so right, that it must be.*

Hakan was awake, just barely. *So, this is what it can be like. I've had my share of sex, but never did it feel like this.* He thought of his wife. *There was duty and release, and I loved her. My needs were met, but she never initiated. This went far beyond. I feel like the poets must when they write of darkness into light, of soaring, and transcending. Oh, by Allah, I want more. I want her.*

When Charly returned to bed, she motioned for him to turn over and commenced to massage him from head to toes. He was very aware of each stroke. It seemed to be something done to each other, not her to him. It was the breeze caressing the tree limbs. When she began the Turkish massage using the quick movements of her cupped hand, he asked himself, *How did she learn that?* He found himself strongly and quickly aroused. Quickly turning over, he placed her over his hips and she encased him with warmth and wetness. They rode with a wildness this time which soon ended. And, surprisingly, they began laughing, which turned into playful tickling. "God, we're just like two kids."

Hakan laughingly responded, "Turkish kids."

For some reason this sobered their mood, as it brought to mind their own children. Reality entered, aided by the dawn call of the *muezzin* coming through the open window. In contrast, a jet from the nearby NATO airbase flew over.

Hakan tousled her hair, and got up. "We'll talk—later."

They were both feeling the need to regain their own space and think about the change in their relationship. They took their time showering, dressing, and packing up their few belongings.

Hakan thought he should be exhausted, but instead he felt exhilarated.

Allah be praised! What a woman. She's not afraid to show herself to me. Once again, the contrast with his deceased wife intruded.

After breakfast they walked along the thick basalt city walls, alternately walking on top and exploring the corridors. "I feel we're walking among the ancients. I wish we could go back 5,000 years when the first people settled here. I wish we knew their stories," said Charly.

"I'm not so sure you would have been happy living here. These walls don't offer the protection you'd think. Until the Ottomans won control in the sixteenth century, there were continuous periods of battles and regime changes."

This discussion served to take them away from themselves and the relationship they were forging. They needed this distance to continue unfettered on their mission. It was dangerous to become emotionally involved with one's partner. Hakan well remembered the admonitions of his training officer that involvement could lead to carelessness because the mind might stray, or steps would be taken to protect the other. Anything that diverted one's attention from the task at hand could be fatal.

Luckily, they were both excellent at compartmentalizing. They could direct their energies to a mission with almost single-minded focus. And just as easily, when the job was over, selectively allow distractions.

Hakan and Charly returned to their car, and were ready to commence their journey to make their delivery.

"Ah, if it were only as simple as Frances had thought when she accepted the package from Besim," lamented Charly. "It certainly started out as a simple task, but now has become part of a covert operation."

"Having second thoughts?"

"No, I was just thinking of other times when I had fallen into doing consulting work with the CIA just because I happened to be in a place where I was needed. After that first accidental time, I surely got hooked. Consulting work, ha! What a benign name for dangerous missions. Maybe it will be a simple delivery after all."

"Dream on, Charly."

- 11 -
If you are an anvil, be patient;
If you are a hammer, be strong.
- turkish proverb -

While Hakan drove, Charly studied the detailed map of the road which Turkish MIT had provided. Their destination was a village in the eastern mountains of Hakkari toward the Iranian border.

"It looks as if this road becomes increasingly narrow and winding. It just ends at the village. I don't like that. We could get trapped. Do you think we should hide our car and approach on foot to see if anything is going on in the village?"

"No, if it is as Cevik's intelligence suggests, they'll have spotted us as soon as we leave this main road. They'll be suspicious enough without watching us skulk around. It's a good way to get shot." Hakan spoke with the confidence forged by experience.

"So, it's best to go in innocently. I'm just doing a favor for a friend—friendly American and all that."

"Right. Just don't overdo it, Charly."

They passed two checkpoints in the twenty miles before turning off to begin their ascent. Their four wheel drive was perfect for the deeply rutted and dusty road, necessitating slowing to a crawl as Hakan maneuvered around huge boulders. As they got higher the road frequently gave way on one side to the valley below, while a cliff loomed on the other. Suddenly, it just stopped.

"What's this? The map shows the road ending at the village. All I see is the dried stream bed."

"Damn," muttered Hakan. "Now we sit and wait. They know we're here. They'll come to us in a few minutes. They're watching us now to see what we do. Look to your right, a ways up the mountain and you'll see what I mean."

Charly saw the man holding a rifle where Hakan pointed. "Look, there are several."

They waited in the car with the windows open. The cool breeze reminded them of their altitude. They were quiet, busy with their own thoughts. Their heightened tension kept them within themselves.

This is it, thought Charly. *Whatever "it" is.* She tugged the shawl she'd bought in Cappadocia more tightly around her shoulders, made sure her scarf was in place, and felt for the package in her pocket.

Within ten minutes three men with automatic assault rifles appeared and approached the car, one on each side. The third stayed several yards away.

Hakan explained in Kurdish. "My friend is from America. She is here to deliver a package from a friend."

"Show me your identity papers."

After looking at them for several minutes, he gave a quick command, and the other two lowered their rifles.

"Come with me. We've been expecting you. I am Mahir."

Mahir was tall and slender with a salt and pepper goatee on his chiseled face. His manner was at once graceful and commanding, calm yet intense. His dark eyes penetrated and were unreadable.

Upon leaving the vehicle Hakan was patted down for a weapon. When they reached the edge of the small village a woman appeared in full *chador* and motioned Charly to come with her. In a nearby hut, she painstakingly searched for weapons. Not finding any, she went to the door and nodded to the leader of the band of three then motioned for Charly to leave.

"We have guests. Come welcome them!" shouted Mahir. Slowly children then women filed into the single street of the village.

"This is my wife, Dilara. These people have come a long way to see you."

"Dilara, my name is Charly. I shop in your cousin's store in America. He sent this present for you." Fortunately Dilara understood Charly's Turkish.

Dilara unwrapped the brightly colored scarf which Frances had thought made it look more like a gift. She let it slowly trail through her fingers. "This is so beautiful, so soft." Her eyes crinkled at the side as she widely smiled.

She immediately handed the CD to her husband who had slipped into the hut and retrieved a portable CD player.

Hmm, state-of-the-art, thought Charly, as she eyed the latest Sony workmanship. Soon the music from The Red Hot Chili Peppers was blasting away and the children started dancing to its rhythm and laughing.

Mahir nodded to Hakan and began walking down the path toward the mountain.

"You need to stay here with the women. Remember your new role." Hakan quietly spoke so the others couldn't hear.

And indeed I do know it well, lowering her eyes when Hakan spoke with her, and reminding herself of some basic cultural differences. Rural Kurdish women had specific roles and viewed the freedom and assertiveness of American women as a sign of weakness in their ability to hold onto a man and marry. Or maybe no man loved them enough to take care of them, so they just wandered free. Charley always thought it must be similar to a goat that had broken its tether, and the farmer never came searching for him so he starved. Since men and women had a difficult time controlling impulses, they were usually segregated by sex. Women covered themselves to keep themselves sacred and not tempt men. And one never looked directly at a Kurdish man, or a Turk for that matter, as it was often interpreted as an expression of sexual interest.

Okay, so I know all this. Go to work!

Charly found herself isolated in the street. The women in the group formed a circle around Dilara, admiring her scarf.

Charly approached Dilara in Turkish. "Dilara, the children love to dance to the music. Do you?"

"Not this. Wait." She dashed into the house and brought back another CD.

With a wave of her hand and a few Kurdish words, the children formed a circle.

"In your honor." Dilara nodded toward the group.

Instrumental Kurdish folk music filled the air. The children began circling, clapping, and weaving amongst each other to the ancient rhythm. Without thinking, Charly began swaying and clapping. Noticing this, Dilara took her by the hand and they joined the children's folk dance, delighting the children.

Looking around as she tried mastering the steps in her less than graceful footwear, Charly saw smiles, laughter, and acceptance. *These villagers aren't fearful or suspicious, which comes with oppression and uncertainty. I'll bet my new boots this is not a terrorist encampment.* She relaxed, enjoying the spontaneous dance.

Hakan was ushered into a cave at the end of the village where it abutted the mountain.

Once inside, Mahir challenged. "Welcome to our war room, as we like to call it. Now, no more nice-nice. Why are you really here? I know who you are, of your standing in Turkish Special Forces operations. You usually work undercover and covertly. Now you bring in an American woman on some frivolous pretext. There is no way you are out for a casual jaunt in the mountains."

Mahir sat staring at Hakan, arms resting on the table, his eyes blazing. Behind him two unsmiling Kurds leaned against the wall loosely cradling their AK-47s. Sensing alert observation in the three men, not menace, Hakan's tension slightly lessened.

Taking a deep breath, Hakan dove in, realizing anything but honesty would be counterproductive. *Limited at first, then I'll see what happens.*

"Charly did bring the package from her friend Besim in America." He went ahead to relate the series of events that drew them to be at this point.

"But why send you of all people with her? For that matter, why wasn't she just arrested for transporting questionable material?"

"My command knows of the recent increase in terrorist activity in the area and wanted me to escort her to keep her safe."

"Allah Kahretsin!" exploded Mahir, pounding his fist on the table. "You came after me!"

"Now why would I do that?" countered Hakan with mock seriousness.

"Stop talking nonsense. *Saçmalama*! What have you heard about me, of us?"

"You have led the fight, instigating action against the Turkish military for the duration of the fifteen years of conflict. Granted, most of it was insidious action, such as disabling their trucks or alerting a village of their arrival. But, you were there in the middle of it all. You have great respect of the villagers in the Hakkari region."

"And the rumors?"

"PKK affiliated."

"And what have I been doing recently?"

"There's the rub. No one is certain. Either you have turned pacifist and mind your goats or you are being especially clever not to take credit for your activities."

"Ha!" scoffed Mahir. Even the two guards smiled at this.

"Okay, enough of this sparring. I need you. I've already talked with Cevik about a joint mission and your command has approved. It's a test of our loyalty of support for the Kurds, not the terrorists. A lot has happened in the twenty-four hours it took you to get here."

He's right about that! Hakan smiled to himself.

"I need to verify what you're saying."

While Hakan placed the calls, Mahir retrieved the CD from Dilara in order to begin their own analysis.

Hakan placed two satellite calls. Cevik verified the latest intel and urged cooperation. "It may be our best chance. We've had no success on our own."

Hakan's contact at headquarters agreed to take advantage of this opportunity to join the local mountain group who had inside information in a way they could never get. "It could be the beginning of a very helpful relationship in fighting the terrorists."

"What about Charly?"

"She'll have to go along, Hakan. No choice. It's taking her recon skills further than either of you had in mind, but she's been on similar missions. Do you think she'll balk?"

"Quite the contrary! But she's not Turkish and shouldn't do it without American special ops knowing and approving."

"That's out of your bailiwick, Hakan. Don't worry about it. It will be handled."

Hakan rejoined the group. They removed headphones and continued talking quietly while working with some graph paper.

When they looked up Hakan confirmed, "Okay, I'm in."

"Charly isn't just a tourist, is she? How does she fit in?"

As Hakan related some of Charly's background, Mahir's eyes grew wider. "You have a woman for a partner now?"

"Oh come on, don't sound so shocked. We both know that the all female terrorist groups are the most cruel and cunning. And have some of the best results, too. Who better for a partner?"

"Are you saying Charly is a terrorist?"

"Of course she's not. But I'm betting that she can hold her own."

"We'll see, won't we? I assume you will join our team together? Or, we could leave her at the village with the women until we return."

Hakan laughed aloud, startling the three Kurds. "Clearly you don't know Charly!"

"Has MIT broken the code on the CD yet?"

"Only part of it—some coordinates but we didn't know to what they relate."

"Looks like we'd better revise if MIT got even some of it." Mahir frowned.

"We just finished listening, Hakan. They're coordinates all right. Let's bring in Charly and tell her our plans."

Mahir instructed one of the guards to bring something to eat and ask Charly to join them.

Not knowing what to expect, Charly paused at the door of the room, raising her eyebrows in question at Hakan, who nodded. She stood at the entrance to the cave room with her hands on hips, silent, looking at each man, directly holding Mahir's gaze.

"Why was I left standing in the street alone?" she demanded.

"Did you stay alone?" Mahir countered.

"No." *Jeez, I sound petulant. Stop it!*

"So?" Mahir sidestepped a confrontation. "We didn't know you, Charly, and hadn't heard of you until yesterday. We know Hakan by reputation. Strangers here are treated with respect but not more until we know their intentions."

Charly nodded. What Mahir said made sense.

Hakan was relieved to see that some of Charly's tension, evident in her rudeness, visibly lessened. *We don't need that today, Charly*, he thought.

Hakan motioned her to sit down and explained the change of situation.

"Well, let's look at the plans, then I'll decide."

Charly felt a mixture of relief that these villagers posed no immediate danger. In her first impression, she had sensed no threat other than the weapons themselves. The reference to Cevik's verification was reassuring. However, it was a lot of change to absorb. Whether her command approved or not did not concern her. She guessed they eventually would do so. *I'm here now. This is what's most important.*

Tea and snacks were brought, quickly consumed, and the remains pushed aside.

Topographical and road maps were spread onto the tables. Mahir identified the area where his informants had told him terrorists were massing, which had been confirmed by the insertion of information in the modified CD.

Mahir further explained to Hakan and Charly, "It's a copy of what Besim's group in the U.S. had intercepted. It reveals the location of terrorists and designated targets in the Sat-Cilo Mountains, but no dates. The only specific plan my intel heard was of an imminent coordinated plan to begin destroying oil and gas trucks coming across the borders to Turkey from Iraq and Iran."

"Thus the urgency."

"Right, Charly. We need to move out tomorrow."

Several plans and approaches were considered. As they narrowed their choices, plastic sheets were placed on top and three emerging plans were marked. They narrowed their approach to two. In case one failed, they would have a backup.

They debated whether or not to have Charly use the false identification papers which were given to her by Cevik. There would be less questions at checkpoints if she carried Turkish ID. It would be the same passing through checkpoints manned by the official groups of Turkish military or Kurdish legitimate forces. In the hands of terrorists, she might be held for ransom if they saw she was American. If Turkish, she would likely be shot like the rest of them. The discussion of which would raise the least suspicion went back and forth. For her safety, it was decided to have her dress as a Kurdish boy. But, if questioned, she would use her own papers.

They didn't get much sleep that night, only catching a couple of hours, and rising before dawn.

Charly and Hakan were given clothes to help them pass as Kurdish villagers, as they would surely run into checkpoints and other travelers. In this land so familiar with terrorism, it was not unusual for travelers to openly carry weapons, so they didn't need to worry about concealment.

As Charly was slim and athletic, her transformation into a Kurdish boy was easy. *At least from afar*, thought Charly, unconsciously touching her eyes where fine lines had formed. Charly's deep russet hair was hidden beneath a fez.

For the first part of the journey, Hakan and Charly took their jeep, concealing their weapons in the compartment of the floor. They were registered by checkpoint personnel as being in the area, and it was just as well that they surfaced now and then, which showing their own papers assured. Mahir rode with them. Two of his men took a second four-wheel-drive vehicle, leaving thirty minutes later. The rendezvous time had been set with a two-hour leeway because they were taking slightly different routes.

Charly and Hakan had not had an opportunity to be alone since their visit to Mahir's encampment. Their discussion of the mission had been with the other team members. The others had not noticed that their relationship was anything but professional. Since Hakan and Charly had compartmentalized their feelings when they arrived at the village, their intensity was singularly focused on the mission ahead. Charly rode in back, and let Mahir take her place in front.

Finding it difficult to hear and enter their discussion unless she sat leaning forward, Charly spent the long drive dozing and speculating on what she was doing and why. She had always been very good at visualizing and did so now. She cleaned, oiled, loaded, and handled her guns, feeling increasingly confident each time she ran though it. She imagined herself climbing a rocky mountain trail so as not to dislodge rocks. She thought of each of the team members, and of their strengths, whom she thought she could trust the most and in what circumstances. Over and over Charly went over the outline of what they intended to do.

Hakan frequently glanced at her in the rearview mirror, fascinated by the varying facial expressions and intensity. She was obviously reviewing everything in her mind, a trait not foreign to him or most Special Forces troops. His mind flashed back to his buddies just before they stormed a house where terrorists resided. Each of his companions had the same active and intense expression. They did not talk and held themselves still. Communication was by eye contact. Then he chuckled to himself, as he thought, *Charly and I won't have any problem there.*

With this thought he had a strong image of her eyes filled with wonder after their first kiss. Automatically he glanced into the mirror and found Charly looking at him with love. It was as if she could read his mind. *But, love? Where did that idea come from? Much too soon for that. Or is it? Kes! Stop with these thoughts, Hakan!* Out loud, Hakan groaned.

Luckily Mahir had been lost in his own thoughts, and merely turned to him, "Huh? Sorry, I missed that."

Hakan muttered, "Ah, nothing, I'm just getting a little stiff." As Hakan shifted in his seat and rotated his shoulders to verify his words, he caught Charly's eye once more and her silent laughter.

After passing through five uneventful checkpoints, they arrived in a small village just before dusk. Finding the designated two-story small hotel run by family of Mahir was not difficult. They were immediately shown their two rooms, which were on the same floor. Hakan and Mahir were to share one. The only other room was designated for Yasar and Akam who had not yet arrived.

After depositing his pack in the room, Mahir dashed to the local mosque for prayer, as dusk was quickly falling and he just had time to make it. Just as quickly, Hakan stepped across the hall to Charly's room. She had left the door ajar and he quietly slipped inside.

As he locked the door, Charly turned from the window. From this distance they held one another's gaze, and both could feel their hearts beating faster and their bodies flush with awareness. Slowly they crossed the room. Charly put her head on Hakan's chest as his arms closed around her, his hand removing her *fez* and running his fingers slowly through her hair.

"We haven't much time," warned Charly.

"I want you." Hakan's grip tightened and Charly raised her lips to his.

What began gently turned rapidly into a blaze of passionate longing as their bodies strained toward one another. They turned as one toward the bed and Charly pulled back the covers in one motion. There was no ceremonial removing their clothing, as haste was the master. Their hormones had done their work and their bodies were damply flushed and ready. Hakan sat on the edge of the bed and Charly did not need the encouragement of his strong hands at her waist to lower herself onto him in one firm movement. There was no pause to savor or extend, as they moved passionately in unison, their bodies burning along the path to fulfillment. As they stilled, with their moist faces touching, Charly breathed into his ear, *"Sevgilim."* Hakan's arms tightened upon hearing the endearment in his own language, my darling. *I never want to be separated from her*, thought Hakan.

They silently readjusted their clothing, stealing looks at one another.

"This may be the last time we can be together like this for a while. It would be insulting to our team if they knew we were lovers. Much more than that, it could disrupt this mission," Hakan said.

Charly agreed. "I know we can't take that chance. We shouldn't have just now. But I miss you already."

- 12 -
A cup of coffee commits one to forty years of friendship
- turkish proverb -

The team ate together that night at their lodging. They needed to talk and did not want to draw attention to themselves by going out in public. The appearance of strangers in this remote Hakkari village would raise curiosity and suspicion. Even though they were legitimate as far as the Turkish government was concerned, there were ears and eyes everywhere for the PKK or one of the offshoots. Plenty of Kurds, even if not a member of a terrorist group, were hostile to anyone they thought might upset their precarious balance. It was best to avoid this potential problem.

Mahir's cousin's wife, Hale, had prepared classic hearty dishes of stuffed green peppers, rice and vegetables, grilled lamb served with *ezme*, a fiery hot tomato and onion dish. Her *pide* was especially delicious. Charly never could get her fill of this chewy, elongated flatbread. Besides, she loved the custom of mopping up juices with it. In too many countries, such as her own, it would be considered poor manners. *I fit right in*, she thought with not a little pride.

It was difficult for Charly to follow all their planning, as they spoke in rapid Turkish, using idioms at which she could only vaguely guess the meaning. To complicate understanding, explanations were sometimes given in Kurdish.

Charly was not able to contain her curiosity any longer. "Just how well armed are these PKK?"

Mahir elaborated. "It's not unusual for the various renegade Kurdish groups to have shoulder-held RPGs, Kalashnikovs, and a variety of other weapons, both which NATO used as well as the Russians. Some even prefer the Israeli Desert Eagle, politics be damned! The illegal gun trade is fairly common from both Iran and Iraq into Turkey. The many caves in the area lend themselves well to storage. It's rare to locate them without good intelligence or through interrogation."

Charly pondered. "But I thought there was a ceasefire. The European Union has that as part of the criteria as they look at Turkey for membership. "

Mahir scoffed. "Tell her, Akam. You live with it daily."

"Too many of our families have been killed in this war between the Turks and the Kurdish terrorists that is supposed to be over. Bitter feelings do not die simply because the government and PKK leaders say 'cease fire.' It's been inconsistent over the years. Öcalan continues to run this terrorist group from jail."

Hakan shifted uncomfortably. "Partly true. His brother is the leader of another contingent whose goal is to resolve differences using peaceful measures. Interesting and very disturbing is our information which tells us there are several splinter groups of terrorists operating in Iraq, Iran, Syria, and Turkey."

Mahir summarized. "To put it mildly, Charly, we must watch our backs and try to stay one step ahead."

With this pronouncement of what they all knew to be true, a pall fell over the group. One by one they dispersed to their respective rooms.

The next morning they were up before dawn for a simple breakfast of bread, honey, yoghurt, nuts, and tea. Hale had prepared food for them to take along—*pide*, cheese, walnuts, and dried apricots, figs, and dates which they added to their backpacks.

They each secreted their knife and handgun of choice under their clothing. Their high-frequency mobile units would carry at least three miles, even in the mountains. Mahir and the second team leader, Yasar, also strapped on plastique and pencil detonators. Their layered clothing was perfect for concealment. Akam, a tall, slender man with a sharp beak nose and little facial hair, would join Mahir and Yasar.

Mahir elaborated on the relationship among the men. "Yasar and I have been like brothers in this conflict over the last fifteen years. I trust him with my life. Besides, we may need his explosives expertise. Akam recently joined our group when he married my cousin. He grew up in the Cilo Mountains in a village near Yuksekova."

Mahir, Yasar, and Akam carried AK-47s, Hakan his new M16A2, and Charly a lighter version with collapsible stock. They would appear more natural trekking through this part of the country with them slung over their shoulders than without.

The only traffic they were likely to meet were trucks going to market or carrying the workers to the fields. The cotton was ready to pick and the wheat to be cut, so that was a logical guise to use. They piled into the back of the truck, which had a wooden bed and high sides. Sitting, they could not be seen from the side of the road. But, just in case, Hale gave them each a colorful scarf to wear, which fluttered in the breeze. If they kept their heads bent, any passerby would believe them to be women workers on their way to the cotton fields. In spite of these precautions, their driver took side roads as soon as he left Hakkari to avoid the police checkpoints.

What a shock they would get if they were stopped and someone peered in, thought Charly. *I'm surprised I'm not more concerned. Is it delusional to feel such trust in these people I've known for such a short time?*

The four men looked roguish, the kind of people she would go to the other side of the street to avoid if she were home in Oregon. They would be terribly out of place there, though, and here they fit right in. She had to laugh at herself as she admitted she and Hakan looked just as rough as they did. *Um, I'd better start thinking of "us" instead of "them."* This reflection of obvious reality gave Charly an instant since of pride. *I feel my backbone stiffen, as my mother used to say. I'm not afraid because I have faith in their skills as soldiers. And in mine. I'm just glad they trust me, an outsider.*

What warriors we have in our women, thought Mahir. *The women in the PKK terrorist organization have the reputation of being the most effective and fierce. We have highly skilled professional women who could go up against them anytime. I just hope Charly is one.*

He spoke softly to Hakan. "I hope you don't take offense, but before we left I spoke again with Cevik about both you and Charly."

"I would have expected nothing less than to discuss us with your contacts. You could not take the word of just one person about Charly."

Especially not when you have feelings for her. Mahir smiled to himself and gazed at his new friend. *You better be cautious.*

Mahir continued. "Of course, you I know by reputation. Have you heard that in the field you are referred to as Efe? They say the meaning suits you because as a team member you are as their brother, defending them courageously. That is a high compliment among a group of Kurds who often squabble among each other."

Mahir referred to Charly by quoting the Turkish proverb, "thorns and roses grow on the same bush."

Hakan laughed. "That's true enough. But luckily her thorns only prick you if you're her enemy. Or, so I've heard. I investigated her, too." Then he related the story of how she had outwitted the soldiers at the training camp a few days ago.

"I was skeptical of Charly at first, but I was immediately impressed with her bravery and tenaciousness when delivering the package evolved into a mission of a different kind. She never even flinched at being in such a place as our camp, and adapted to surroundings immediately. Too bad you can't access her security report. She's had a lot of related experience. She's much more than what she appears."

"Ah, then that explains it. They said not to worry about her doing her part, especially if it involved evasive tactics or a sniper shot. I'm afraid we'll likely be seeing some of both."

At the point Hakan started to respond, the truck turned off the secondary road and headed toward the mountains. They lengthened their trip going this way, but they needed to avoid any possibility of checkpoints. Some were legitimate military and others were village guards, PKK, or another local armed group. Each sought a "tip" for letting travelers through, but that wasn't the problem. There was a good chance they would alert those they sought. This was going to be a long ride and seemed longer because the road, if one could call it that, was deeply rutted from spring runoff from the higher elevations. The empty feed sacks provided poor protection from the bouncing truck bed.

They were lulled in to weariness, not even trying to peer over the side of the truck after the first thirty minutes. Most fell into a stupor-like doze. When the truck stopped, they shook themselves into full alertness. They were behind a large outcropping of rock. The team hopped out, AK-47s shouldered. The last one tossed out their backpacks before leaving. Taking advantage of the last of darkness, the truck was soon lumbering back down the rutted road.

Charly caught her breath as she looked at the mountains standing tall and proud with snow-capped peaks. The brisk breeze reminded her that winter was rapidly approaching, particularly in the higher elevations. The stars seemed exceptionally bright this far from any village or city lights. It was so quiet the occasional truck could be heard on the road between Turkey and Iran. *Even the goats aren't up yet,* thought Charly, as she strained to hear their bleats.

Out of the stillness, but from an unseen source, came the Kurdish greeting in a firm, commanding voice. "Welcome to our mountain." The click of safety-off weapons could be heard, as they dropped to their knees.

"Goats have three legs," Mahir oddly countered.

"But only because the mountain is so steep." Deep, booming laughter resonated.

"It's okay," Mahir assured their group who then all stood, shouldering their weapons.

Emerging from the darkness of a cave's entrance Charly had not noticed was a short, sturdy, heavily bearded man with a brightly patterned long shawl over his long *jakarta*-style shirt and baggy pants. A deep red *pakol* was perched rakishly on his head.

"I am Balaban." He eyed each of them, nodding as they introduced themselves.

At Charly, he did a double-take. A couple of red curls had escaped from her hat. "You have softness to your face and no beard. Your eyes are green. And this, this red is lovely. I was not told they were sending a boy along."

"Do not worry, sir. I'm not a boy."

Light dawned in Balaban's eyes as the others roared with laughter.

At his bidding they entered the cave, took two turns and emerged into a fair-sized room. Coals from a fire glowed in the center over which was perched a kettle. "Please sit and have some tea." They seated themselves on the floor around the fire warming their hands on the cup.

"This is Ahmed, my son. He will be going with us. He knows these mountains nearly as well as I do."

Ahmed nodded almost shyly. His dark eyes were gentle, not yet holding the alert suspicion nor the degree of merriment his father's held.

Balaban explained that he was a member of the home security forces, village guards, found in every southeastern city or village, as was his son. "At this time of year, most of those on their summer *yaylak* have already made the journey to *kislak*, their place for wintering from the harshness of the high pastures. We'll hike to their settlement and take shelter in the tents left behind. The mountain peaks received their first snow in early September. Everyone should be out of the mountains by now. We're pushing our luck here at 3,500 feet in mid-October."

When the sky lightened but the sun was still hidden behind the eastern peaks, Balaban led the way, following the sheep and goat trails that wound around the mountainous terrain. He looked as his name in Kurdish implied, a large and very strong mountain man.

The seven silently headed up the barely perceptible trails winding up the side of the mountain. The climb was made difficult by alternating terrain of varying sizes of rock, sometimes deteriorating to scree. Charly was glad her new army hiking boots fit well and tightly around her ankles. Even so, she still slipped occasionally. *At least I haven't fallen yet*, she thought.

They kept a steady pace. Up ahead were the mountains leading to Yuksekova and the nearby border to Iran. "Up ahead" was about twenty miles ahead, "as the crow flies."

By midday they had passed two deserted *yaylaks* and had seen no one, as Balaban had predicted. Charly's feet were starting to blister in her new boots, but she quietly endured. *To say anything would be wimping out*, she thought. *None of the others hesitate as they skirt around steep crevices or leap over boulders, and damned if I'll be the first.*

Charly was more than ready when they stopped for lunch. They loosely gathered close enough to talk and share their food, each taking walks away from the group to relieve themselves. It was such singular occasions that Charly wished for the male apparatus, as she tugged down her trousers. She longed to remove her boots and look at her blisters, but fear of showing weakness kept them on. They ate lightly of bread, cheese, and figs before continuing. Wild goats scrambling across the rocky terrain and birds seemed to be their only companions.

The sun was behind the mountains and only the highest peaks cast shadows by the time Balaban stopped and identified the plateau below as his.

It was somewhat eerie to look down upon the river flowing through the still green valley and see only the remnants of a tiny village. There were cleared spaces which must have housed individual tent homes. Now there were just two remaining, as well as three structures made of stone which were used for a gathering place for celebrations, a mosque, and a school.

Seeing nothing amiss, they wound their way down the mountain. Instead of feeling tired after their long trek, relief at finally arriving lent a festive air amongst them. They gravitated to a pool of still water which had been diverted from the river. It was shallow and the sun from earlier in the day had warmed it. Each sat on a rock, removing boots and immersing feet, socks and all, in the water. The conversation was more casual than on other occasions, with several sharing memories of previous such moments of pleasure after a long day. Topics widely ranged from whose wife made the best *pide* to the joy of eating fresh bear steaks after a kill. And so it went, with laughter and teasing.

Wringing out their socks and draping them on a line left by the recent dwellers, they donned their only other pair of fresh ones. Hakan noticed Charly's blood-spotted socks when she took them off, but as she was doing her best to hide them, he made no comment. *The rest of us have been in the field so long, our feet have developed tough calluses. Charly put up a good front. No, actually, she pulled her own weight, not asking for special accommodations. She's kept up her basic fitness and firearm skills, but still hasn't built the toughness which only comes with regular field work.*

Balaban had a surprise awaiting them in the meeting house: fresh goat cheese, *pide,* and a delicious, thick hot soup with vegetables from their not long ago abandoned garden.

After their repast, tiredness quickly settled into their bones. The men spread their sleeping bags on the floor, and one by one quickly fell asleep.

Balaban led Charly to a hut nearby, where she was surprised to find a goatskin pallet and a colorful woven blanket to keep out the cold.

"Ahmed found these among the extras left behind."

Charly was touched by the young man's thoughtfulness. "You raised a generous son, Balaban."

All of the improvised bedding plus her own sleeping bag provided unexpected comfort and warmth. Her last thoughts were of Hakan. The physical closeness they had shared seemed far in the past, so much had happened. But she wrapped those warm thoughts around her and fell asleep.

In the middle of the night she was awakened from a deep sleep and thought she had heard a gunshot. Hearing only silence, she was quickly asleep again.

Am I ever sore! Charly stretched as she slowly awoke. Her nose was cold and she could see her breath. It took a strong will to struggle into an upright position. Luckily she had slept in her clothes. Sitting, she dragged her pack closer, found her antibiotic salve and bandages and proceeded to treat her feet for the upcoming trek.

Donning her boots and coat she made use of the primitive facilities. The sky was dappled with streaks of light from behind the mountains to the east and by striated clouds from the northwest. The mountains surrounding the high plateau seemed ominous in their stillness. An apt Turkish proverb came to mind. *A heart in love with beauty never grows old. Well, I feel old this morning!*

Charly went through some of her yoga practice, which seemed very awkward in her bulky clothes, but it helped ease some kinks. By the time she had made her ablutions at the river, the smell of roasting lamb enticed her to join the others around the fire. Exchanging a direct and almost too lengthy gaze with her, Hakan scooted over to make room for her to sit on the *kilim*. She took the remaining stick with lamb and began slowly roasting, grateful for the well-stocked underground storage.

"Did you sleep well?" Ahmed politely asked.

"Like a log, and very comfortable. Thank you. But I thought I heard a gunshot in the night. I must have been dreaming."

"No dream," Ahmed remarked. "I was on guard duty for the first shift last night. There was a glow from what looked like a fire, maybe five miles away—far enough to see but not smell. There were a few shots, too. I would never had heard it if the wind weren't from that direction. I didn't see anything else. I woke Mahir at 0300 for the next shift."

"I didn't hear or see a thing. But it felt as cold as a glacier coffin."

"Was it in the direction we're heading this morning?" Charly inquired, inwardly smiling at Mahir's analogy.

"Our route will take us by the next *yaylak*, where I think this shot came from. I didn't think the terrorists came this deep into the mountains."

The PKK were continually patrolling the mountain roadways and commonly used paths. It was rumored they had cached not only weapons but heroin in caves in these Sat-Cilo Mountains near Yuksekova. Heroin smuggling had long been a primary means of funding their activities, and apparently a lucrative business. Even though the PKK had been greatly diminished in this area, they still had a strong foothold.

The group quietly finished eating, each lost in thought. If the terrorists being sought were scouting, it could mean they were aware of them. On the other hand, that gunshot could simply have been a random act. But whichever, each knew their vigilance should be stepped up several notches. They had not expected to engage their prey so soon.

Within thirty minutes they had cleaned up camp, checked their weapons, donned their packs, and were ready to go. Movements seemed more precise today, awareness higher. Charly felt more tension in her muscles and tried to relax them. *There is no better way to develop tendons that scream at you at the end of the day than to trek with unreleased tension,* she reminded herself.

Hakan fell in beside Charly as they walked along the valley before beginning their ascent. "How are you doing? Sorry you got involved with all this?"

"No, not at all. The planned terrorist action must stop, and I'm happy to help."

"That sounds a bit glib."

"Aw, come on! This isn't my first and it won't be my last. I need this kind of excitement. I thrive on it, if I believe in the cause. "

"But it is so different from what you do in America."

"And that's what keeps me sane, having that balance. I need both the routine and the quiet of the intellectual challenge, as well as the physical. That's why I run ten miles, six days a week, and train monthly at the army post. How about you?"

"I see what you mean. I won't be able to maintain my disguise as a bus driver for long. I'm quite ready to be assigned to the field. Yes, I need both, too. But it doesn't leave much time for normal life."

"We could spend all day defining 'normal' for us!" They both laughed and fell into amicable silence.

In a few minutes Charly broke the silence. "I miss you."

Hakan nodded, not looking at her. "I miss not being able to have the closeness with you, too. Just not possible now."

With this mutual acknowledgment, Hakan fell back to take the rear lookout position, just as Balaban began the trek upwards.

Hakan mused to himself. *I have to keep my feelings in check. She's doing the same thing. When the others are around we act like strangers, and that must be. There is no place here for romance. I should not have allowed our attraction to flare. Ha! As if I could have stopped it! But I could have, I just didn't want to. And I sure didn't think we'd end up on this mountain, taking this action.*

They walked at a strong, steady pace as the path was free of loose stones and their footing sure.

Charly let her mind wander as it didn't need to be engaged in this easy part of the trek. *Just keep alert to my surroundings.* Her home in Oregon seemed far away. She thought of the thick pine forests which surrounded her log house, giving it privacy. The creek which ran through it was only three feet wide in most places and ran gently into the Alsea River. At home now her mums and shasta daisies would be standing proudly in the early coolness of fall. All this she could see in her mind's eye. It was so very different from the harshness of these mountains. Charly felt, for the umpteenth time, as if she was meant to be here in Turkey, that this was her other home. She was so deep in her thoughts that she had been unaware of their progress. She felt the sun hit her face as it came over the peaks, and its warmth cheered her and brought her back to reality.

They were climbing higher and more steeply, and she breathed more deeply. The oxygen was a bit less, but certainly no problem. Charly could feel the muscles in her legs as they took her weight in climbing a steep path with knee-high boulders alternating with loose rocks. Her attention needed to be sharper here, as a misstep could lead to painful fall or turned ankle.

After a few hours, Balaban paused, and they grouped around him. "We will be able to see the *yaylak* in a few minutes. I have seen no sign of others on this path, but we need to walk silently and be alert. We don't know what or who we'll find."

They paused frequently to listen, hearing only the call of hawks. Surprise registered on their faces at what they saw when coming over the crest and looking down upon the *yaylak*, or what remained of it. Stones from one of the two structures were scattered widely about and there was a deep depression in the ground. The remaining one was still standing, but at a tilt, with loose stones. They squatted and silently observed the area. Listening. Looking. Sensing. Finally satisfied no one else was about, they made their way downward.

Hakan searched the wreckage. "Looks like a rocket hit it." This was confirmed by the smashed metal at the bottom of the impact point. "RPG-7, I bet. Someone was target practicing."

"Pretty heavy duty for just practicing without a goal in mind. I doubt new recruits are being trained up here. Father, what do you think?"

Balaban checked the cache in a small cave where the summer dwellers kept their food cool. "Nothing has been touched; the usual stores remain. They always leave some for fellow nomads should they get stranded and need nourishment."

"Okay, so we know they weren't travelers in need nor were they looters. I agree with Hakan. Let's look for evidence they've even been to this site." Mahir assigned each an area.

Nothing else was found which would indicate intruders. They agreed someone had likely used the launcher from the cliff above, viewed the damage, and left. If that was a correct supposition, they could still be nearby.

"The effective range for a stationary target like this is 500 meters." Hakan sighted in the distance with his scope.

They pooled their expertise in deciding on the direction from which the rocket came. Their best estimate was from mountains to the east, farther to the north, but in the same direction they were traveling.

Mahir was getting restless. "We have a choice. We can look for their camp, or continue our mission. We can't do both, as we need to be in place by tomorrow."

They quickly and unanimously agreed to proceed with their mission. Whoever had done this did so without hurting anyone and may or may not have been the group slated for convoy destruction. As it was late in the season they probably correctly assumed that the *yaylaks* were deserted.

Using his satellite phone Hakan called to report their decision. Charly checked coordinates with the PLGR and relayed them. Regional Command asked them to pursue looking for those who struck the deserted village after their mission was complete. There hadn't been any other reports of related activities in the area, either by the PKK or military.

"I got a weather report from HQ. Increased clouds are expected in our area, bringing on the first storm of the season." Hakan looked concerned as he relayed this information.

"Then we move out quickly. We don't want to get caught. Does anyone need any other clothing? We have extra stored here."

Charly noticed that Yasar and Akam pulled out *pakols* like Ahmed and Balaban were wearing. "This *kufi* I'm wearing isn't nearly warm enough. Do you have another like you all are wearing?"

"Not like my pretty red one!" Balaban posed, the big burly fellow looking ridiculous. Continuing the charade, he minced away, returning with a brown one for Charly.

Appreciating the tension relief, the group catcalled through their laughter.

Charly donned the *pakol,* easily pushing her curls underneath and rolling the wool brim over her ears. "Much better." She packed it away for use when the weather changed.

About twenty minutes after leaving the valley Ahmed pointed. "There ahead, do you see it? The scrub grass is scorched."

"Sloppy bunch. Dirtying up our mountain like this." Balaban picked up the launch casing. "From this point they had a clear line of sight for the *yaylak*. It would have been no problem to line up their target as the stars and half moon lit the valley last night."

"They must have been staying close by. This is not terrain conducive to night travel."

Hakan marked the location on the map and transmitted it to headquarters.

Continuing, they avoided the draw of the sunny valley. For hours they walked the narrow paths forged by people and animals who inhabited the mountain valleys in spring and summer. There were no further signs of intruders.

They sat in the shadows as they ate their lunch. They were experienced enough to be wary that the intruders might still be around. Their surveillance maps did not show any more *yaylaks* on the way to Yuksekova. This was the highest elevation they would travel. The trekking from here would be more difficult as there wouldn't be the well-worn nomadic paths to follow. With luck, they should run into some wild goat trails.

The rest of the afternoon was tough going. There were no cliffs to climb, but it was slow picking their way around jagged rocks sometimes so high it was easy to get disoriented as to direction. Without compasses or GPS they would have been lost. Each seemed to have a different pace, and for the first time spread out over a half-mile distance. They were going slow as they looked for recent evidence of anyone else having been in the area.

As the afternoon wore on and the sun went behind the mountains, the breeze freshened. Clouds were on the increase. *There will be no stars out tonight. Damn, it's getting cold.* Charly gladly donned the pakol. *How can I be sweating and yet cold?*

Night closed around them and each put on night goggles. They climbed together now, as the mountain's dangers had increased. Light snow began to fall. Although all were breathing heavily, they did not stop to rest. To get caught without shelter now could be fatal. They rounded a bend, and the biting wind was now at their backs.

"It's only another thirty minutes," Ahmed shouted back to them.

I wonder where "another thirty minutes" takes us? A steaming bath, massage, a warm bed, maybe just Hakan and I, alone, with the steam swirling around us. Thus went Charly's fantasies. At this point she was just putting one foot in front of the other, and hoped her thoughts of something warm would become real. She had found this worked for her before with some modicum of success: think warm, be warm. At least this last leg went quickly for her as she toyed with eroticisms.

"Here we are." Balaban stopped at a wider than usual area. A natural rock platform jutted out over the valley below, leaving a sheer drop. They couldn't tell how far because the wind swirled the accumulating snow. They could barely see five feet.

"Be careful of the ledge; it's a thousand foot drop to the valley," Balaban added.

"Well, that answers that, but what is the significance? Are we staying here?" piped up Mahir.

Balaban turned and walked toward the mountain. With Ahmed's help, a large rock was pushed aside.

"Welcome to your five-star hotel for the night," Balaban taunted and disappeared as he stepped forward.

There was just enough space for each of them to enter and huddle near the entrance as it was pitch black inside. Soon they saw a glow but not the source of light. In following it, they found Balaban holding up a kerosene lantern. Hanging it from the side of the large room, he lit two more.

"Wow!" Charly spied a pile of woven rugs neatly stacked along one wall. Stones were piled in a circle, next to which was an old copper kettle. There were also wooden crates with the Turkish crescent and star.

With a slightly amused expression, the men watched her explore the room and its contents. They knew of the hidden caves, which would be well stocked in case of such an emergency, but Charly did not.

"Good old MECKs, I see. American dining at its best. I'm not even going to ask how you got these!"

Even Hakan was amazed at the variety. "How many of the twenty-four entrees do you think are here?"

By then, all were gathered around the crate to see what they'd have for dinner.

"Quite a bit different than the usual army issue we get from the 1980s. The packaging even looks good. Look at this 'Hooah!' bar." Yasar took a bite. "Not bad for a nutrition bar."

"I haven't seen you so excited about anything this whole trip," Akam teased as he playfully punched Yasar on his shoulder and reached for one himself.

They all laughed and continued their search for favorites.

"Great! There are snacks-on-the-go. I need these to keep up with you guys," Charly said. *And because I have to eat every few hours to keep the shakes away.* "They even have nutrition tablets."

Hakan explained, "They were designed for the highly mobile units, the commandos who need an energy boost without the time investment. Just pop-and-go. I hear the high carb mint ones aren't bad."

"We have some of this stuff, but not the variety you do. Please tell me how we can get it," inquired Mahir.

"Just put in a requisition form, Mahir. Ask for the latest shipment and list some of the types specifically. Then, the guy supplying it will know that you know the difference, and will probably get it to you."

"Akam, you heard the man! Do it."

"*Evet*, right, boss. I just think we need to hook up with these guys more. That'd be more likely."

There were also several bars of shortbread, chocolate chip, granola, and cornflake cereal. Each pocketed a couple for the next day, along with a couple of sandwiches in self-heating packages.

They had the most fun with the packaging of the entrees. Hakan and Mahir explained to them how the eight-ounce packages could be heated with the FRH, Flameless Ration Heaters, which were included. "The food had been thermostabilized in packets, kind of like a canning process. The FRH is a water-activated exothermic chemical heater. One package could heat in twelve minutes."

"Let's try one," encouraged Charly.

"But we don't need it, Charly. We have provisions with us," Hakan cautioned.

"Ah, come on, just a couple. We need to see how it works.

What if we're caught sometime and don't have the time to sit around and figure it out?"

They all laughed at this and at themselves acting like kids in a candy factory. Ahmed and Akam joined Charly's crusade, and they finally agreed to try two. Much debate and cajoling occurred in the decision of which ones, deciding finally on jambalaya and one of the vegetarian dishes.

Ahmed filled a pot from the stream coming down the mountain just outside their cave, while Balaban was busy getting a small fire going in the stone pit.

"This should be clean, as according to the map there are no pastures higher up on this side."

"Well, I'm not taking any chances. All we need is for us to come down with intestinal problems," warned Balaban, as he tossed a couple of iodine tabs in the pot.

While the water was heating, with Balaban and Mahir quietly talking and tending, the other three explored the cave. There were two other rooms leading from the main area. Stooping to enter them, they shined flashlights around, estimating one was seven feet deep and the other ten. There were no other exits from either. In one corner of the room, two boxes were propped off the floor about three inches. Lifting the lid they discovered various ammunition, and in the other, guns with a few gun cleaning kits.

"I guess we know what our job is tonight." Hakan picked one gun up after the other. "These are in remarkably good shape—new and no rusting." The dampness of the cave had not affected them at all. It helped that they were packed in wood chips.

Hakan dragged a crate into the main room of the cave. The difference in temperature was noticeable even though their fire was small. They each got their own gun carefully cleaned and oiled before eating. They would take care of those stored after dinner.

Charly was pleased to notice that the FRH did not take any special expertise. The pouch was placed into the bag with the heater, and just a small amount of water added, keeping it upright so the heater could absorb the water. Then they stuffed it into the carton, folding the top.

"I sure didn't anticipate the chemical smell. That's toxic!" Charly complained.

Hakan chuckled at her surprise. "No, but it would be if we had more going. That's why they say no more than ten if you are in a confined space."

The other packet was put in the now boiling pot over the coals. In about ten minutes they were both ready. The staples they had brought with them of bread, cheese, nuts, and dried dates supplemented the MREs very well. They shared tastes of the peanut butter, crackers, pretzels, and toaster-type pastry which had been mixed in with the military rations.

"And for dessert let's try the spice pound cake!" enthused Charly. "And hot chocolate, too."

Enthusiastically agreeing, they enjoyed every crumb and drop.

Charly thought their dichotomy of playfulness and dead-on seriousness was interesting. *Every special ops guy I've known has been like this—often near the limit of both extremes. It seems difficult for some to find a middle ground or ever just relax. I guess I have some of this restless intensity, too.*

After this frivolity of feasting, the weightiness of their task descended once more. With heads bent over the topographical satellite maps, they went over their path for the next day. The trucks were due and the terrorists would be ready to destroy. So must they be ready to counter, extreme if necessary. The snow amounts could change their plans, but they wouldn't know until morning. For now they were planning as if it were not a factor in preventing them from reaching their goal. It did, however, mean some changes in equipment. They made these adjustments from the supplies within the cave. Luckily they found a cache of balaclava, which snuggly covered the face and neck except for the eyes and mouth. Charly and Hakan needed to appropriate warm parkas, as climbing in the Sat-Cilo Mountains had not been part of their plans when they left the tour.

The temperature in the cave really wasn't too bad, perhaps 55 degrees Fahrenheit. After all preparations were made for the next day, they sat back, cleaning the stored weapons and told stories of previous ops.

Happy to just listen, Charly took in the excitement, pain, success and failure of previous missions. Several had been in conjunction with American reconnaissance. *Interesting, I hadn't thought Americans were participating in this PKK war of terror. Surprise! But on second thought, maybe not. Turkey builds U.S. fighter jets, purchases weapons, and has a long standing relationship through NATO. It seems logical then that America would engage in missions with Turkey. They sure aren't talked about, though.*

Putting a couple of rugs underneath, each unrolled their bedroll and crawled inside. A few candles were lit to take away the total darkness.

Charly was in a room of the cave by herself. Through the opening there was a faint glow from the candles, just enough to take away the total darkness. Shadows played on the walls. The dampness of the cave had left her chilled and she was glad to pull her bag snuggly around her.

Hakan slept near the entrance. At first Charly was resentful at his thinking she needed his protection, but this feeling soon was lost in the reality that she did indeed feel safer with him there. *Of course I'd like it better if he were cozied up next to me, where I could reach out and touch him.* With this thought, warmth born of unbidden arousal stole over her. She let thoughts of their togetherness wrap around her. Charly thought of how his body felt pressed into hers and of his inquiring hands. Rising up she could see him lying quietly just a few feet away with his back to her. *Probably asleep already. How dare he go to sleep so easily!* She squirmed around trying to find the non-existent soft spot on the hard-packed floor.

The next thing of which Charly became aware was the rustling sounds in the main area of the cave. As she slowly awakened to her surroundings, she held onto her sensuous dreams of the night before. *She had been sleeping nude in a large feather bed with the lightest of covers as it was warm and pleasantly humid. Gossamer curtains floated in the jasmine perfumed breeze. Hakan slowly pushed the door open and got into bed with her, laying on his side, pressed into her. She awakened feeling the pressure from his arousal through the light cotton robe he wore and his gentle cupping and kneading of her breas*t. So thus she woke to reality: alone on a hard, makeshift bed with cold from the damp floor seeping through. Purpose took over from sleepy druthers.

Balaban poured her a cup of tea, and she stood with the others as they sipped and stretched out their soreness from the hard cave floor and yesterday's climb. They munched on breakfast from the military rations.

"There are even eggs!" Charly was delighted to tuck into such an ordinary breakfast under these extraordinary circumstances.

"And pancakes, too." A respectful Ahmed shared some with her.

Maybe it's not home cooking but it's mighty good, Charly thought as she ate her share.

- 13 -
It's easy to say 'come', difficult to say 'go'
- turkish proverb -

After donning their winter gear and shouldering packs and guns, they gathered at the cliff's edge outside the cave. The sun was still low in the sky below the mountain peaks, but bright enough to magnify the blinding whiteness. Quickly putting on sun goggles, they looked at the beauty before them. Fog was coming up from the river in the valley far below, giving a soft eeriness to the landscape.

The charm and mystery of winter never failed to entrance Charly. The craggy rocks had perky white hats adorned with sparkling diamonds. A heavy blanket of snow capped the peaks that only yesterday had been merely dusted. *Luckily for us there is only about five inches of powder. A heavier or deeper snow would have meant snowshoes and slower traveling.*

Despite the frigid air, within an hour their inner linings were wet from their exertion. Although the goat path was still easy to see, the snow covered what was underneath. The need for quiet and stealth were vital, which errant rocks could break. It always took more energy to climb when the temperatures were below freezing.

They gradually made their way around and down, hoping to come in behind the terrorists. This all depended upon the accuracy of their intelligence in pinpointing the best spot for the ambush. Balaban continually checked GPS readings.

With luck they could use their altitude in spotting their target. Having crossed the Iran-Turkey border at Esendere, the ambush of the oil lorries would likely be on the outskirts of Yuksekova, when they would be going slowest due to the steep grade. The roads in the mountains were narrow, with the few vehicles proceeding at a slow pace. Having crossed the border safely, the convoy's guard would be down somewhat.

The team's destination was only about a two-hour hike away. They stopped periodically, listened, and swept the area with binoculars and the handheld thermal imager. They were using the 150mm lens, which would allow them to detect up to 4800 feet away. The imager could be used in total darkness, mist, fog, and smoke. It was powered by a four-hour rechargeable battery.

Balaban was the first to spot a path worn in the snow. It seemed to come from nowhere but closer scrutiny revealed an area worn in the snow in front of a cave entrance.

With even more care, they worked their way toward the cave. There was no way to approach it without being in the open the last twenty-five feet. Although they listened intently, they heard no sounds inside. Balaban took out his Lugar with silencer already attached and thumbed off the safety. Hakan did the same, and covered for Balaban while he stealthily made his way toward the cave entrance. He positioned himself to one side as Hakan came up on the other. They paused, listening intently, and detected the smell of fresh cigarette smoke. Holding up a hand, Balaban indicated that Mahir, Ahmed, Yasar, Akam, and Charly should remain in place, hidden from view from the entrance.

After about ten minutes of waiting, they heard faint footfalls and the clank of metal on metal. A bearded figure wearing a fez stepped outside the entrance, his Kalashnikov hanging loosely from his shoulder. He put his arms up to stretch, twisted, and saw Balaban from the corner of his eye.

With a broad smile, Balaban greeted him in Kurdish. "Hello, friend. Beautiful day."

At the same time Hakan kicked his feet from under him while jerking the gun from his shoulder. The fall and Hakan's knee in his back did not allow a breath to be taken to shout. There was just a whoosh of expelled air as he landed belly down on the rocky ground. Dragging him from the cave entrance, Balaban cuffed his hands behind him, tied his ankles together, bound hands and feet together, and gagged him. This all took place within a matter of a few seconds with no words spoken, giving the man no time to put up a fight.

Using the imager, Balaban scanned the cave's interior while Hakan kept watch, and found no one else. It was a simple but effective hideout for a limited stay. The one room contained several bedrolls, remains of a fire, foodstuffs, one backpack, and several rifles. A topographical map was left behind which marked the site of the ambush.

Charly and Mahir joined them at the entrance; Yasar, Akam, and Ahmed remained on lookout. "Take a look." Balaban showed them the map. "Looks like our intel was right on target. It matches what they left behind. Time's short, we need to go. Who is going to stay behind with our new friend?"

Not surprisingly, no one volunteered. Balaban continued, "Well, we know they are expecting to return here. If we fail in capturing them we should have someone stay here as our second line. We have to come back and pick up this one anyway."

"But our plan calls for all of us to maximize our success. Come on! We're going to get the bastards! Let's go!" urged Mahir.

Thus agreed, their captive was dragged inside the cave and

induced to take a sedative to knock him out for a few hours. Charly observed Hakan's gentleness in giving the terrorist water and not banging him around. *Well, at least that is more humane than a whack on the head.*

Knowing where they were headed as verified by the maps eased their minds as did their snowy path, which led predictably toward the target site each had identified.

The best spot for good line of sight as well as protection for the ambush was behind large boulders from which the terrorists could see the approaching convoy. Unfortunately, there were many such rocks in the area where one could hide from the road as well as being difficult to detect from this side. They also supplied good support for their shoulder-held RPG or Stinger missile.

"Almost there. Any questions?" queried Mahir, who was the designated team leader for this part of the mission. Balaban was the most knowledgeable in the mountains, but now leadership reverted to Mahir.

As there were no last minute clarifications needed, they continued very slowly. Around the next outcropping they caught sight of five terrorists. One man in each of two pairs held a shoulder weapon. The fifth man was perched about fifty feet away, alertly watching the road with his AK-47.

"It looks like one team is going with a Stinger and the other with an RPG. One good hit would cause an explosion igniting the oil." Mahir was puzzled by the amount of fire power.

"Sounds a bit like overkill. Maybe a trial-run for something bigger? " Charly observed.

In the distance they could hear trucks lumbering up the winding road.

In a few minutes the convoy came in sight. *Now or never,* thought Mahir. With a hacking motion of his hand, he indicated to his group to take out the terrorists. They had agreed beforehand to wound only unless personally threatened. The information they would be able to ferret out of them could prove very helpful in preventing future ambushes.

As the fall-back sniper, Charly positioned herself behind a large outcropping, her rifle resting securely. If the rebels tried to escape the way they came, they would run past her.

Loud staccato sounds assaulted the silence of the mountains. Rock shards flew in front of the four manning the weapons. Shouts of surprise and pain arose as three fell to the ground. The fourth took off running back into the mountains, his AK-47 waving in the air. Charly took careful aim and shot him in the arm carrying the weapon. He dropped it and kept running in her direction. It was impossible for the others to get a shot as the rocky terrain prevented a direct line of sight. Charly crouched down from view. He continued running, holding his arm.

He won't get far with that arm; he's running on adrenalin now. Charly proceeded to cautiously follow him.

The machine gun fire had stopped. The three trucks had kept going without knowing the reason for the commotion. Two of the rebels were dead, a third was groaning in pain from a wound in his chest. Hakan stanched the bleeding as best he could with a pressure bandage. The fourth had surrendered and was spread eagle in the snow.

"Where's Charly?" Mahir scanned the area.

"Heading after the fifth, most likely. I'll check." Hakan trotted off in Charly's position.

Charly was rewarded in her stealthy efforts, as she soon came upon her prey, who thought he was safely out of sight behind a rock. Having lost his assault rifle, the usual second weapon carried, a pistol, was beside him and he was busily trying to tie a tourniquet around his arm. Tears streamed down his face. He was oblivious of Charly silently watching.

My god, he's just a kid! There isn't even enough beard growth to begin to cover his chin. He can't be more than thirteen.

She pulled her Glock and greeting him good morning in Turkish, *"Günaydın."*

He reached down toward his gun, and Charly spun it away with a silenced shot.

"On the ground, face down," she commanded in Turkish.

He just looked at her. *Oh, shit,* she thought, *and me with only a little Kurdish.* She made a downward slicing motion with her gun and flung her arms out, shouting "Now!" in Kurdish, one of the few words she knew. After she repeated it twice, aiming her pistol at him, he complied, and groaned as he tried to straighten out his arm.

Hakan came up behind her. "Well, I see you have the runaway. Let me cuff him for you."

Cuffing, then jerking him to a seated position, Hakan sat back on his haunches and spoke to him in Kurdish. The boy was openly groaning in pain. "Let me see your wound, son."

It was obvious that the boy's youth had made Hakan more kind-hearted as he quickly cut through his jacket and shirtsleeve. It was barely bleeding now, but was an ugly wound. The bullet had gone through, chipping bone and tearing flesh. Hakan disinfected it and wrapped his arm.

"It needs stitching. Let's put him with the others before the local police come, Charly."

Charly followed at a distance with the Glock at the ready as Hakan walked the boy toward the others.

"Okay, here's the fifth." Hakan briefly related where he had found him and Charly.

"A good stop, Charly. If he'd been able to call in what had happened, it would have revealed our presence and not given us time to clean up." Mahir used his mobile to call the gendarmerie in Yuksekova, giving them the position to pick up the prisoners.

"Now let's get out of here before the locals arrive." Mahir led the others at a trot back the way they had come.

Quickly arriving at the cave the terrorist group had used for shelter, they went through everything more thoroughly this time and gathered it into a pile, confiscating maps and other papers. Certain they had everything, Mahir laid C-4 explosive and a timer for thirty minutes. They didn't wait to watch the destruction.

Between the wind and sunshine, the mountain steppes were fairly well swept of snow by now, and darkness was approaching as they made their way toward Yuksekova. Their prisoner from the cave was staggering with a lot of the sedative still flowing through his system. They left him beside the road, again alerting the gendarmerie to pick him up. He would remember nothing of the events of the last few hours.

Using what remained of light, they silently followed an animal path as it wound its way around the mountain. In the distance they heard a faint "thwunk," and gave each other a thumbs-up.

They momentarily stopped every fifty feet or so to listen before continuing. There was a good possibility of other terrorists in the area.

From their elevation the coming darkness allowed them to see occasional lights from several tiny villages dotting the valley, at the end of a dead-end road. Yuksekova was evident by a glow of lights from the town near the border, and from trucks lumbering along to cross over into Iran.

The cover on the mountain was sparse, with occasional large boulders. They gained the height they needed to see the border crossing clearly with their binoculars. As the moon rose, they continued to work their way to the south side of Yuksekova. They were able to move fairly quickly as they blended into the brown rocks of the hillside and negotiated their way according to the plentiful cover.

Charly was enjoying a calm sense of purpose stimulated by the physical exertion and the camaraderie she felt with the others. It was satisfying to actually be doing something rather than merely preparing for it. Since becoming involved in these occasional actions with security forces, she felt more intensely alive. *Guess I'd better be or we all could be in deep trouble.*

As planned, by dusk they came to a spot where they needed to descend into the valley. The cultivation of the land was sparse and the huts randomly located and isolated. For this section they donned dark colored long scarves which concealed their guns but provided creative slits for quick access to them. Now on the outskirts, they kept to the trees, avoiding huts. This was obviously a poor section of the city, with heavily rutted dirt roads and chickens and cows roaming free. The occasional dog would begin barking, but would soon give up when another didn't join.

Because of the closeness to the pass, they had been informed that armed guards were patrolling the road and monitoring all who passed. Their safe house for the night was on the nearest side adjoining a field of olive trees. The road that passed closest was about a football field distance from the house. It was now fully dark, and clouds occluded the moon's brightness.

They quietly and safely made their way to the house, huddling on the side farthest from the road. Seeing no one, Mahir went to the door and softly knocked. A light from inside went out. After a few minutes, a figure came from around the side of the house with rifle pointed at Mahir.

Not dropping his weapon, Mahir exchanged with him their code of regional proverbs.

"For every wise man there is one wiser."

To which the stranger replied, "A good companion shortens the longest road."

With motions to hurry, the others jogged across the street and into the house.

The man who welcomed them introduced himself as Arun. He was short and burly with a thick white mustache, broad grin, and a fez perched upon his head. Heavy sheepskin curtains were pulled and a single lantern lit. He directed them to put their packs in one of three adjacent rooms. Each kept weapons at hand.

When they were settled on cushions in the living room, hot tea was passed around along with thick soup made with potatoes, turnips, and cabbage. They alternately detailed the mountain engagement and assured him of their invisible passage into town.

Arun had already heard about the men who had been picked up along the roadside. "Word passes quickly in a town where so much happens. It seems like every day there is violence, arrest, and scandal. The local gendarmerie assumed it was an ambush that had been disrupted and the wounded are currently being interrogated. But there is some confusion as to who thwarted the attack.

"By morning I should get word about the location of their cell," assured Arun. "Until then, you'll hunker down here and relax. It looks like you could use rest."

Arun placed a *narghile* in the middle of their circle on the floor. They nibbled on sweet date cakes while taking turns enjoying the Turkish tobacco and thick yoghurt drink. After one polite draw on the water pipe, Charly left the ritual to the men.

About an hour after they arrived, they were all asleep in the large room where they had placed their packs. Comfort was not an issue, as they were all too tired to notice. At a gentle knock sometime in the deep of night, Arun slipped out the door to speak with his contact.

The next morning Arun informed them that the gendarmerie had learned during interrogation that several other ambushes were planned. "I'll show you the locations we know about as soon as we've had some breakfast."

"We'll look at them now, eat later." As a group they were tensed to move. They pored over maps, identifying the ambush sites.

Mahir encoded the information into his PLGR receiver and transmitted it to his command post. Within an hour there was a call back on his satellite phone. After listening for five minutes, making only one-word responses, he called Hakan to the phone.

As Hakan listened, he kept stealing glances at Charly, who was certain the conversation involved her. She could feel her gut tighten with anxiety. *Has something happened to my son? To Frances? Some tragedy back home?*

"Yes, I understand. I'll talk with her. I'm not sure." Hakan was clearly agitated as he clicked off the phone.

Settling back into the group, Hakan explained, "Command wants Charly out of here and the rest of us to continue."

"Like hell! What are you talking about?" Charly was indignant.

"Your government wants you to return to home base near Diyarbakir. From there they'll arrange transport to Istanbul. "

"But why? I thought all this was cleared through them."

"It was cleared through the counter-intelligence command with which you've previously worked. Evidently the American ambassador's office got wind of the information somehow and is furious that a U.S. citizen is involved, one without official standing, I might add. Captain Blanchard apologized but says it has something to do with ongoing negotiations with my government. Turkey is refusing to have U.S. involvement in their country's scrimmages with the Kurds."

Mahir scoffed. "Scrimmages? He actually used that word? Sounds like Charly's foreign office thinks we're playing games. Little wonder we have so much difficulty with our two governments communicating about internal affairs."

"Remember, Mahir, that the military have always had a lot of clout with the government officials in Ankara. I bet that's where the difficulty arises, another of their power struggles." Yasar shook his head. "We've run into this before."

"That's all very interesting, and certainly consistent with what I've seen and read. But it sure as hell doesn't help me any," said Charly. "Hakan, did you get any feeling for why now or did the ambassador just hear? And what is it the rest of you are supposed to be doing?"

"They've received intel about a major action planned in Yuksekova to dislodge the PKK who they think have a stronghold here. The reason for your presence will be very embarrassing for the Turkish government. And there is always the possibility that if the PKK got hold of you, they would use you for extortion or kill you. They said it was just too dangerous. Yuksekova is too volatile. We are to call back and give them our plan for your extraction. A helicopter can pick you up well away from the village in a valley."

"Too dangerous," voiced Arun. "If the PKK see the army helicopter, they'll know a mission is in the making. There would likely be reprisals in the village, a witch-hunt, as you would say."

Charly had been feeling very much a part of the group and wanted to stay the run. What had started out as a simple delivery of a package and helping out with reconnaissance had woven into a team effort for a cause in which she now deeply believed. She loved the Turkish people and was in empathy with the Kurdish plight of fighting for recognition by the government of their rights as Kurds. Too many lives had been lost already.

After this mulling, Charly looked up and found the others focused upon her. Hakan softly addressed her. "Charly, it's up to you."

"Will I handicap your mission? Can I be of some use to you?"

"You have shown that you not only can hold your own, but can be relied on during a mission. You pursued and took down a terrorist while we were engaged with the others. That saved us from discovery." Balaban nodded in agreement with Mahir.

"Hakan?"

Hakan grinned before replying. *I sure can't tell her how I feel in front of the team. But just wait until we're alone, then she won't have to ask.* "We succeeded in our original mission, Charly, and went on to another. You can leave with knowledge of that success. But there is still more we can do. There are only those of us in this room who have infiltrated the village. If you are willing, I'd like you to team with us."

Relieved, Charly grinned at each man broadly. "I'm staying. Thank you. Hakan, will you call my answer in, please?"

All business, Hakan moved toward the phone, feeling a sense of lightness because they wouldn't yet part. Besides, he always liked the original team to stay together until all aspects of a mission were completed. He thought they would have to split up here to focus on different parts, and they'd need her.

"Well, what did Captain Blanchard say?" They had all heard Hakan's voice rise and fall with emotion but hadn't been able to discern the upshot of the conversation.

"Captain Blanchard said he had already guessed Charly's response. Evidently someone with whom she's worked before was in the office and gave him an earful about their mission together in Jordan. He wouldn't give me details, just said she knew her mind, that once it's set in a direction, is almost impossible to divert. He said he had relayed the government's message, and what we did with it was up to us. "

"And that's it?" Charley was incredulous at how easy that had been.

Hakan mischievously grinned. "He added that it was too bad communication would be down between Diyarbakir and Ankara for awhile."

The men congratulated Charly and voiced pleasure that she would remain with them.

Ahmed teased her. "Charly, tell us about the mission to which Captain Blanchard referred!"

"Maybe later. But now my remaining is settled, I'd like to know more about Yuksekova and what we're up against with the people who live here." *I know I'm blustering a bit, but I don't want them to know how pleased I am. If only I could wipe this telltale grin from my face!* She glanced over at Hakan, who responded with a smile in kind.

Arun was happy to oblige. "Yuksekova has more than doubled in size since 1991, going from less than 30,000 to 66,000. The reason for this increase is due to so many families in surrounding villages being turned out of their homes by the Turks, their villages and homes destroyed. Or, perhaps they were caught in the crossfire between the Turks and PKK. Whatever, they found us a safe haven, and a place where families on the run could find relatives to house and protect them.

"We're also the center for smuggling of weapons, heroin, and oil. Many families have become rich through this trade, but you won't see it from the outside of their houses. Around a poor hovel will be the usual chickens running loose in the yard and paint peeling, if there is any. Inside many houses, it is a different story, a fortune within, every convenience and beautiful silks. Let me show you."

He led them through a door they hadn't noticed because of the woven cloth they assumed was decoration.

"Oh, my!" Charly was awestruck at the difference. The two rooms where they had eaten and slept were clean, tidy, and rustic. "Well lived in," her mother would have said. This room held beautiful silk carpets, not the more typical wool or simple kilims. Copper and brass gleamed. Colorful silk embroidered pillows adorned low-slung divans. Although small, this room would fit in any urban upscale home.

"You've made your point, Arun. You have gathered beautiful treasures here."

Arun shyly turned back into their previous living space, adjusting the wall hanging to camouflage the entrance to the room very few knew existed.

Arun continued, "In addition to many homes here having such rooms, lavish homes in other cities such as Konya, Ankara, and Istanbul are kept by some. But here in Yuksekova, discretion is key to survival.

"Our roads are rutted, dusty, and full of large potholes. At the end of the Turk-Kurd war, the Turkish government gave us and nearby villages approximately three hundred bricks apiece to rebuild our homes. Three hundred! The Turks widened the road into a huge turnaround. It's an ideal place for their planes to land. To appease us they are building a new complex with indoor and outdoor swimming pool, billiards hall, and a bar. We are waiting to see if it is ever completed. In the meantime, we are a mishmash of modern apartments and hovels, sports cars, and donkey carts.

"We are a very clannish people, and are suspicious of outsiders. Although we like our riches from smuggling, we do not like the PKK. We want to achieve peace without violence. We want to be left alone. You need to help rid us of the PKK.

"So, with that in mind, you'll be staying another day or so in my part of Yuksekova, a small village within the city, unto itself. I have just the cover, which will let you scout the area without being noticed. Tomorrow there is a wedding..."

- 14 -
There is darkness at the bottom of the candle.
- turkish proverb -

Before you even think of leaving the house today, you must know that our town is not what it seems. You need to be wary."

Basic information about Yuksekova was known to the group, but having Arun put it into perspective illuminated the dangers. Each attentively listened, having learned from experience not to ignore local intelligence. To do so could prove fatal.

"Killings, torture, and kidnapping are not foreign to us. Amongst us are gendarmerie, PKK, terrorist sympathizers, and village guards. After the arrest of PKK leader Abdulla Öcalan, most of the terrorists relocated into Kurdish Iraq and Iran. Those remaining have made themselves scarce, but are still here. House raids are not uncommon to ferret them out. We are suspicious of strangers. It is common for the visitor to be detained and interrogated, often not gently."

Shuddering, Charly nodded to herself. *Turkish prisons and detention centers are notorious for inventive torture. Definitely something to avoid.*

"We have a large contingent of *peshmerga,* our Kurdish irregular soldiers. There is often conflict between them and the gendarmes who are seen as an arm of the Turkish military. What would we do without them? They have Kurdish interests in their hearts, not those of the Turks or the PKK. They protect our rights.

"So, you can see, there are many competing forces in our town. In many ways Yuksekova consists of separate villages, each with its own subgroup. One has to constantly be alert and keep a low profile when outside of our own area. Within, we protect each other.

"You need to only speak Kurdish, be Kurds. If they suspect you are Turkish, Hakan, and part of the Turkish Special Forces, you will be arrested and likely tortured. You are hated and feared here. Your Kurdish will pass, don't slip."

"What about me?" asked Charly.

Arun looked at her curling, dark red hair. "Why, you are Hakan's wife, the infidel from Ireland. Definitely not American! We admire the Irish because of their fighting skills against the British who are seen as repressing religious faith. They are fighting a holy war, too. We will go together to my cousin's wedding. Most people in our sector will be there plus many visitors. We have so little to celebrate that we take advantage of every opportunity."

Arun brought out colorful vests for the men to wear over their long full trousers with full-sleeved long shirts. The vests were in patterns using the Kurdish colors of green, red, and yellow. He had borrowed a dress from his sister for Charly, a beautiful long georgette yellow *abaya* heavily embroidered in red and gold around the cuffs, neckline, and in a panel down the middle. Charly immediately went into the other room to try it on.

When she came back, Hakan's eyes widened. "That dress will have everyone staring. She can't keep a low profile that way!"

Charly tied the deep red matching *shayla* loosely around her waist so the long ends would blow in the breeze.

Yasar, Akam, and Ahmed were openly staring in admiration, feeling a bit guilty for looking so directly. Charly looked so different that it was difficult to reconcile her with their fellow soldier.

"But that's not our fashion to do that. The *abaya* must hang straight. You look too, too...well, foreign." Balaban caught himself. "Unless that's the intention..."

"Exactly! Someone trying to be invisible would not dress like that. She will draw attention, but as your wife, Hakan. She'll provide legitimacy for all of you."

"Of course! I am foreign and all will know it when they see my red hair. Besides, according to you I'm Irish and should be allowed some latitude for the fanciful."

"I give up!" Hakan threw up his hands and shrugged. "You are right. You will be noticed anyway. And I agree that anyone with something sinister in mind would not dress to evoke attention."

Arun continued his litany of blending in with the wedding party. "Only take your handguns. I'll hide your others here. Although some will have guns openly, it is best to not arouse suspicion. They'll be watching you as strangers closely enough."

Despite Arun's advice, Mahir and Hakan took their AKs, easily concealing them under their full robes. The others took their pistols. Only Arun openly carried his rifle.

Around noon, they went out into the brisk sunny day and began to slowly walk around the town. Arun boisterously greeted everyone, introducing his cousins who came for the wedding. They were readily accepted with admiring glances cast Charly's way. Several jested good naturedly with Hakan about his choice of wife, that with that color hair she must be really fiery. Charly had the good sense to look down and away during these exchanges. It was clear that Arun was a respected member of their village and well liked.

Charly shivered as she looked around, thinking of how she would describe it to Frances. *Yuksekova's location was striking, deep within the beautiful mountains, yet there was a feeling of bleakness. Gendarmerie and peshmerga importantly patrolled the streets with their AKs slung in front of them. Buildings were begun only to be abandoned. Roads were dusty, one side-stepped cow dung, and dogs chased the chickens. On the other hand, smiling, laughing children dressed in their finery were on their way to the wedding. Happy greetings were shouted across the street at one another. Among men, cheeks were kissed. Yes, there was a definite festive air today, befitting the beautiful mountain and sunny day.* This was definitely a Frances kind of day.

After a bit of walking around the village, they went with the flow of people toward the growing, brightly clothed crowd of laughing merrymakers. All the while the group were surveilling for anyone or anything suspicious. With the wedding, that meant someone who wasn't partaking in the festivities.

"I'm worried that the PKK might try to rescue the three in custody before they reveal too much. And we need that information. It is difficult to resist talking under torture. Our village guards can be vicious," said Arun.

"I've heard stories about that," commented Charly. "What do they do?"

"Let's just say they will be lucky to come out in one piece. Beatings are the norm. Prisoners may be stripped, blindfolded, and hosed with high-pressure ice-cold water. Hanging them from their wrists behind their backs or by their feet for long periods is not unusual. Beating the soles of their feet, electric shock to sexual organs, and putting a block of ice on their bodies are just some of the more usual of the tortures. The rape of women is common."

Charly was concerned about the young boy she had captured and turned over to the gendarmerie. "What about the boy? Surely they won't torture him?"

"Charly, we have children as young as nine or ten who join in terrorist activities. When they do that, they automatically are treated the same as anyone else. And why not? They wreak just as much destruction. They can kill just as many."

Aw, that poor kid. Charly fretted. *I wonder how his childhood was stolen. He likely was born into a family group of extremists, and believes deeply in their cause. To him, they are probably "in the right." Frances would be picketing the detention center in protest if she were here. Lucky she's not, or she'd get us all killed.*

Shifting gears to more pleasant thoughts, Charly observed, "Something smells delicious!"

"Roasting lamb. Hungry? I know I am," responded Mahir. *No matter how tough she seems on the outside, she really is just a neophyte in our business. We treat her like our tough little sister, knowing she can take care of herself but feeling protective at the same time. Yes, we're all rather taken by this red-headed tornado.*

"Starving!" Charly quickly responded. Even though there was a great potential for danger and their mission was ongoing, they all felt more relaxed, and were actually smiling. The warmth of the greetings they had received and the lively music had worked its magic. *Ah, our wonderful dichotomous personalities asserted once again!*

They were gathered at the bride's house, where soon she was put on a decorated horse which led the procession of well-wishers, drums and *zurnas*. The children danced and skipped in the street. The procession picked up the groom and, joined by his relatives, turned around and returned to the place of feasting and dancing.

Charly was thoroughly enjoying herself, entering into the folk dances with enthusiasm. Dancing had long been her outlet; she loved it. The tension she'd been carrying since she and Hakan began their trip east evaporated with the rhythmic movement of these ancient dances which somehow seemed familiar to her. The red scarf swirled in abandon. The women good-naturedly laughed at her attempts to follow the footwork of their folk dances, and then laughed with her as she skillfully followed their steps. They nicknamed her Dervish the Red.

Charly thought that was amusing as she had admired the Whirling Dervishes' grace as she observed them in their religious ceremony in Konya. *Nice company to be placed in!*

No one asked Charly where she was from or why she was there. One old woman whirling around asked, "where's your husband?" and was satisfied when she pointed vaguely toward the group of men. With a smile she nodded. "Ours, too."

The men began clapping to the rhythm and began a dance themselves. Mahir, Balaban, and Arun moved away from the dancers. They needed to keep alert to their surroundings and not be tempted by the frivolity. The three younger men entered into the spirit of the celebration, knowing it would be rude and noticed if some of them did not.

Hakan hung back to keep an eye on Charly who now blended in with the group. *How relaxed she seems. And beautifully happy. How can she then turn around and be perfectly at home in immersing herself in hardships of the hunt, of our kind? But she does. And I'm beginning to fall in love with this complicated woman. Just beginning to?*

Charly and the others drifted together and were looking

on as the festivities were drawing to a close. In a traditional final burst of good cheer the men of the wedding party raised their rifles, shooting into the air. Nearby there was another volley.

Arun quietly alerted his companions. "That was in the direction of the detention center. Yasar and Akam, stay here with Charly, see if anyone else follows us. Let's go."

No one paid attention to them as they silently eased themselves from the edge of the crowd. Once around a building and out of sight, they quickly ran in a circuitous route, keeping to the cover of buildings. To go directly may have put them in danger as their mission would have been easily detected.

Three men leaped into a jeep and were off in a hurry. There was no other movement. In the distance they could hear the music interwoven with the celebratory gunfire, which was now sporadic. They crept to the open doorway, guns drawn.

"Cover me," Arun directed as he entered the building, gun first. Mahir and Balaban quickly followed. Hakan covered the rear of the building to prevent anyone from leaving. All of their weapons had silencers.

After a few minutes the three emerged out the back. Arun shook his head. There was tacit agreement to postpone discussion until they returned to Arun's about thirty minutes later.

They quickly and unobtrusively made their way back to the edge of the party, now mostly dispersed into small groups not quite ready to go home yet. Charly and Hakan, as the "married couple," broke off in one direction, and the others joined groups smoking *narghiles* and drinking tea.

When they all had returned to Arun's, Mahir related

what they had seen when they went inside the jail. "The young boy was lying naked, dead, in his own blood. He had been badly beaten and there was evidence of torture with burns on his genitals and armpits. The one with the chest wound was also dead. Not many marks on him. He probably died before they could administer much in the way of persuasion. It looked like the bones in his face had been crushed. The third prisoner was gone."

"A boy so young—it is terrible to torture, but to do so to one so young is just too brutal," Charly said angrily.

"I agree, Charly, but such is the way when information can mean life or death. We are concerned because the forays the PKK is making into Turkish territory are increasing. Actually, we are not sure if they are the PKK or a newly formed group. If we could discover their base or even who they are we could protect ourselves better." Arun spat his distaste.

Hakan sensed Charly's outrage, and expanded to help her understand what was considered routine practice to them. "Torture is common within Middle Eastern countries. It has been a successful method for centuries. The Turkish government is putting on a lot of pressure to eliminate it, which is a joke, as it is the method of choice for the military. Or at least it has been. Wanting to join the European Union has wrought a lot of new human rights directives."

"Okay," interrupted Mahir who had just gotten off the satellite phone with Command Center. "Let's decide what's next. Command wants us to pick up a trail on the terrorist group operating in this area. They have no idea how big a cell it is, or what they plan next. But it's rumored they plan to hit the diesel trucks at the border. Since Turkey has a quota on how many they admit per day, there is usually a queue of several dozen waiting for permits. This would cause a massive disruption of oil flow and traffic at the border. There are also rumors about sabotage of the oil pipeline from Iran. No details, though, as to where. Whatever specifics the gendarmerie may have learned overnight are dead with them."

"How much time do we have?"

"Their best estimate is three days from now for the hit."

"What did they say about weather? It looked like the clouds are beginning to build over the mountains." Balaban was concerned, for he well knew the dangers the first heavy snowstorms could bring.

"Beginning by morning, heavier by midday. Looks like this one has several pulses to it."

"Do we have a place to overnight if we leave now?" Ahmed could see the advantages of saving their energy expended by gaining altitude tonight, being fresh to track in the morning.

Hakan was nodding agreement. "I see where you are going with this. It'll be a tough go if the snow gets really deep on us tomorrow. Better to start fresh."

"Right," Mahir confirmed. "Tracking with night goggles isn't the best by far. If the satellite weather report is on target, we'll have a couple good hours of visibility in the morning."

"Arun? You know these mountains better than we do. Anything in place?"

"There is a nomad encampment in a valley an additional 2,000 feet elevation in the mountains. That would give you a very good head start. It's about three hours from here. They abandoned it several weeks ago so no one will be around. There won't be any tents, of course, but there is a crude rock structure that might do."

Mahir turned to the others, who nodded their agreement.

"Yasar and Akam, I need you to stay with Arun for a

couple of days, blend in, and keep your eyes open. See what the repercussions are to the raid on the detention center."

"You'll have to wait until dark," warned Arun. "There are still too many in the village for you to slip away unnoticed in the light. Wait until after prayer call at sunset, then be off. Most will either be at the mosque or home for the night. It'll be too cold tonight for much outside socializing."

Agreeing, once more maps were spread on the floor and options considered. Arun marked the route to their shelter for the night.

"What do you think of the possible PKK caves our ops map shows?" Hakan asked.

Mahir pointed out at least four sites.

Arun added two more to the mix.

Looking at the maps after these additional caves were included, Hakan was concerned. "There are two groupings of the possibilities, too divergent in location for one group."

"Okay, so let's think about this in a different way. Our goal is to find their central command site for this operation at the border and prevent the action. To attempt to waylay them at the border is too risky."

Hakan agreed with Mahir. "If we waited at the border, they could be too spread out to get all of them before they have a chance to set up or plant detonators. Will they fit explosives onto the waiting trucks or explode with RPGs? Too many unknowns."

Charly piped up. "I can see your points, but finding just the right cave is tricky, too. And how about multiple cave areas?"

Balaban exaggeratedly puffed out his chest and boomed. "Ahmed and I are mountain ferrets."

Charly burst out laughing at the image of this large,

boisterous man as a polecat searching for rodents, with his son close behind. Ahmed started to take offense until she explained.

Hakan chimed in his agreement. "We've got the best. Let's use them!"

Balaban poured over the possibilities again, checking distances and elevations from the GPS information, boldly marking two. Ahmed sat back, the excitement of agreement on his face. He clapped his father on the shoulder and grinned.

Charly thought Ahmed's grin was almost as infectious as his father's. *He's so clearly proud of his dad!*

Balaban looked questioningly around the circle. "Mahir?"

"Agreed. These are the most likely. I see your logic. It provides them the most protection in descending to the border crossing."

Mahir turned to the others. "What do you think?"

Agreement was unanimous.

They busied themselves in the hour before sunset checking their packs for survival gear, leaving anything extraneous. Arun surreptitiously slipped a small flask of brandy to Charly. "This might help if anyone gets in trouble."

"But how did you—"

Arun stopped her question by shaking his head and walking to the kitchen area.

How sweet, and what a welcomed surprise. Charly gazed fondly after her host.

Arun fed them well with *patlicanti pilav*, a favored eggplant and rice dish, along with *salçase*, Turkish yoghurt. None of them were very hungry after the feasting earlier in the day, but they knew they'd need the calories later. The sour cherry juice was particularly welcomed.

Warmly dressed and ready to depart, Arun handed each a small wrapped bundle of food to take with them. Balaban winked at Charly, as he had noticed the earlier exchange and guessed it wasn't juice in the flask.

- 15 -
Even the highest tree has an ax waiting at its bottom
- turkish proverb -

By the time they began their ascent at the edge of the village, there was a brisk breeze and temperatures below freezing.

"Smells like snow." Charly breathed in appreciation of the familiar moist bite in the air.

"Good nose, Charly," Balaban said. "Alaska or Turkey, the signs are the same."

"Don't worry, Charly. We'll get there before it starts," Ahmed reassured Charly.

He's so sweet. He was the same age as her son, and she felt a tug of compassion as she once again noticed his shy, protective manner toward her. He was on his way to developing many of his father's characteristics, but she doubted if he would be able to duplicate his robust good humor. His gentle nature didn't have the edge of self-assurance. At least not yet.

They bent their heads to the onslaught of wind as they began a gradual climb. A steady pace was easy to do as they took the path up the valley, well worn by the nomad's livestock over the years. Lights from Yuksekova were blocked by the mountain as they twisted and turned upward. The night was dark, no moon. Stars were obliterated by thickening cloud cover. Time quickly passed.

The nomads' encampment was nestled in the valley against the side of the mountain which formed a natural wind block. There were four free-standing small stone huts. Looking in each, they chose the largest which had a stone fireplace in the middle, with an air vent for smoke in the roof. They didn't even look around to see what extra stores the nomads had left as they carried what they needed.

No one was hungry, so after building a fire they spread their bedrolls and settled in for a short night. For the sake of propriety, Charly was on one side of the fire, the other four on the other side. Charly smiled at the courtly manners of the Turks and Kurds in even the most primitive of circumstances.

The fire took the edge off the freezing temperature, but not by much. *More than anything,* thought Charly, *it provides an artificial ambiance of warmth and coziness.*

The large stones were roughly laid, not intending to be a winter refuge. Through these openings the freshening wind raced, occasionally setting up eerie howling sounds. *A good night for ghost stories,* thought Charly. *But I'm not even going to mention it. I don't even know if ghost stories are part of their culture, although fanciful tales are certainly freely generated. No, too somber of a night. Tonight is for gathering strength from our ancestors, for tomorrow will likely be very rough. Tonight is for being alone, with our own.*

The next morning each was still cocooned in his or her own armor. The give and take of sharing the breakfast Arun had packed for them was done in silent acknowledgment. No jocularity this morning. Only intention, soberly focused inward.

Quickly gathering their bedrolls they geared up in their warmest. Snow was lightly falling. The clouds were low and looked heavy in their greyness. The five acknowledged this in silence, each knowing it meant rough going.

Balaban took the lead, followed by Mahir, then Ahmed. Charly waited until Hakan was even with her. Each reached out, touching gloved hands, then putting their own hand to their own chest. Of one heart, you are in my heart, what did it matter? It was a silent contact of caring, a human touch which intruded into their aloneness of the day.

The weather put them at a disadvantage. In all likelihood the terrorists would be holed up in their cave of choice and not making tracks to follow. As they had planned a few hours ago, their goal was to seek their camp, gather intelligence and destroy. Balaban, in the lead, made a swirling motion with his hand indicating to pick up the pace.

Instead of climbing higher into the steeper part of the mountains, which was perhaps safer from detection, they chose the lower landscape. By keeping to the side of the mountain, there was some modicum of protection from the rising wind and snow. The ground was more level, which made walking easier and a faster pace possible.

Within a couple of hours their balaclava and scarves covering most of their faces were white with snow, and ice had formed at their mouths and noses. They had to walk within a few feet of each other because visibility was very poor. Balaban stopped periodically and checked the compass coordinates, turning his back to the sting of the snow. The temperature was rapidly dropping.

Slipping into the shelter of a crevice in the rock of the mountain, they brushed off snow and took a few extra moments to have a packet of self-heating beverage. Balaban explained that from here they would begin to work their way to higher elevations.

Charly inhaled the aroma of the hot cocoa and remembered many times at home in Alaska enjoying it around the huge stone fireplace which kept out the cold. She could see the flames and hear the crackling of the fire—almost. At this she chuckled, and the others looked at her with wonder.

"What good spirits, Charly. Hovering at zero degrees Fahrenheit in a snow storm, and you are laughing." Mahir gazed at Charly in wonderment, admiring her spirit and spunk.

Charly laughed again, this time at Mahir's puzzled expression. She punched him on the arm, which took him aback more. *Not exactly your traditional Muslim woman, am I?* thought Charly. "Well, why not? Actually I was just remembering warmer times."

Hakan raised his eyebrows. "Ah, I can remember some, too." He chanced a glance at Charly.

Charly felt welcomed warmth come into her face in embarrassment and memory of the warmer times to which he referred. *Am I glad my face is red from the cold already!*

But the reminder was enough to have her reliving memories of Hakan's devouring mouth on hers, his hands teasing...*Lucky I only have to keep watch on Mahir in front of me,* she thought. *Gives me time to dream a bit. Odd how my mind wanders even when faced with possible danger. It must be this cocoon of snow, making me feel an unnatural security. It keeps immediate reality away.*

Charly remembered many other occasions on hunting trips when the snow would sock them in, sometimes so bad they had to huddle on the side of a mountain until the worst had passed. It had been a special time of closeness with her father; fear had never been part of the experience of snow, ice, and storms. Concern, yes, just not fear.

Hakan was doing his own dreaming as he brought up the rear. He liked the position he was in, keeping his eye on

Charly's back as she walked in front of him. Not much shape to her now with all the heavy clothes, but oh, what's underneath. Hakan imagined he had x-ray vision, looking at her firm hips and how they tensed and relaxed with each step. He remembered his hand taking both mounds into his hands and kneading as they kissed before falling into bed, of how he drew her closer, ravishing her mouth. And her response had been to press closer. To move one of her hands, which had been around him, downward to tentatively touch him, then to grasp firmly. So into the daydream was Hakan that he groaned aloud. At the sound, Charly whipped her body around, promptly slipping on the narrow path the three ahead were making and stumbling in the deepening snow. Reaching out to steady her, Hakan also lost his balance and they tumbled down a slight incline, catching on an outcropping of rock before the cliff plunged to the bottom. The others were unaware as the snow muffled their fall. Charly and Hakan were well enough trained not to shout out. They were now fairly near the first cave where the terrorists might be.

Charly landed squarely on top of Hakan. Going on instinct, she lowered her face to his, lips gently touching. "I've missed this." For only a moment they felt as if a *fusun,* or magic spell, had been cast.

Within a breath, the reality of where they were and why intruded. They helped each other up, brushing off snow, and picked up rifles which had been partially buried in the snow.

So much for our compartmentalization! Charly chastised herself. *How can we feel so alive when danger is so close? This certainly goes beyond the find-it-where-you-can attitude of most ops guys.*

Hakan and Charly regained their path with little trouble. It seemed as if they had been gone a long time visiting another world, but not enough time had passed for their tracks to be obliterated or even filled. They plodded ahead, single file, focusing on signs of the trail and listening for sounds out of sync with the howling wind.

Both abruptly stopped when they heard a cracking sound. Thinking *"rifle shot"* each automatically touched their rifles. Almost simultaneously they felt a slight tremor and heard a whoomph, whooshing sound, which they immediately recognized from winter maneuvers and hunting trips.

"Avalanche!"

Judging by how short lived the rumbling, it was not a major one, and not far away.

Another few minutes of hiking and they came across a bank of snow about nine feet high blocking their trail. There was a narrow vertical chute to their right from which the snow had cascaded. Visibility was too limited to determine the altitude of origin. To their left the snow had tumbled down into the valley far below. The width looked about thirty feet.

They walked over to the edge and looked down, fearing Balaban and Mahir had been caught. "No traces, Hakan, but I can't clearly see." The heavily falling blowing snow as well as puffs of snow still settling handicapped their vision. "If we hadn't fallen..." Charly left the thought unsaid and shivered.

Focusing on the real problem at hand, Charly inquired, "Should we go through or over?"

"And use what as a shovel? Let's try over. With luck it packed heavy enough to hold our weight."

"Let's be safe." They discussed the best procedure while they waited for the snow slide to settle. They were avoiding the hazard of getting caught in a secondary one, which occasionally hit the same area. Charly unpacked the climbing gear she carried.

Hakan tied the rope around his waist while Charlie hammered a piton into a small crevice of the hard rock, canting it downward into the groove in a crack. She cringed at every sound, realizing how it might echo, alerting the terrorists. It went in easily, so telltale sound was minimized. Attaching a carabiner, she secured one end of the rope around the loop.

Charly held the rope so Hakan would feel slight pressure as he began his climb up to the top of the snow berm. In case it cascaded farther at least he wouldn't be caught up in the rush to the valley floor. On the sides the snow was loose, but once on top it held his weight as he slowly inched across.

Once over, Hakan secured his end of the rope as Charly had done and tugged for her to proceed. Tying the end around her, Charly had no trouble scrambling over the top.

Stowing the equipment they used, they cautiously continued. There was no way to know how much farther ahead Balaban and Mahir were, but the first and most likely cave was very near.

They heard the distant soft crack of a rifle, then the brief stutter of a machine gun on automatic. In the silence after the shots, they heard shouts in Kurdish. Then silence again. It was difficult to judge the distance as the heavily falling snow and wind distorted the sound.

Hakan and Charly secured their weapons in front of them and took off the safeties. Taking a minute or two, they checked the coordinates for the terrorists cave, less than a mile away. They worked their fingers to limber their stiffness from the cold. They tried to pick up their pace, but paused periodically to listen. The lateness of the afternoon and heavy snow brought on an early dusk. Reflected by the snow, they saw a lightening of the darkness.

Sidling closer to the mountain, off the path, they made their way closer. Much trampling of the snow in front of a rock face meant they had arrived. One sentry was hunching his shoulders against the cold, swiveling his head from side to side. Nearby was a hump in the snow. Hakan touched Charly's arm, pointing. Looking closer they saw blood seeping into the snow. Both had the same thought. *It must be Mahir, Ahmed, or Balaban; they would have moved their own inside.*

Hakan pointed to himself, then to the sentry. Understanding, Charly waited as he slipped forward. The snow and the sentry's head-covering muffled footfalls. Hakan waited until his head was turned away, then grabbed him by the neck, twisting hard. This should have broken it but the protective clothing made the movement awkward. Instead the man fell sideways, bringing up the butt of his gun against Hakan's head. Whether reflex or intentional, his weapon discharged.

Charly unleashed a burst of fire, knocking the terrorist off his feet. Rushing in, she pushed a stunned Hakan to the side. They had just gotten out of sight when two men burst though the entrance of the cave. One kept his machine gun fanning the area, while the other grabbed the dead sentry and pulled him inside.

Hakan and Charly quietly pulled away farther, behind an outcropping of rock. Again, the snow kept them from being detected by sound, and the sudden emergence from light to dark gave them an edge from being spotted. Hakan took advantage of the confusion of the others remaining in the cave by slipping the silencer on his 9mm. His aim was on-target as the bullet imploded into the lookout's head. Silently, he fell.

Dashing to the entrance, Charly was ready with the heat

imager, reaching the entrance even as the body was falling. Getting a clear reading, she showed it to Hakan, who had joined her. Three standing in one area. It looked as if one were lying down. In the second room there were two images.

The first room was empty, but light was showing from an entry to the left. With hand motions they determined to both go in, firing. Peering around the corner they quickly ascertained that the three had their submachine guns shouldered and in hand. The one they had killed lay motionless on the floor.

In one swift motion, Hakan stepped into the room and crouched, opening fire. Surprised, the three did not have a chance to raise their weapons. It was over in seconds, with only the echoing sounds from the walls of the cave and their ringing ears. Charly was at the door of the other room when the firing began. Her weapon was leveled at the terrorist who looked up, startled, from his seated position.

"Sit on your hands," Charly ordered in Turkish.

Instead, he made a sideways leap and grabbed his gun in one motion. Charly shot, hitting the arm that held his AK-47. Louder, she shouted her order once more. He complied. A few seconds later Hakan dashed in, took the weapon and two knives the man had hidden in his belt. Dragging him into the larger room with his dead comrades, Hakan quickly tied his feet behind him, binding them to his thighs. His elbows and hands were tied in front.

With barely a pause, Hakan raced out the entrance to see about the body in the snow.

Charly made sure each of the three were dead, stacking their weapons in a pile away from the bodies. Her hearing was just returning when she heard a groan. There were two rooms leading from this one.

Mahir was in the smaller, hands tied behind him and

hung onto a hook, dangling. Blood was caked to the side of his face. When he saw Charly, he managed a weak smile. "I thought it must be you. Who else would shout 'sit on your hands!' Allah! Where did you get that?"

"For that I'd leave you up there."

"Go to Ahmed first. He was hit. They might have left him outside."

"Hakan's on his way to Ahmed right now. Where's Balaban?"

Mahir nodded his head to the left. "He was a wild man when Ahmed was hit. He's probably very upset. I am worried. I haven't heard anything for awhile."

While he was talking, Charly began getting him down. Stooping, she draped Mahir's legs around her shoulders, and holding them, stood up. It took pressure from his arms and he was able to unhook himself, half falling from her shoulders. Not for the first time she thanked God, Allah, or whoever for strong legs kept in shape with skiing, running, and use of the weight room at her local gym.

Charly untied him, giving him a quick once over before hurrying to the small opening she hadn't noticed before. Mahir was beside her as they knelt at the opening. It was too dark to see inside. "Allah help us, it looks like a black hole."

Hearing a groan, Charly shouted, "Balaban, where are you?"

"Get a light!"

While Charly dug in her pack, Mahir felt around the edge of the hole, finding a thick rope. Charly returned with the flashlight, illuminating a natural-made hole in the cave floor. A rope was wound around a sturdy stick and placed across the top.

Urgency increased in Mahir's tone. "I've seen this before. We have to pull up on the stick simultaneously or else one end will fall into the hole and Balaban will tumble. It could be a thousand feet or more deep."

Balaban boomed, "Easy does it, but do it! My arms are falling off."

After briefly talking it over, they decided to tie a rope around each end of the stick, tying it together, and securing it around a natural outcropping. Feeling a bit more secure, they tossed a looped rope in the hole and asked Balaban to feel for it with his legs.

"What am I doing? Riding a phantom goat?" Balaban roared with humor despite his pain.

"Something like that, only one-legged." Charly quipped.

After a few minutes they heard Balaban. "Okay, I've got one foot through the loop."

Slowly Mahir pulled the rope up until he felt tension.

"Easy there, friend. I still might want more fun in life!"

Tying this rope to the one going to either side of the stick, they slowly winched Balaban up until his shoulders were even with the cave face. From there, Mahir and Charly were able to pull him out.

Charly was shocked at his face—red, raw, and oozing. The fingers on one hand hung loosely. He was clearly in considerable pain, but still he blustered. "What took you so long?"

Assisting Balaban, they went into the larger room. Hakan was there with Ahmed. Balaban fell to his knees beside his son.

The cold had slowed the flow of blood, which was now congealed on Ahmed's jacket. Removing it revealed wounds to chest and shoulder. Ahmed was in and out of consciousness, mostly out.

He grimaced as Hakan cut away his shirt. "Easy, my friend. I don't need a knife wound, too."

Balaban held Ahmed's hand while Hakan worked quickly

to clean, bandage, and administer injections of morphine and antibiotic. They piled blankets to warm him from lying in the snow for nearly an hour. Ahmed let out a long sigh and slipped into unconsciousness.

"Now, let me look at you, Balaban." Hakan carefully cleaned and put antibiotic salve on his open facial wounds. The bullet graze at his temple was not deep, but might cause some disorientation. Feeling Balaban's torso revealed broken ribs. Fingers on one hand were broken, which Hakan wrapped as they were with a protective bandage. Noticing how Balaban held one shoulder and was grimacing in pain, Hakan asked, "May I?"

"Only if you know what you're doing."

"Do you have an option?"

Before Hakan got his answer he had snapped his dislocated shoulder in place.

"Thanks, Hakan. It feels better already. Do the same for my son."

"You know I'm trying. But..."

"I know." Balaban smoothed his unconscious son's hair back from his forehead.

Next, Hakan turned his attention to the terrorist Charly had wounded. The bullet had gone through, smashing the wrist bone. It was more painful than it was dangerous. The terrorist said nothing but his eyes flashed with fear. He expected to be shot or tortured. Hakan cleaned and bandaged the wound. He helped the wounded man down two pills for pain and a strong dose of valium to force relaxation. He next put a headset on him which emitted only static, which was unpleasant but masked conversation. He was turned, lying down, to face the wall to prevent the remote possibility of lip reading. Humanely, his damaged hand was placed side-up.

As they gathered around the fire, Charly pulled out a flask of brandy, which got raised eyebrows from Mahir and chuckles from Hakan. "Medicinal, I'm sure."

"Thanks, Charly. This is very welcome. I wondered if Arun had slipped something to you before we left the village. He knows I am a better Turk than I am a Muslim, and enjoy our rules on such things." Mahir held out his hand. With the three alternately taking swigs, Mahir explained what had happened.

Knowing the first possibility for the terrorist's cave was just ahead, Mahir had paused to take out the thermal imager, and Balaban had stopped with him. Ahmed had continued past them, presumably just to look around the corner. He had startled a sentry, who was equally as surprised as evidently he had just stepped away from the cave entrance to pee. He was the first to get a shot off, and Ahmed had gone down.

Balaban had already started after Ahmed and got hit on the temple by a bullet ricocheting off the rock. Balaban had staggered and fallen to his knees beside Ahmed. Mahir had shot the terrorist, but another appeared at the cave entrance, getting the drop on him. Mahir had been directed to first assist Balaban, then drag the dead terrorist inside.

"Lucky bastards! Never should have happened."

But that's just the way it sometimes does happen, thought Hakan. *That's how we lose our best, not focusing on the tiny details.*

Unbidden, a Turkish proverb came to mind, which Mahir recited. *"Tekerkirilinca yol gosteren cok olur."* For Charly, he translated into English. "Many will point to the right way after the wheel is broken."

Mahir had tried to bluff it out when not so gently

questioned by the terrorists. He had assured them that they were simply coming back from a recon mission. "Who else would be out on such a night? They chose us because we're the lowest rank."

"And dumb, too, for getting caught so easily," one of the terrorists had said. "Behir, guard the entrance, and no peeing. See if he tells the truth."

They had proceeded to beat Mahir for more information, and eventually tied his hands, made him stand on a crate, placed his tied hands over a hook about two feet taller than he was, then kicked the crate beyond his reach.

"Thank Allah they didn't tie your hands behind you," commented Charly. "Your arms would have been wrenched from their sockets."

"Yes, instead they just feel like they were!" Mahir continued to rub his shoulders while Hakan cleaned his face, exposing what would become nasty bruises and a few minor cuts.

The blood had stopped, so he just left the wounds open to the air.

Mahir nodded to Balaban, who was sitting with his son. "As I hung there I could hear them beating him, asking questions, to which they only got silence, then more body blows. He was very brave." Mahir stopped, shaking his head.

Hakan moved them toward action. "We need to get to our cave. The satellite phones will work in another hour. We need to get word to Command about what we found and request an emergency extraction."

They thoroughly searched the cave before leaving, finding satellite photos and plans for the next missions. They took photos with their digital camcorder and camera of the terrorists and the materials to send on as soon as they reached their destination.

Ahmed was unable to travel. It was decided that Charly would remain behind to care for him and stand guard over the prisoner while Mahir and Hakan climbed to their shelter, perhaps an hour away.

"Balaban?"

"You don't need me. I want to stay here."

Charly walked to the entrance with them. The wind was whipping the snow into drifts, obliterating the distinction between the path and cliff's edge. Shivering, she wished them well and a speedy return. It was unlikely there would be anyone else wandering the mountains in this storm, so there was little to fear from humans.

Charly returned to stoke up the fire and check Ahmed. He was still unconscious and had developed a high fever. Occasionally moans would erupt and he would thrash about. Charly tried to get him to take in some water by forcing a few drops into his mouth.

She and Balaban sat, feeling helpless. Ahmed was in a restless sleep and they could not rouse him. There was little to do for him. In another two hours he could have another injection of antibiotics and morphine. Balaban was in obvious pain from his crushed fingers and broken ribs and finally agreed to a mild dose of codeine along with some soup. He seemed dazed.

The fire crackled. The only other sound was the wind, which occasionally would find an opening at just the right angle, and a howling reverberated in their enclosed space. Finally, Balaban dozed.

Charly's mind wandered. She thought of the caves she had explored in Cappadocia. As she had wandered through she had felt as if she weren't alone. Around each corner she half-expected to find someone eating, napping, or cooking. She allowed imagery to once again take her through their labyrinth, feeling the calm and connection she had felt there.

A groan from the wounded terrorist brought Charly back to reality and she shivered.

Taking a packet of soup from her stash of MREs, she warmed it, drank a little. Balaban still dozed beside Ahmed.

Cautiously, she approached the prisoner, who had been moving restlessly in the limited fashion his bindings would allow. *He's really just a boy,* Charly thought, *probably the same age as the one he tried to rescue in the Yuksekova jail. His clothes are a little ragged. I bet he's hungry. What am I thinking about! He seriously wounded Ahmed and almost killed Balaban. He would just as easily kill me if he had a chance. Boy in age, but not in experience or ideology.*

Charly poked him with her foot and he forced his head back. His eyes flashed, but his lids were droopy. He blinked in fighting sleep. Charly flipped off his headset and held out the cup to him. "Would you like some soup?" She could almost read his mind in confusion thinking, "Soup? Poison more likely!" She smiled. *Maybe I look like his mother with my red curls covered.* He just stared at her.

"I'll drink some first. It's really quite good."

The second time she offered, he nodded assent. Charly helped him sit, leaning at an angle against the cave wall. He awkwardly held the cup in his bound hands and sipped. Thinking he might throw the cup at her, she scooted out of his line of movement.

The three dead men to one side of the cave kept drawing her attention. Somehow it seemed rather macabre sitting in the same room with them, like a wake. There was a side of her who believed in the spirit of the dead remaining around awhile. With her lively imagination, she could "see" them rising and falling with the shadows cast by the flames of their fire. It was silent but for the occasional crackling of the fire. The wind sometimes found something to vibrate and it made eerie sounds.

Finally deciding to be proactive, Charly dragged each of the dead to another room of the cave. She was tempted to drop them down the hole that went an unknown distance below, but decided that wouldn't exactly be honoring the dead. She laid them side by side, folded their arms, and closed their eyes. Charly placed a blanket she had found over them, which at least covered all three from the waist up.

"I know you were brave soldiers. You must have been to have broken your friend from the jail, and to be wandering in the mountains. Had you lived, you would have taken my life, or worse. We are on different sides today, but tomorrow we may not be. May Allah look kindly upon you."

Charly bowed to them and returned to the fire to sit beside Balaban and Ahmed.

Hakan and Mahir had gotten through to Command and relayed the request for extraction and the information regarding the plans they found, including a computer which needed to be perused with a fine-tooth comb. The photos of the terrorists they faxed had been in the main files, and were "known and wanted." They received orders to come back to base with the confiscated materials. A pick-up site was designated farther down the mountain in a narrow valley which provided enough room for a helicopter to land. Satellite imagery indicated there would be a brief break from the heavier snow before it socked in again. They would try for that window.

Mahir and Hakan returned to the cave to gather up Charly, Balaban, Ahmed, and the prisoner. Coordinates had been given to the inbound team to retrieve the bodies. They each pulled an aukio, a version of the smooth curved bottom sled used for rescues in mountainous regions, which had been stored in their cave quarters to transport Ahmed and the materials more easily over the snow. They also took three extra sets of snowshoes as by now the snow accumulation was about two feet.

There were no new footprints in the snow around the cave's entrance. Hearing no sounds from within, Mahir and Hakan cautiously entered. Their shoulders brushed an unseen wire and they were startled by the crashing down of falling metal. Dodging and falling flat, they crept around the debris, rifles at the ready, inching around the corner.

Charly was on the floor drawing a bead on the entrance. Hakan's recognition was instant. "Hey, Charly, what was that all about? Afraid you'd fall asleep and need an alarm?"

"Yep, and you were it." Charly got up and stretched out the kinks the snooze on the cold floor had wrought.

Balaban rose stiffly and stood beside her.

"Ahmed?" Mahir softly inquired with concern.

Charly's voice cracked with sorrow as she responded, "He didn't make it."

Ahmed's face was turned toward Mecca, his eyes closed. Balaban had placed his son's feet together and laid his hands side by side and on his belly, in the tradition of Islam.

The three men gazed upon Ahmed and recited an Islamic

prayer, asking Allah to extend mercy and forgiveness. They knelt and helped Balaban wrap Ahmed closely in his sleeping bag, covering him completely. The required cleansing would have to wait until they brought Ahmed home. They were each quiet with their own memories.

Mahir seemed to go deep within himself as he closed his eyes and whispered prayers. Balaban and he had been friends and fellow soldiers fighting for Kurdish rights for many years, bloody years. And now that fight had taken the life of his friend's son. He had died a soldier's death and would be honored. Mahir's feeling of loss extended beyond Ahmed. It was for all who had died over these twenty years, the innocents, the soldiers, the unborn.

Charly had seen Ahmed as a sort of nephew, someone to tease. He had lightened her day and had always made sure she had a cup of tea in her hand, or room in the circle. Charly had seen some of the same characteristics in him as his father, a true mountain nomad. Although Balaban was tough on the outside and a sweetheart underneath, Ahmed hadn't yet developed the tough exterior. She wondered if he would have had the deep rumbling laugh of his father in a couple dozen years. He had already had a twinkle in his eye. She had found his reference to her as little sister endearing.

Hakan had grown to greatly admire Ahmed's quickness to learn. Sometimes his unflagging energy had been impetuous, but he had had the enthusiasm of youth, so that was expected. He couldn't imagine how difficult it must be for Balaban to lose his son. No doubt Balaban had made *du'aa,* supplication for his deceased son.

| *Inna lillaahi wa innaa ilaihir raaji'uun.* | *To Allah we belong, and to him is our return* |

Allaahumahajirnee fee   O *Allah reward me in my*
                               affliction and
museebateewe akhlif lahuu   *let him be succeeded by the best.*
khairanminhaa

Hakan cleared his throat of the lump which had gathered as he said his private goodbye to Ahmed. "We need to return him to his village."

"Yes. Today," Mahir agreed.

Stepping outside, Hakan called Command alerting them to Ahmed's death. "Alert the pilots we'll be diverting to take Ahmed home." He listened, growing annoyed. "We **will** honor Islamic law by permitting an earliest possible burial. Give the pilots the order." *Why do things need to be so difficult sometimes! Just do it. He died for our mission, damn it!*

"Okay. Yes, I understand the pressure the Americans are putting on you. Fine. Thanks. Alert the imam of the village we are coming, and ask him to break the news to Ahmed's mother."

Hakan listened, tension slightly lessening. "Yes, the snowstorm may sock us in by the time we get there. It's predicted to hit with full gale force winds. I'm sure his family will put us up. Right. The Americans will just have to wait another day for Charly. Good luck explaining! See you tomorrow."

Hakan snapped shut the mobile phone, tucking it away.

- 16 -
The world is a building with two doors
- turkish proverb -

They coordinated their arrival with the Black Hawk so it wouldn't be waiting on the ground in case other terrorists were around. They wanted a quick in and out.

Ahmed, wrapped in his bedroll, was carefully laid in the aukio. For the trip home, his rifle was placed by his side. The heavy white waterproofed canvas sides were pulled over him and securely fastened.

Balaban picked up the triangulated metal tongue of the aukio. "I will take my son."

Charly began a protest, "But your ribs…"

Balaban looked at Charly fondly but resolutely. "You may come behind us."

Charly picked up the ropes on either side of the back of the sled, determined to keep it balanced and to relieve Balaban as much as she could.

Hakan and Mahir looked upon this lead duo with tenderness. In "civilization" a woman would not have been given this honored role. In the field, things were different. They mentally shook themselves back to the task at hand and completed securing their aukio with the most relevant of the confiscated materials.

They unbound the prisoner, put snowshoes on him, and tied a rope around his waist. He was placed behind the second sled, with Hakan bringing up the rear, holding onto the other end of the rope attached to the prisoner.

Slowly and with care they began their descent. Snow was lightly falling and the clouds less dense. A fairly stiff wind drifted the nearly two feet of fresh snow. Their bear-claw type snowshoes held a firm grip. Going down a mountain trail was always trickier than coming up. The smooth, scooped bottoms of the sleds with two wooden rails as runners made control difficult. The only sounds were the swish of the sleds, very soft footfalls, and the occasional call of a bird.

As they approached the small plateau they heard the whirring chop of the helicopter before they saw it appear over the mountain top and quickly settle in a cloud of snow. The snow had diminished to flurries which opened up visibility to one thousand feet.

Four men quickly hopped out. One held his assault rifle at hip level, scanning the area. The others started unloading equipment, including two more aukios.

By the time they were finished, Mahir's team had reached the helicopter. Ahmed was released from the protective covering of the aukio, gently handed into the plane and placed on a litter. With great dignity and clenched teeth, Balaban got in with no assistance and sat near his son. With the advanced warning two litters had been added, removing troop seats to make it possible. Charly and Hakan were next, passing up the equipment which had been confiscated. The complaining prisoner was loaded next, placed in the very back, and bound into silent immobility.

While the Black Hawk was being loaded, Mahir talked with the clean-up team, making sure their map was correctly marked. "Since the snow has diminished, at least for a while, just follow our path."

"You're making it too easy on us!"

The small group donned snowshoes. Each pulling an aukio, they immediately started across the clearing.

Soon after the helicopter lifted off, clouds obscured the narrow landing area and they lost sight of the disgorged soldiers. With the limited visibility they flew the valleys toward Balaban's village.

Charly found the vibration of the Black Hawk soothing. She'd never been bothered by it as were so many. The noise precluded conversation in a normal voice, and no one felt like shouting. Her body was still tensed with the efforts of the past ten days. Sorrow for the loss of Ahmed seeped in and Charly felt loneliness. *It is easy to feel that way when other senses are blunted with fatigue and ambient noise. Maybe it's a kind of protection. Death is lonely.*

Why do I toy with risk which brings death closer to the realm of possibility? The simplicity of the answer did not surprise her. *It makes me feel more alive. And it's always measured, controlling the dynamics as best I can—fitness, well-trained colleagues, and careful planning. But it's the unexpected, the misstep that changes the course. I've never been on a mission that went completely according to plan. Glitches, minor or major, were a part of each. That's what makes it dynamic. It's the unknown element and mastering it which energizes me. But today we didn't succeed. We lost Ahmed.*

Charly looked around at Hakan, Mahir, and Balaban. Each looked deep within his own reverie. Alone.

Mahir's shouts instructing the pilot where to land brought her out of her own thoughts. Coming over the crest of the foothill, a small village appeared. Roofs were lightly covered with snow. The smoke from chimneys was going straight up, a sure sign the wind was calm and temperatures low. At the sound of the helicopter, people were emerging and walking toward a cleared area which had been marked for landing.

With slight rocking, the helicopter gently settled, the motor turned to idle. They watched as the blades turned more slowly. The co-pilot opened the door, jumped out, and stood by the door. Balaban joined him, and both grasped the litter as it was lowered by Mahir and Hakan.

They walked under the now barely moving blades to the approaching imam, the village priest. Two white-robed assistants took the litter from the soldier. As soon as he re-boarded, the helicopter immediately took off again, returning to meet the clean-up team.

Mahir, Hakan, and Charly observed from a distance. After the imam prayed, the three walked on. The villagers watched, and did not follow.

"Where are they taking him?" Charly asked. "Should we go, too?"

Mahir explained Muslim ritual surrounding death and burial. "Ahmed will be ritually cleansed, *ghusl*. It's a very specific procedure ending with him being wrapped in a white shroud. I suspect Balaban will wash his son, with the village expert assisting to be sure it is done correctly. So, no. That is private. Afterwards we will join the procession to the cemetery."

As Charly was taking this in, a young girl walked up to her and in Kurdish asked if she would please join her. "The others will go with the men."

Mahir translated. "This is Ahmed's sister. She's offering you her family's hospitality. Please go with her."

Charly followed her to a house where women of various ages were preparing food or solemnly sitting and talking. There was a quiet air of expectation. Most stopped what they were doing and stared at Charly when she entered.

I must look a fright. Dirty, blood spotted, and probably smelly. She hung back at the door.

A woman of her age approached, speaking in Turkish. "I am Ranya, Balaban's sister. Would you like to get cleaned? There is enough time before prayers."

With relief, Charly nodded her head vigorously.

Saying something in rapid Kurdish, she led Charly to the bath. When finished, she was pleased to have a clean, hooded *abaya* and socks given her by Ranya. She would put her boots back on when they left the house.

This time when she entered the room of women, there were welcoming nods. Ranya stopped before a woman in full *chador*, introducing her as Ahmed's mother, Derya. Charly did not know the Kurdish words, so simply said in Turkish, "I am sorry. Ahmed was my friend."

Derya looked up with great sadness in her tear filled eyes. She simply nodded, then patted Charly's hand.

Ranya led Charly to a grouping of pillows on the floor, onto which she gratefully sat. She was happy to just sit back and relax awhile with a cup of tea as the activity flowed around her. Charly noticed that the other women treated Derya with great respect and deference, but Ahmed's mother remained detached, seemingly in her own thoughts and world of sorrow.

A procession began at the place of cleansing, with Balaban and a few male relatives holding the funeral bier carrying

Ahmed. Derya walked slightly ahead of the other women, to the side but very near the bier. An increasing number of villagers joined them, walking alongside, or taking a turn carrying the bier for a while before relinquishing it to someone else. As they proceeded past the mosque to the cemetery, Mahir and Hakan took their turn as Charly walked along with the others. There was no open crying or wailing, as that is forbidden in Islam, as was music at funerals. There was a low murmur of chanting prayers. Charly felt badly that she did not know them and could not join. In the mountains she had felt equal as a team member. Here, she felt out of place.

As they paused outside the mosque, the imam led the community in the funeral prayers, *SalaatulJanaaza,* asking for God's mercy and blessings. They proceeded to the cemetery.

Ahmed's shrouded body was laid in the awaiting grave on his right side, facing Mecca. Balaban gathered loose soil and tossed it into the grave. Other men joined in this ritual, using both hands, starting at the head. After each of at least three scoops, they said a prayer.

With the first scoop:

Minhaakhalaqnaakum	Out of it we created you
With the second:	
Wafehaa nu'eedukum	And into it we deposit you
With the third:	
Wa minhaa nukhrikum	And from it we shall take you out
Taaratanukkraa	once agin.

Water was sprinkled over the grave when it was full.

Charly was remembering that at burial, an angel would ask Ahmed three questions. "Who is your lord?" "Who is your prophet?" "What is your book, the source of this knowledge?" When they were correctly answered, a cry came from heaven of acceptance of his soul.

The wind came up again the snow flakes began to fall as they stood by the grave. It was cold, but no one left until burial was completed. Outrage, grief, shock, and bewilderment were etched into the faces of the villagers. More prayers were said before the villagers dispersed to rejoin for a meal before the evening prayers for Ahmed.

As they proceeded back toward the village, their helicopter returned.

Hakan approached, inquiring, as the pilot hopped out. "Captain, you're back earlier than we thought."

"It's starting to sock in again. We thought we'd better make use of the little daylight we have left before the storm hits full force. Looks like another heavy snow fall."

Mahir inquired, "Can you still take me home on the way?"

"We should have enough time if we get right off. I'll get the prisoner loaded while you say your farewells. Sorry you won't be staying over."

"Disappointed?" Mahir asked Charly as they walked back to Balaban's house.

"A little. But I'm really tired. It's time to go. Are you okay with it?"

"Yes. Balaban and I will stay in close contact. And I really want to see Dilara."

- 17 -
What you give away you keep
- turkish proverb -

The safety of the Turkish helicopter and the presence of troops allowed Charly to relax and she was grateful. She was able to finally allow exhaustion to seep throughout her body and thoughts. Images of Ahmed floated in and out of awareness. Charly fell asleep, the noise muted by earphones. The pilots talking to base only lulled her further. She dreamed of being rocked by gentle waves as she peacefully floated. Occasionally a wave would roll over her and she'd take in water, splutter a bit, only to return to her peaceful space. The rocking became more insistent, then stopped. The lack of motion awakened her instantly to the landing.

Mahir gave her the Turkish cheek kisses usually reserved between men, holding her gaze and saying thank you in his Kurdish language. Unbidden tears swarmed her eyes as she watched him jump out and run to the waiting Dilara, heart adorner and lover, as her name conveyed. The helicopter almost instantly lifted off. Looking on the mountainside where she had trained with Mahir's men, she could see several standing, leaning on a rock or lifting their rifles in firing salute.

Another hour and we'll be at the base. Charly looked upon the desolate mountainous area now covered with snow, broken by beautiful valleys with streams and rivers. *It's truly a country of contrasts. Istanbul with its teeming millions and pollution from cars and this stark beauty populated by tribesmen, nomads, and villagers. Horns blaring versus goats bleating. Western dress mixed with the traditional in Istanbul, in contrast with the dress here—the consistency of robes, headcovers, scarves, and baggy trousers common to these Hakkari mountains. Heart-to-heart connections, that's what I feel here.* With something of a shock, Charly realized she did not want to return to what the Western World would call civilization. As she glanced at Hakan, she shivered, realizing he was part of it, but not the basic impetus for her feelings in southeastern Turkey.

I wonder what Megan would say to these thoughts—not as a friend, but as a psychologist? For that matter, what is my self-analysis? Huh! Probably the same thing. That I'm too close to the situation now to know how I really feel. That my emotions are hovering too near the surface, and I'm identifying with those with whom I've faced death.

Megan suspected I was attracted to Hakan. Knowing we are together, I bet her imagination has been working overtime these last ten days. I can almost hear Megan ask, "Well, where are you and Hakan now?" And how would I answer? I don't know; I just don't know.

It was easy to tell they were nearing base, as the air space became active with jets, transport planes, and helicopters. There was an almost palpable excitement one could see in the activity. The markings of both Turkish and American planes could be discerned, although they were the same types of aircraft. Soldiers in camouflage were moving about purposefully, perhaps a war game exercise or something real in Iraq or Afghanistan. Looking around, Charly noticed that both she and Hakan were sitting taller, looking out, no longer lost in their own thoughts.

They landed at the edge of the field, away from the activity. Jumping out, she grimaced with the reminder of her tired and sore muscles and joints. After the hooded prisoner was helped from the helicopter, Hakan and Charly walked briskly behind them toward the hanger.

Hakan's shoulder accidentally bumped hers. Their eyes met and held. They did not share a smile this time. Now that they were back into the "real world," the doubts of what would happen to them as a couple were surfacing. They both knew that at the very least, they could be highly censored if their intimacy were known. But that wasn't their future with which either was most concerned.

After a quick shower and change, Hakan and Charly walked to the mess hall for dinner. They joined several of Hakan's Special Forces friends who were eager to hear more about the mission-that-wasn't-supposed-to-be. Knowing the formal debriefing had to happen first, they turned their attention to Charly. After getting out a few curiosity questions about her, to which she responded generally without details, Hakan asked what all the activity was at the base. Charly gave him an appreciate smile. She just didn't feel like focusing on herself right now. Maybe after the debriefing.

Alec, the Special Forces team leader assumed the role of spokesman. "It's rumored that the Taliban in the mountains between Pakistan and Afghanistan are engaged in a major offensive against several bordering villages which have been harboring our and Afghanistan's Special Forces. Our infiltration of the villages has been a gold mine of information, and they've developed a wary trust."

"Of course that is to the detriment of Taliban. I've heard you've had surprisingly successful counteroffensive missions." Hakan edged forward in his chair, intently listening.

"Yeah. We thought we had dislodged them from at least that tangled web of paths between countries, and cleared some caves, too. But the Taliban can't countenance that kind of success. They've sharpened their talons and want to teach us a lesson."

"Contentious bastards. No respect."

Everyone chuckled at Hakan's truism levity.

"On a serious note, Hakan, it looks like we may be the ones following up on the information you found. We'd all like to know firsthand what you encountered. We're scheduled to meet with you tonight, after your debriefing."

"If it can't be us, then I'm glad it's you guys. But tonight? We're exhausted!"

" 'Fraid so, Hakan. We're up against possible action by the terrorists in twenty-four hours. Coming with us?" Alec looked expectantly at Charly and Hakan.

Hakan again responded for he and Charly. "You know the routine. When there have been deaths on your mission, Command wants you to sit out the next one if there is a replacement team ready to go. And it looks like there is."

The director of clandestine missions was housed in a highly fortified building two stories underground. Also located there was the air traffic control group monitoring the radar and all incoming and outgoing flights. It was purely a safety move; in case the above ground tower was destroyed, there would be no pause in the flow of planes.

"What should we expect, Hakan?" Charly asked as they headed toward the director's office. "The debriefings I've had in the past were tokenisms—the group sharing information with whomever was in command of the unit at the base."

Hakan looked at Charly, her nervousness visible in the tightness with which she held her shoulders and the preciseness in her speech. "I wish I could relieve your mind, Charly. This won't be as friendly as you've experienced before. You engaged in a mission with a Special Forces MIT team in a foreign country, without prior approval of your government. Plus, part of your team included a former PKK member. Add the deaths of the terrorists and Ahmed who was not one of us but part of the team. We both have a lot of explaining to do, Charly. Don't try to hide anything, embellish, or rationalize."

Charly groaned and shook her head. "Don't hide anything?"

"Anything related to the mission." Hakan grinned at Charly.

Hakan opened the door of the building, beckoning Charly through first. He noticed that she took a deep breath and rolled her shoulders to loosen them. Hakan relaxed a little. *She'll be okay, but it will be rough on her. We're both so tired—maybe that's why they're debriefing now, to catch us off guard, not just for the benefit of the next mission.* Hakan admonished himself. *Stop being so paranoid. They'd pick up on that in a flash!*

Showing ID, they were passed through three guard stations with metal detectors at each. An escort attached himself to the pair as they entered the elevator to the basement offices.

Stopping outside a door, he knocked, and then indicated Hakan was to enter. Charly stepped forward, too, but was told they would be interviewed separately. Managing a nod at each other, Hakan entered.

Farther down the hall the procedure was repeated. Charly opened the door to a conference room, which contained a round table, where three uniformed men stood as she entered. She soberly scanned each face, recognizing the third. "Major Prater! This is a surprise!" Her relief at seeing a familiar face with whom she'd previously worked was obvious in her big grin. She walked forward to shake his hand.

"Hello, Charly. I've been in on this since the beginning.

When I heard you were returning this afternoon I flew up from Dubai. Thought you could do with a friendly face."

"For sure!"

Major Prater introduced the other two, both from the counter terrorism branch, Turkish and American.

"Let's get right to it, Charly. We've reviewed the papers, computer and maps you found. We have formed a preliminary opinion which indicates our team needs to move immediately. After we are finished here, you and Hakan will meet with them. They need to be on their way by midnight, if nothing to the contrary is found by our analysts while we debrief you."

The three seemed genuinely interested, asking piercing questions while leading Charly through the mission from the time they left the tour group in Konya. They did not let her get away with generalities and used a map following their path. They spent a lot of time questioning her about Mahir's compound, training, and the personnel she had encountered.

The debriefing team thoroughly covered attitudes she had had at each step and descriptions pertaining to the others on the team. Rationale pertaining to each decision to use their weapons was challenged. It was impossible for Charly to guess their reaction about what happened as they were stoic and professional. The only way she could judge was how quickly they moved on to another aspect versus time spent lingering.

The last question dealt with her mental state. "How are you handling wounding the boy who subsequently died at Yuksekova?"

"I couldn't have prevented it from happening. What I am not 'okay' with is the way in which he was tortured in the custody of the village guards. In fact, it pisses me off!"

"Is this why you killed the terrorists instead of counseling caution and wounding them instead?"

Chary just sat there and stared at the Turkish interviewer, trying to process the implications of the question.

Major Prater interjected after a minute went by. "Charly, what was your first response to the question?"

"No!"

"What was going through your mind after that?"

"I was thinking of what could have been done differently. That of course they didn't have to die. We could have taken a chance on getting shot and gone easier."

"In the cave, why did you opt for wounding your target and Hakan killed his?"

"I told you, we agreed within a minute, non-verbally, then went."

"You said earlier that Hakan suggested it. Why?"

"I didn't think of an alternative at the time. He's much more experienced. Counter-terrorism and working with Special Forces is his life's work. It was logical that he would make the decision. There was not a chance to discuss the situation."

"Was he protecting you?"

"If he'd been protecting me, he would have left me outside the cave!"

"We mean emotionally, Charly."

"I can't speak for Hakan."

"Did you endanger the mission because he felt he had to protect you from killing?"

"I don't know. I think I pulled my own weight and served a supportive roll. I never felt 'protected' by Hakan or anyone else."

The three men glanced at each other, nodding.

"Charly, do you need to speak with psychological support?"

"Right now I just want to go to bed!"

"Charly?" Major Prater admonished.

"No. I need to work it through myself. Right now, I'm just tired."

The three stood up. Charly followed suit.

"Charly, we'd like you back in two hours, at 2100, to meet with the team who will be following up on your information."

"Major Prater, I'd like to go along."

"Negative. I knew you'd ask, Charly. I think you pushed the limit and need a break. There will be another time. Besides, we can keep the ambassador's office at bay only so long. You'll be getting an eyes-only commendation for what you've done, so it will be more difficult to give you grief about your cavalier behavior."

"Cavalier! Now just a minute, I...."

"Charly, leave it!"

Charly went to the room assigned her in the adjacent building housing transient personnel. She felt drained of energy. A shower invigorated her somewhat. Tossing on a clean t-shirt to ward off a slight chill in the room, she sat cross-legged on the bed with a towel underneath her to cover the scratchy wool blanket. She plugged in the laptop the military provided on loan, and accessed her email.

Charly had three sites for different purposes, junk/commercial, personal, and secure. The amount of mail went down drastically as the site became more private. Not bothering with the dozens she knew would be in "junk," she looked first at her secure host. Although it would be very time consuming to break into, she had no doubt that it could be done. If national security computers could be broken into, anything could. It helped tremendously that she used Linux as an operating system as the firewalls were the most impenetrable.

On the secure site she only had one message, and that was

from her agent in the CIA. "Hear you're alive. Job well done. Contact me!"

Oh, well, Bob wasn't the most loquacious in written word. But it sure felt good to have that contact. Charly sent out a brief message.

She was delighted to learn that Frances was still in Istanbul. She had thought by now that Frances would be comfortably and safely ensconced at home in the routine of friends, walking her dogs, gardening, and consulting jobs with the local university. Her email message only said she would be arriving in two days in Diyarbakir with Megan in tow and not to make reservations yet back to America. Charly chuckled at this, as she was clearly not ready to leave Turkey.

Still smiling, she lay on the bed, intending to review the afternoon's debriefing.

"Charly, answer the door. I know you're there." Concerned that she didn't respond to his knocking, Hakan tried the doorknob. Finding it unlocked, he slowly and quietly opened it. *Oh, God, she looks exhausted.* He eased the door shut and sat in the only chair, watching her deep breathing, her tousled red hair tugging at his heart. He longed to sit beside her on the bed and run his fingers through its tangles, his finger across her lower lip. Her t-shirt had ridden up to her waist, and the towel immodestly draped over her hip.

With a start, he brought himself back to the task at hand. *I wish I could just let her sleep. But we need to meet the next team soon. She's going to throw a fit when she finds out I'm going back with them.* He cringed just thinking of her outrage he anticipated would be coming. *Just as well, though, for us. I need some space to think about us as a couple, of our time together. And I sure as hell know Charly does, too. From the time we got on the helicopter, I felt her distancing herself from me, from us. Whatever we end up doing, it's not going to be simple.*

Charly slowly became aware of another's presence in the room. It didn't frighten her; she knew it was Hakan. *Just don't ask me how I know, I just do. I wish he'd come closer. I wish he'd touch me again.* Her cheeks grew hot.

Hakan noticed that her breathing was shallower. *Her cheeks are flushing. I bet she knows I'm here. Maybe I should lock the door...*

Charly's voice was sleep laden and hoarse. "Hakan. Lock the door, please."

"Are you sure?"

"Very."

Stifling a groan, Hakan did as she bid and sat beside her on the bed, brushing her hair from her face. Charly touched his mouth with her finger, teasing his mustache with the tiniest of tugs.

"How much time do we have?"

"We meet with the others in forty-five minutes. Do you want anything to eat or drink first?"

"Not now."

Charly opened her arms as Hakan stretched out over her, bearing his weight on his forearms.

"No, I want to feel your weight. All of it."

For a few moments they laid thus together, with each touching point increasing in sensitivity. They lay without moving but both felt as if their bodies were intensely active, seeking, meeting, responding.

"Hakan, I need you. Okay?" Charly reached down, trying to unbuckle and unzip. "Damn it, help me."

Hakan quickly undressed as Charly tossed aside her only garment.

Urging him, Hakan was immediately immersed in the warm moist welcome that was Charly.

Their union reflected the embedded sweetness of their care for each other as well as the violence of what they'd just been through. Simultaneously they were there for each other and themselves, as both seemed to work through their own demons, their own feelings for the other.

They lay, catching their breath, sweat gleaming. Tears rolled down Charly's cheeks. When Hakan noticed and gently brushed them away, his own eyes misted. An almost overwhelming sense of tenderness toward Charly welled up inside. He firmly held her hand.

Charly was the first to break their silence. "Hakanin, my dear one. What are we to do?"

"Gulperi, you'll always be with me now, *Kalbim senin kalbine yakındır*, in your heart, as you will be in mine." *But do we have a future? I can't ask that. It's too soon. I'm too much on an emotional rollercoaster right now. But I wish I knew. I want there to be one, but how is a huge unknown.*

Instead, Charly asked, "What happens tomorrow?"

Hakan shifted to capture her eyes. "I'm going back with the team. They feel my recent good contacts in Yuksekova might smooth some rough spots. And I know the area a bit better now than do several of the replacement team." He tensed, expecting fury.

"I asked, but was refused. I'm glad you'll get to follow-up on what we discovered. It's a way of pay-back for losing Ahmed. Just come back safely."

"You never cease to amaze me. I thought you'd be upset."

"You are doing something I would if I could. I'm pleased for you. And you are very good. You'll help get the job done." Charly began to tickle Hakan's chest hairs, calling him her warrior. They giggled playfully for a few minutes, then drew apart with deep regret, and dressed.

"Hungry, Charly?"

"It's the best snack I've ever missed!"

On the walk to meet their cohorts they shared what happened in respective debriefings. They had been strikingly similar.

"They must have found consistency in our stories, or we would have been called back within thirty minutes. Did they offer for you to see a psychologist?"

"Yes, and at first I was offended. But I'm thinking it might not be a bad idea to have someone help me sort things through. I'll have to guard against allowing overt feelings toward you to come into the conversation. My lack of being forthright might come across as having something to hide, which of course I do."

"I agree that a perceptive psychologist would most likely pick up on any ambivalence in feelings."

"Yeah, and neither one of us could afford that, you less than me, Hakan."

Several minutes passed in silence. "I do have an idea, though. I heard from Frances that she and Megan will meet me in Diyarbakir day after tomorrow. Megan is a clinical psychologist also trained in Reiki."

"I see where you are going with this. Might be a really good idea to have someone around for a few days with this sort of training. Do you trust her?"

"I've only known her for the few days of our trip, but we immediately felt a close connection. I'm not sure yet, but it's a possibility. And just being around Frances will help me ground again."

Arriving at the building, their professional personae reasserted. The next two hours were spent with maps spread in front of the Special Forces team as they planned the mission, relying on descriptions from Hakan and Charly to flesh it out. The five commandos, including Hakan, would be leaving before dawn. Prior, they were going to check over their equipment and weapons.

Alec carefully refolded the maps and directed his group to the next task. "We almost have it all assembled, but want you to go with us to check it over, Hakan. Then, we'll have a few hours to sleep before take-off."

Outside, Charly shook hands with each, wishing them a safe mission. As they walked away, she turned to Hakan. "Later?" she asked softly.

"Leave your door unlocked."

Charly lay in the dark, too tense to sleep although she was exhausted. Hakan quietly slipped in the room, sitting on the bed to remove his shoes. "I set the watch alarm for three hours from now. May I stay until then?"

"I was hoping you would."

Hakan gathered Charly into his arms, snuggling from behind. No words were spoken until Charly said softly, "I'm falling in love with you, Hakan." Hakan did not respond. Charly felt his chest rising slowly, steadily, and she, too, finally gave herself over to sleep.

The alarm rang all too soon, and they slowly awakened from a drugged, dreamless sleep. Hakan quickly showered and dressed in the clean fatigues which he had worn to her room. Charly sat cross-legged on the bed, watching. Before Hakan left they faced each other, placing a hand first on their own hearts, then each other's.

"Please come back safely. I want to see you again."
"We'll be together again, Charly."
Charly cried herself back to sleep.

JEANNE REEDER

- 18 -
Whoever is fond of cream should take the cow around with him.
- turkish proverb -

Charly awoke at noon, feeling ravenous. *A good sign, I guess. I better hurry or I'm going to miss lunch.* The needle spray of the shower refreshed her, and she found herself humming. *Humming? Why?* She gave voice to a few words of the lilting ditty she had written years ago. "Away and once again, the band began to play. Let the maiden find her way among the roses blooming." She laughed at the obvious reference. *Prophetic. I guess I'm ready to get on with it! Whatever "it" is, and wherever "it" leads.* She smiled broadly as Hakan's faced floated in her memory. *With you in my life, I hope.*

Later in the day Charly caught a ride to Diyarbakir with a pair of soldiers dressed in Kurdish casuals.

"Recon?"

They responded affirmatively to her in Kurdish, and they all laughed.

"Diyarbakir Dedeman, wow! You're going upscale! We don't even want to be seen around here." The driver shook his head in wonder at the fancy façade of the hotel.

"No problem, let me out at the driveway turnoff." Charly quickly jumped from the car with backpack in hand and they sped away.

Dedeman was a chain of five-star high-rise hotels favored by international tour groups who knew their clientele enjoyed the amenities of home. The members of Frances and Charly's tour had stayed in two already before Charly had left on her mission. As Charly entered, she noticed several restaurants and cafés. Glancing through the list of services as she waited to register, she was pleased to see the usual for the Dedeman: Turkish bath, beauty salon, internet connections, fitness classes, skin and body care, and the list went on. *Yes indeed, a hotel for Frances. Not at all surprising that she booked a suite. If no Hilton, the Dedeman will nicely do.* Looking around she noticed the sign for Diyar Bar, another necessity.

Once settled in her room, she ordered a light meal from room service plus ice and gin. There was only Coke, juice, wine, and whiskey in the mini-bar. Waiting, she surveyed the lovely, if standard, appointments of the living room and lapsed into reverie. *Lucky for me they have full room service available. I don't feel like moving. It's day and night different than the one in which Hakan and I stayed not that long ago. Probably a good idea, or his absence is all I'd be thinking about. Ha! Isn't it already? I'm glad I came early. I need this time by myself to regroup. Lucky in a way Hakan's gone, otherwise I'd be resentful of Frances' intrusion. And poor Frances, she wouldn't know why. This is something I just can't share with her. Not yet. Funny how we are very close and have the highest regard for each other, best friends, really. But yet we know so little about each other's intimate lives. I've been curious, but haven't asked. I'm sure it's the same with her. How different with Megan, to develop closeness nearly immediately knowing her for only a week. It's a bond born of a feeling of shared souls, an intimacy in itself.*

And then there's Hakan. Is there a future? If so, what dimensions will it take? Sex, for sure. Charly felt herself grow warm with remembrance of his touch, his eyes devouring her. But more. Charly thought of the last few hours together as they had slept, just slept, within the cocoon of comfort the other provided.

After eating and limiting herself to one glass of gin, Charly decided to take further advantage of the hotel's fine services, and called for an appointment at the Turkish bath. Unfortunately it was full. They suggested she could have a masseuse come to her room in two hours. In the meantime, she took advantage of Dedeman's health and beauty care services. Shampoo, trim, facial, and the advertised "painless epilation" which didn't quite live up to the claim.

Feeling bright and shiny, she returned to her room for a long bubble bath. As she was toweling off, she heard an abrupt rap at the door. Two hours had passed quickly. Using the heavy white toweling robe provided, she opened the door to a stern, sturdy woman who bid her good evening in heavily accented English. Charly indicated where she wanted the table set up, and agreed to the one-and-one-half-hour option.

During the first hour of the massage, Charly's every aching muscle was awakened and protested. *She is good. If there is a sore spot she not only finds it, she delights in working through it.* In the last half hour, Charly succumbed to the rhythm of the massage and entered a state of relaxed bliss, drifting inexorably toward sleep.

Charly barely awoke enough to sign the authorization slip, add a tip, and double lock her doors before falling bonelessly into bed. *If only Hakan were here,* were her last thoughts.

The first call of the *muezzin* awakened her in the morning. She smiled and went back to sleep.

At nine the requested wake up call with tea arrived. As Charly answered the door, she was surprised that she felt no soreness and was wide awake, and ready for a huge American-style breakfast.

She bounded down the stairs, eschewing the elevator for the nine floors, and burst through the exit door into the lobby. Across the way she saw Frances and Megan registering.

"She's here already? When did she arrive? Last night?" Frances inquiring voice floated across the thirty feet from the desk.

Tears sprang to her eyes as she saw her old friend. Part of her past, reasserting Charly's reality. *And Megan. Gwen is here too!* Charly quietly slipped up behind, putting her arms around them. The four enthusiastically greeted one another, with unasked questions sparkling from their eyes.

"Why don't you guys run your stuff up, then join me for breakfast? I'm starved!"

Frances grinned at her old friend. "Well, Charly. True to form, I see."

Charly turned with a wave. "Diyar Café!"

Charly was tucking into her eggs, pancakes, and sausage by the time Frances, Megan, and Gwen joined her. Pouring them each a large glass of freshly squeezed orange juice, Charly waited until they had placed their order before asking to be filled in on just what they were doing there. "I thought you three would be home long ago. What's the deal?"

"Whoa! First, Charly, we want to know if you are okay. Did you deliver the package without incident? Where's Hakan? How did you end up at the base? All Kamil would tell us was you were flying in there yesterday, but nothing else."

"Ah, Frances! I'm just fine, and the package was delivered to a very nice lady. The whole village enjoyed the music. And Hakan left already for another mission."

"You mean another tour?"

"Not exactly. More like a continuation of our excursion into the mountains. But what about you guys?"

Megan knew this was a clear fob-off but as Frances seemed to have accepted it and was ready to go on, she would also. At least for now. *Something's up with Charly. There is way too much that she's not saying. A sadness is lurking under her exuberant facade.*

Charly ignored Megan's inquiring look. "Tell me why you three are still in Turkey."

Charly learned that when the tour had ended, Frances was tired. The rush-rush and early morning starts of the tour had taken their toll. Frances needed the relaxing pace of staying in one place at least a few days at a time. She admitted that the tour routine of frequently moving to a new scene wasn't her idea of fun anymore.

"I decided that the three days we spent upon arrival before the tour in Istanbul weren't nearly enough. There was too much I still wanted to see and I hadn't even been to Roberts College yet. I couldn't leave without seeing how my home area had changed over forty years!"

Gwen continued. "Megan and I had already planned to remain in Istanbul for a few more days. When we discovered we all had this in mind, we decided to hook up. We switched to the Hilton so we could be together with Frances awhile longer. We'd had such fun together on the tour swapping stories over our before dinner drinks. It's amazing what we have in common!"

Each day in Istanbul, Frances, Megan and Gwen got up at a more civilized hour and leisurely toured one site. Over late afternoon tea at the Hilton, which merged into scotch at happy hour, a plan had emerged.

"It began with Megan talking about her research into the effects of war on children," Frances revealed. "And you know, Charly when it comes to children, I'm a lost cause!"

Charly smiled at her, recalling what a terrific early childhood lab school teacher she had been, and the causes she had taken up for their wellbeing over the years, through local and national organizations. "Children at-risk was your particular interest."

"Megan took her interest into the field more broadly than I did. Tell her, Megan!"

"My research took me into war torn areas, where I studied children. Soon, just researching about children's responses to war and disruption wasn't enough. There was such inadequate care for them in the camps. Sure, they had a roof of some sort over their heads, tent canvas if nothing else, and subsistence food, but that was about it. Fifteen years ago I began to work almost exclusively in Afghanistan in the refugee camps. Being part Arab and speaking Arabic and a smattering of Pashto and Farsi was invaluable in building trust."

"But where does your clinical practice fit in with all this?" Charly inquired.

Megan grinned. "That's how I earn money for my research! I have an active practice through the hospital attached to the university where I teach. It's ideal in rounding out my life."

"But no family life?"

"Right. No time. I tried marriage once, but felt too constrained. Close friends and work sustain me."

"And you're now broadening your sites in the Middle East to include Turkey?"

"It seems like a natural progression. I've met Red Crescent workers who have been associated with Turkey's Kurdish refugee camps set up during and after the major Turkish-PKK war and subsequent devastation. Even now, four years after the so-called cease-fire, displaced Kurds still live in the camps. Red Crescent is running most of them."

Having worked in their camps elsewhere, Megan knew how sorely short of funds they were. Basics, yes. Frills such as an educational program for those under seven, none. She knew children needed normalcy, needed a home with their parents, and safe routines. Unfortunately, that reality was far down a bureaucratic road. Educational or organized play programs could go a long way in providing security for them.

This immediately had whetted Frances' interest, as she would melt when faced with the cherubic face of a three-year-old, her personal preference. From her days at Roberts College, she had become interested in the plight of the displaced children in Turkey. While there she had become friends with Sulah who became a stalwart leader in promoting Red Crescent work with children.

Gwen's interest was genuine, too, and consistent with her experiences. She had worked in a school of nursing in London, specializing in pediatrics. Since retirement her services had been in demand in whatever Third World country she traveled. She eschewed large cities, preferring small villages, and would take local transportation. Usually she would check in with the local doctor to see if her help would be needed for a few days. The response was always affirmative. Often there were children with infected wounds, ear infections, life threatening diarrhea, or a knee that needed to be bandaged or stitched. But other times, like a few months ago in a remote village in Thailand, she had found tuberculosis running rampant. Too often supplies limited what she could do. But sometimes she could help facilitate obtaining them, and always she could employ her nursing skills.

Enthusiasm radiated from the three women. "Sounds like

you three fit into a puzzle of some sort. Your common interest is obvious. I sense a plan. Give!"

"When I was in Istanbul I tried to find my old friend Sulah. Roberts College gave me her last address, but that was years ago. I contacted Red Crescent and was referred to someone who had worked with her. She is retired and living in Istanbul. She couldn't believe I had returned after all these years!

"We met for lunch and caught up a little on what we'd been doing. Sulah regaled me with stories about her work with Red Crescent. She has worked with a variety of disaster programs. But she particularly warmed up to the subject when she described the need for programs with children in the Kurdish refugee camps. By then Megan and Gwen wandered into the lounge and joined us."

"Uh oh, Frances. And you just couldn't resist, right?"

"Right! Not only I, but these two immediately became embroiled with the problem."

"So…?"

"From there the doors opened wide to us with contacts in the organization. We are going to meet with the regional Red Crescent director tomorrow, here. And, then we'll tour the two nearby camps in this region."

Frances sat back. Charly thought all three women looked like the cats who had found an undefended nest of canaries. They were clearly excited about a cause about which they were passionate.

"Do you want to join us, Charly? Or do you plan to return to the States right away?"

Charly looked at the three faces shining with expectation. She considered options before responding. *This will keep my mind partially occupied for awhile. Frankly, I'd rather be by myself but maybe I need this diversion to give me time to put my life into perspective again.*

"I'm planning to remain in Diyabakir for at least one week. No definite plans to return to the U.S. yet. But why are you meeting with Red Crescent? Do you have something specific in mind? Just fact gathering? Or are you committing yourselves to work?"

Before responding, they glanced at each other. Megan responded. "We don't know, Charly. We need to see the conditions and what they have set up already. Then we can see if we have a role or not."

"Right!" chimed in Frances. "And we thought you could help organize the fact finding."

Charly rolled her eyes.

"And when we arrived in Turkey we all had to pay our twenty dollars for a visa. It's good for three months and we have two left. We could do a lot in that time to help!"

Frances sounds like she's more than halfway committed. "Slow down, woman!"

Charly continued along a practical line. "Yeah, Frances. But if you work for Red Crescent you have to have a residency work visa. You can't work on a tourist visa."

"Oh, Charly, that's just a minor point."

"Tell it to the Turkish Consulate's office!"

Megan spoke up. "Charly's right, Frances. I looked into it online. We have thirty days from when we entered the country to apply for the residency visa, and our time's almost up.

And if we overstay our visa, we have to pay a fine."

"We can work through those details." Frances was not deterred by mere bureaucratic paperwork.

"What about your two dogs at home, Frances? And your house?"

Frances grinned. "My sister's already gotten Tammy and Scrappy from the vet. Her granddaughter wants to move out of the dorm at the university and was looking for a place. Ta-daa! I gave permission last week for her to move in with me."

"So, she can take care of your dogs and your house. Frances! You've moved right ahead. And Megan and Gwen? Have you gone this far in freeing yourselves from your home bases?"

They both nodded, widely smiling. All three looked a little chagrined.

"Well, then, let's get to it!" Charly got up from the table signaling a change of venue was in order.

They spent the rest of the afternoon and evening devising a series of questions and observations they wanted to make the next day. Each had their own for which to be responsible.

Charly felt like she was being swept up in a whirlwind of social action. *But I have no intention of participating beyond this meeting tomorrow. I've been so caught up in their excitement I haven't even had a chance to talk privately with Megan.*

As the evening came to a close, Megan and Charly bid them goodnight and adjourned to the hotel's bar.

"Just one rakı, Megan, I'm bushed."

"Then you'd better talk fast!"

"What do you mean?"

They both laughed at her feigned innocence.

"I don't want to go into details. Let's just say I'm in deep."

"With Hakan? Of course I knew of a major attraction. Did it blossom?"

"Oh, how sweetly put! Yes. And he seems pivotal to everything that happened."

"It wasn't just a simple delivery, was it? Frances told me about some of your other missions, and I assumed it might develop into one. Particularly with the Delta alert still in place."

"You are on-target. Suffice it to say that the trip was physically challenging and emotionally taxing because we lost one of our team. I don't dwell on it, but I feel a little 'flat.'"

"It could be because of the toll on your soul as well as your body. Any nightmares?"

"None. I replay things in my mind during the day, but know it was a pretty typical mission."

"How does Hakan fit? What do you mean 'pivotal'?"

"He was part of the mission beginning to end. I couldn't have asked for a better partner. And throughout there were undertones of deep caring and passion we had to compartmentalize."

"You need to look at each aspect separately, before you can see the whole and its meaning for you. It's my guess you've experienced this before since compartmentalization is how you frequently handle dissonance."

"I know, Megan. Right now it's all too entwined."

"Want me to help?"

"Thanks. I need your magic right now."

Megan returned to Charly's room with her. Charly relaxed in the lounge chair, fully trusting Megan to help her find balance again. For the next hour, Charly felt varying energy pulses as her body responded. Sometimes she could sense her body's resistance, and she practiced deep relaxation techniques to help them surface. Finally, she sensed wholeness again.

Charly opened her eyes and gazed upon Megan, feeling

something akin to love. She had benefited from Megan's finely honed skill and art. Although she herself did not practice Reiki, Charly had the utmost respect for its healing properties. As she had said before, "magic." And Megan was a highly developed practitioner.

"Thank you." Charly took her hand, and they quietly sat for a few minutes.

Almost simultaneously they rose and hugged.

"See you tomorrow. Be alert"! Megan gently closed the door as she let herself out.

It was amazing how at peace Charly felt once again. Like every thing had clicked at the correct resonance.

After a long soak in the tub, Charly checked her email. Her heart leapt when she saw the brief one from Hakan. "My *gulperi*. Please wait for me. Day after tomorrow, I'll come to you. Your Hakanin."

Charly melted at his use of the endearment at the end of his name.

Lines from Turkish mystic poet Yunus Emre kept running through her mind as she was falling asleep:

'Your love has wrested me away from me,
You're the one I need, you're the one I crave.'

I miss him.